KU-673-709

GOING ALL THE WAY

BY
ISABEL SHARPE

MILLS & BOON®
Pure reading pleasure

All th _____ le the
imagi _____ nyone
bearin _____ spired
by an _____ all the
incide

® and ™ are trademarks owned and used by the trademark owner
and/or its licensee. Trademarks marked with ® are registered with the
United Kingdom Patent Office and/or the Office for Harmonisation
in the Internal Market and in other countries.

First published in Great Britain 2007
by Harlequin Mills & Boon Limited,
Eton House, 18-24 Paradise Road, Richmond, Surrey TW9 1SR

ISBN: 978 0 263 85588 3

14-0907

Harlequin Mills & Boon policy is to use papers that are
natural, renewable and recyclable products and made from
wood grown in sustainable forests. The logging and
manufacturing processes conform to the legal environmental
regulations of the country of origin.

Printed and bound in Spain
by Litografia Rosés S.A., Barcelona

1

"MY WIFE PATTY has done a lot of needlework in her time." Mr. Jed Baxter sent the sour-faced woman beside him a look of adoration.

Ryan Masterson raised his eyebrows as if this was the most exciting thing he'd heard in nearly forever, mind spinning over the absolute nothing he knew about needlework to try to come up with a follow-up question. He'd been sitting in the Union Square Café for the better part of two hours with Jed and Patty Baxter, a middle-aged couple who'd just moved to Manhattan from Dallas. The point of the meal was to get to know them, let them get to know him, and to interest them in his firm's latest venture-capital fund, for female- and minority-owned businesses in the city. However, the ebb and flow of conversation had been heavy on ebb and light on flow. He'd already struck out on the topic of rodeo, a passion of Jed's. Ditto barbecue, because what could be said after your guest emphatically denied you could have an opinion being from the North? They'd had to resort to a discussion of tax law, a subject he could only b.s. his way through at best.

"Needlework. Really. What kind?" That had to be a safe and relevant question, didn't it? Wasn't there more than one kind of needlework? He was pretty sure Jed wasn't talking about tattooing or body piercing.

Patty flicked a glance at Ryan and went back to staring at something past his head. "Needlepoint, knitting…"

"Sweaters?" He took a sip of water. *Sweaters?* He was scraping absolute bottom. Times like this he needed a woman beside him, maybe someone like Christine, the woman who lived across the hall. That might sound sexist, but while he was sure there were men into needlework, he was just as sure he didn't want to date any.

"Yes. And embroidery. Crewel tablecloths." She glanced at him again and almost smiled, which was the closest thing to an expression he'd seen all evening.

Ryan put on his most impressed face. Whatever cruel tablecloths were, they clearly deserved a reaction. "Well. I'm in awe. Did you ever think of starting a business?"

She blinked in apparent alarm. "No."

With that chatty and fascinating response, the waiter brought back the signed copy of the bill, thank God, and Ryan could end this misery. At the door to the restaurant, he kept a warm smile on while he shook hands, sure this was the last time he'd get that chance. Jed and Patty were old money, liberal, new to the city and in search of a place to leave their mark. Gilbert Capital's newest fund fit their needs perfectly. But why would they give over large sums to someone they couldn't connect with? Trust and compatibility were vital to the process, and Ryan was generally very good at eliciting both, even at first meetings. The Baxters had defeated him. Done in by bucking broncos and table linens.

"Well, it's been a lovely evening."

"It certainly has been." Jed and Patty exchanged glances wearing polite smiles and made their escape, going east on 16th Street toward Union Square.

Ryan went west, turning back once to lift a hand in case the Baxters had the same impulse.

They didn't.

He sighed and pushed impatiently at hair that insisted on ignoring careful combing, and diving over his forehead, aiming for his eyes. He needed to cut it, but he couldn't bring himself to part with this last symbol of his rebellious youth. Maybe the Baxters liked short hair. Jed's had been buzzed close to military-short. Maybe they liked bawdy humor instead of intelligent conversation, maybe they liked beer instead of wine, maybe they'd rather have gone to a deli for pastrami sandwiches. Jed was obviously devoted to his wife, and Ryan couldn't find a single topic to draw her out, maybe that was it. If Patty made the decisions in the family, Ryan and his fund were definitely going nowhere.

A man bumped into him on Fifth Avenue and Ryan instinctively felt for his watch and wallet, then dodged another man aiming too close. New York, New York, a helluva town. He turned onto West 14th Street and a stiff breeze dislodged the rest of his attempt at a controlled hairstyle. Warm for mid-April. Nearly summerlike tonight.

At the Sixth Avenue subway stop, he paused, got a whiff of stale subterranean air and kept walking, straight and brisk, or as brisk as the crowd would allow. The thought of being underground, cooped up in a metal car, squashed among strangers' bodies never appealed, but tonight it seemed unbearable.

Not for the first time, and more frequently in recent months, the country's largest city felt too small, too tight. He'd never be a country boy, but he craved less crowded spaces, a more peaceful pace of life, a motorcycle between his legs, a pair of female arms wrapped around his middle and nowhere in particular to go.

Which would accomplish what?

He needed a change, but he needed to move forward, not back. His motorcycle days were over long ago, and with them, his reckless youth. Instead of high-speed alcohol consumption followed by high-speed driving, his social life consisted of low-key evenings with friends, work-related outings or charity events, an over-thirty soccer league and occasional dates. In short, he'd grown up.

When he left the city, he'd leave it for a commuting suburb, maybe in Connecticut, his home state, a big friendly house with a loving wife and a bunch of kids to play in the green backyard. That would be his next journey. And if his increasing restlessness in Manhattan was any indication, he was due to be starting it soon.

A taxi screeched to a halt near him, horns blared, people shouted.

Very soon.

He reached home, a typically New York nineteenth-century brownstone on Bank Street, and got into the elevator with a middle-aged woman and her yappy little dog who lived a floor above him. The woman looked, as usual, as if she'd just had a horrible fight with a loved one. The dog was one of those jittery bug-eyed ones that always looked as if they were about to explode. Hostility. Suspicion. Stress. Daily facts of life. He'd had enough.

On the fourth floor, he got off the elevator, calling out a good-night that wasn't returned, and strode down the narrow cool hall. The second his key hit the lock of 4C, the door to the apartment across from his opened.

"Hey, Ryan." The soft throaty voice filled the hallway.

Christine. He turned and nearly dropped his key. *Christine?* Wearing the kind of negligee he'd only seen in the pages of Victoria's Secret catalogs.

Er, not that he ever wasted time looking at those. Of course.

"Hi, there." He suppressed his cave man reaction and grinned, glad to see a friendly familiar face after the strained evening. Christine would have been a welcome addition at dinner tonight. He'd bet she could have chatted easily with the Baxters, as she seemed to be able to do with everyone. The tone of the evening and the outcome would have been decidedly different. He'd probably still have a chance at their participation in the fund.

"Just home from work?" She hefted a small bag of trash, her apparent reason for being out in her nightgown. She worked in the office suite next to his firm's and had asked him six months ago, shortly after she started, if there were any vacancies in his building. He'd hesitated when the first one that came open was across the hall. Did he really want to invite a stranger he'd see fairly regularly at work to be his neighbor?

But something about Christine brought out his protective side—maybe that she was relatively new to the city and Manhattan could batter people who weren't used to it—and he'd given in. A few weeks later, she was his neighbor, and had proved to be as friendly and sweet as she seemed, with a knack for baking—and more importantly, sharing what she'd made—that made his eyes roll back into his head with pleasure.

His suburban-house fantasy crystalized. A harborside mansion in Southport, Connecticut. His lovely wife, Christine, not only at his side wining and dining clients, but beside him at home as well, the beautiful, gentle mother of his kids. The picture was pleasant, comfortable and logical. If her face weren't so innocent, the outfit—and the fact that she often appeared when he was either coming or going—would make him wonder if she'd had similar thoughts herself.

Maybe Fate had put her in his path tonight, when he'd been thinking about settling down.

"Yes, I'm just back. I had a dinner with prospective investors."

"Oh, how'd it go?" She appeared all wide-eyed interest and he managed to keep himself from visually exploring her generous cleavage, displayed by cream-colored material that looked delicate enough to snag on his hands. Her blond hair had been twisted up into a clip with just enough strands loose to make her look soft and vulnerable and…luscious.

Luscious? That was a new one where Christine was concerned. Everything about her seemed different tonight. Was it how she looked? Or how he was seeing her?

"It…went." He gave in and examined the negligee and the body in it, not at all sorry once he started. She was tall, five-seven or eight, with endless legs, one of his favorite female traits—physically speaking. "Did you wear that to work?"

She laughed, blushing, and clutched the semitransparent robe closer. "You caught me. I was hoping to sneak to the trash chute and back before anyone saw. I was trying to play it cool when you appeared, but frankly, I'm mortified."

He chuckled, and in deference to her discomfort, dragged his gaze reluctantly back to her eyes, hazel and luminous, looking at him with something primitive he'd never seen there before. His body reacted; he moved backward toward his door. He needed to think this through before he let his other brain take over. "I didn't mean to embarrass—"

"It's okay. Really." She spoke hurriedly and he stopped his retreat.

Was he nuts? Was she sending him a *yes, please* signal? Or was she only being her usual cordial self and her outfit had turned him into a testosterone-driven beast?

"Well, good night." He turned resolutely away, put his key in the lock, jiggled it slightly while twisting and opened his door. Dating someone who worked and lived so close to him could turn into disaster.

He kept the door open with his foot, reached in and flipped the light on in his entrance hall.

Or it could turn out great.

He'd gotten a pretty good sense of Christine over the past few months. He'd helped her out here and there, recommending restaurants, hardware stores, auto repair places, giving her directions and advice. He'd also helped with a few heavy-lifting and handyman chores in her apartment, which he had a feeling would have been done better by Fred Farbington, the building super. Several times they'd found themselves leaving the Graybar building at the same time on their lunch hours and had joined forces. He liked her. A lot. And with the sudden sexual zing in the air tonight, he wanted to get to know her better. A lot.

She didn't strike him as a complicated person, but far from dull, she seemed intelligent and ambitious, already earning herself a promotion at the insurance firm where she worked. And anyone who could move to Manhattan without knowing a soul and appear to thrive had strength in spades. As far as he could tell, there wasn't a mean-spirited bone in her body. She was calm, beautiful and elegant, but didn't come across as snobbish or—

Okay, he'd convinced himself.

He went back into the hall, found Christine at her door again, having gotten rid of her trash. "Christine."

"Yes?" She turned and smiled, not blushing this time,

not clutching the robe closed, and he saw again, more distinctly, that flash of awareness that she looked good and she knew he noticed and was glad he had.

Well, well. The fantasy house in Connecticut suddenly acquired a detailed master bedroom.

"Do you do any needlework?"

She laughed, a sudden nervous burst he didn't blame her for. She probably thought he'd lost it.

"What kind?"

"Tattooing, piercing...I want to get my nose done."

She started to look horrified and he grinned to show he was kidding. "I meant craft needlework."

"Oh." She put a hand to her chest and his eyes followed it enviously. "Sure. I used to sew a lot. I still knit occasionally, when someone in the family has a baby. I never did needlepoint or embroidery—"

"But you know what they are."

"Yes." She gave him a "you-feeling-okay?" look. "I know what they are."

"I could have used your help tonight."

"You're stuck on a knitting project?"

He laughed at her joke, feeling keyed up and happy, the way he always felt when a promising relationship was starting—though it had been well over a year and he'd had quite a few disappointments before this. His decision had made itself for him. "Have dinner with me tomorrow? Been a while since I had a good Thai meal. I'd like to share one of my favorite places with you."

She looked astonished at first, then her sincere delight made him feel as if he'd been crowned king of a small nation. "I'd love that, Ryan. Thank you."

"I'll knock at seven?"

"Perfect." She smiled again, and he watched her go

through her doorway, then pause and half turn as if she
wanted to say something or look back. She must have
changed her mind because she continued on and the door
swung slowly shut behind her.

Christine Bayer.

He lingered, staring across the hall, then went into his
own place and tossed his keys on the cherry table in the
foyer. Interesting. Unexpected. She'd been under his nose
all along, and he'd never really seen her as anything but a
friend. Okay, maybe a few times, he was a guy for Pete's
sake. But after tonight…

Christine could turn out to be not only what this evening
had needed. But what his life did as well.

CHRISTINE WAITED UNTIL the door to her apartment had
closed completely before she let her pleased smile widen
into a joyous grin that verged on outright laughter. Yes! Yes!
Yes!

She leaned back against the door and closed her eyes,
breathing fast, occasionally breaking into a giggle.

Ryan Masterson had just asked her out.

Finally! After six months of putting herself in his path,
of baking him treats, "bumping into him" time after time
in the hallway here or at work on her lunch hour, asking
for favors the odious building superintendent, Fred Farbington, would be only too happy to take care of, offering
to sew on buttons or pick up something for him at the
supermarket… In short, after gradually working them into
a comfortable friendship before she took the next step…

Well, she'd finally taken that next step.

You couldn't ambush men like Ryan Masterson,
tempting as it had been the first day she'd laid eyes on him
to say, "Hello, how are you? I'm Christine. How 'bout it?"

For one thing she might as well get in line. Men like Ryan weren't exactly a dime a dozen, and women definitely noticed. For another, the approach was too obvious, too easily ignored or rejected. Not to mention that if he did jump, it was too easy for him to jump away just as quickly.

Christine wasn't interested in one night or one month or one year with Ryan. She was all for giving forever a shot, and forever had to be approached with caution. Those fools who dived into forever without checking carefully first were in danger of banging their hearts on the bottom and becoming emotional quadriplegics.

The trick with a man like Ryan was to insinuate yourself into his life slowly, nearly imperceptibly, then just when he'd gotten used to having you around, when his brain no longer sounded the "possible female in pursuit of a relationship" alarm, then you pulled out the stops. Not all the stops all at once. Slowly, a bit at a time, one, then two, then the rest, before he even knew what hit him.

Like wearing the kind of negligee that made men weak from lack of blood to their brains. But not acting as if she'd worn it on purpose. No seduction intended, no, of course not. Far from it, she'd been caught on what was supposed to be a surreptitious sneak down the hall. Oops! She was so embarrassed!

Yes, it was sneaky and manipulative, but oh the ploy had worked. She couldn't even stand how terrified she'd been that it wouldn't. Putting on the negligee, putting on enough makeup to camouflage flaws but not seem made-up, looking herself over in the mirror, straining for the sound of his footsteps and his key…she'd been a wreck.

What if he stared at her, then laughed? What if he merely glanced her way and didn't react at all? What if he figured out what she was up to and the last six months of her painstaking groundwork—and their friendship—bit the dust?

She needn't have wasted all that energy worrying. The encounter had been perfect, down to the last detail. Maybe she should pinch herself to make sure she was awake this time. Last night, she'd dreamed the scene again—only it had turned into a nightmare with Ryan morphing into her geeky sixth grade science teacher and then into Fred the super, overweight, balding, blue-collar, the near perfect opposite of her dream man.

This hadn't been a dream. Ryan had been exactly as she'd fantasized him so many times—friendly, at first, and then when what she was wearing hit him…more than friendly. His eyes had darkened, taken on an intensity that—

Well, her heart was still pogo-sticking in her chest. Lord have mercy, was he sexy. Tall, way-masculine and fabulously built—the kind of guy that felt like a fortress around you in bed. Dark hair he tried to keep in a corporate-conservative style, but which kept escaping into a casual tousled mess across his forehead. Blue eyes that delivered heat or cool, depending on what mood he was in.

Don't even get her started on how he looked weekend mornings, rumpled and unshaven, sometimes bare-chested, body stunningly muscled, picking up the paper on his doorstep.

She could lock herself in her refrigerator for an hour and not cool down by so much as a degree.

As if that weren't enough? Pardon her for putting it right out there, but…he wasn't exactly hurting financially. She had a very good job here, yet she was barely meeting the rent in this building after paying less than half this for a tiny dump in Queens. She hadn't been able to furnish this place worth a damn. But it was important to be close to him, especially since her firm was moving early next month so she'd no longer bump into him at the office. Everything and anything she'd had to finagle for the sake of landing Ryan Masterson was worth it.

So far her plan was going perfectly. If she didn't screw it up, and the miracle she so desperately wanted really came to pass—mercy, she could barely think about it without getting dizzy—maybe soon she wouldn't have to pay rent at all.

She laughed again and came away from the door, feeling as if she could float around her apartment. That miracle was so huge and so precious and so out-there, she didn't like to dwell on it. No point setting herself up for devastating disappointment. She'd plan and celebrate one small step and one small victory at a time.

The phone rang, and she drifted dreamily toward it, imagining Ryan's deep voice. *I can't wait until tomorrow, care to come over for a nightcap now? Don't bother changing....*

"Chris?"

Fred. Her fantasy burst and splatted on the lush grey carpet. He persisted in using the short form of her name even though she'd corrected him countless times. Thank goodness he hadn't come up with "Teeny," the nickname her family and friends used in Georgia.

"This is *Christine.*" She chilled her voice enough to freeze nitrogen.

"Got your new showerhead. Thought I'd come put it in now."

"Now?" She gave the phone an incredulous look before she put it back to her ear. "It's nearly nine-thirty. Don't you ever take time off?"

"Aw, you're sweet to worry."

"I wasn't—"

"I'm a hard-working man, you know that. Building full of tenants I gotta keep happy."

"I'd rather you came during the day." *When I'm not home.*

"Can't do that. This is a special favor to you—on my own time."

Her stomach lurched. She did not want to be indebted to Fred Farbington.

"Right now isn't convenient, how about…" Inspiration. "Tomorrow night?"

"Tomorrow night it is."

"Excellent." She felt like giggling. She'd be out with Ryan. *With Ryan!* "Thank you."

"Anytime, Chris."

Christine. She punched off the phone disgustedly. Maybe if she started calling him Frederick he'd get the message.

Eight steps to her dining room and the bottle of Early Times she kept on a rickety table found on the curb. She poured herself a shot and downed it as if she were trying to wash out the taste of Fred, then poured herself another and raised it in a toast to her success tonight—to her and Ryan—before downing that one, too.

Three more steps toward her living room, and she paused in front of a print of one of her favorite paintings, *Lovers Over the City* by Marc Chagall. The picture was cheerful, colorful. In the foreground a round table with a meal set on a red-checked tablecloth. In the background, a romantic hilltop city with distinctive tiled orange roofs. And in the upper left-hand corner the lovers, colored passionate red, facing each other improbably astride a huge bird.

The symbolism and the message were probably deeper than anything she could get. She just liked the picture. She liked to imagine the bird's immense wings beating, carrying the lovers in effortless flight. She liked the woman's hand on her lover's chest, his suggestively touching her hips.

Was he flying her to the hilltop city, away from their meal? Or whisking her away from the city and to the private bliss of a lovers' picnic? Or bringing her the world on some global journey, and this was just a snapshot of their travels? She didn't know. She didn't even know why the picture called to her so strongly.

She'd seen it the first time on a school trip to the library. Mrs. Chandler, who'd ended up as Christine's mentor and had encouraged her in a way her parents wouldn't have known how to do, had shown it to the class. The kids had laughed at the big bird and the red people. Christine had laughed, too, but that night she'd dreamed for the first time of flying away from the too-small, too-crowded house, out of Charsville and out of Georgia forever.

The print was the first thing she'd bought when she got her first paycheck in New York, even though she had no room for luxury purchases. But here she was, out of Charsville and out of Georgia, and if luck kept going her way and Ryan fell in love with her, the forever part would come true, too.

She touched the couple lovingly, imagining Ryan's hands at her hips, hers at his magnificent chest. He was everything she'd ever wanted. If they worked out, she'd have security, respectability, a stable family life, children who'd have enough to eat every day of the year and double on holidays, who'd own whatever kind of sneakers and dresses and toys they wanted—within reasonable limits, of course. More than that, she'd have Ryan.

Christine had overcome a lot of challenges in her life. Been the first in her family to attend college and graduate, the first to leave Georgia, the first to tackle a big city. But now at twenty-seven, she'd be the last in the family to get married, the last to have those children her brothers and sisters had been popping out for years.

Ryan was among the toughest challenges she'd ever faced. But that was fine; she still had time to win him over. Anyone as amazing as Ryan Masterson was plenty worth waiting for.

And, unless Christine was letting her fantasy run too far away with her, if the look in Ryan's eyes this evening had been anything to go by, she wouldn't have to wait much longer.

2

"THE SINS OF WOMEN are many." Jenny Hartmann raised her voice. "Repeat after me, 'Jenny, I have sinned.'"

The ninety-nine percent female crowd at the Marcus Center for the Performing Arts in downtown Milwaukee boomed out a delighted response. "Jenny, I have sinned."

"I have sinned the sin of making myself too available to men. I have kept weekend evenings open in case they want to see me, I have stayed off the phone in case it rings—" she waited a beat "—even if I have call-waiting."

Laughter from the crowd.

"Yes, Jenny, I have!" shouted a voice.

"Confession. One of our sisters has made a confession here." She raised her hand in the general direction of the voice. "Forgiveness is yours! Next time go out and have your own fun, girlfriend. Live your life as if it's your only chance, because 'men' is not the answer to the question, 'Who are we?' 'Men' is not the answer to the question, 'What do we need?' and 'men' is not the answer to the question, 'Who can we become?'"

The crowd cheered. Pumped to the max, Jenny strutted stage left in sky-high-heeled pink sandals, clutching the mike she'd yanked from its stand ten seconds after she started speaking.

It was glorious when her lectures went like this, when

the crowd was with her, when her adrenaline was at its helpful best instead of its crippling worst.

"'Jenny, I have sinned.' Say it." She waited until they were done, wiping sweat off her forehead with a pink and black sequin-bordered handkerchief that matched her cami lace top. "I have sinned the sin of changing my plans, changing my hair, changing my body, changing my life to suit my man or the man I want or the man I imagine I'll meet someday. Say it with me, ladies, one more time, 'I have *sinned.*'"

The crowd chanted enthusiastically, "I. Have. *Sinned.*"

"I have sinned the sin of putting up with questionable sexual technique and I have not said what I wanted instead. I have faked orgasms to avoid teaching my man about what my body needs."

Nervous laughter and a shout, "You go, Jenny."

"I have sinned that most vile and evil of all sins— basing my self-worth on whether I have a man to call boyfriend or lover or husband. I have sinned by feeling attractive only when a man finds me attractive, feeling witty and charming and sexual and worthwhile as a member of the female race only when a man finds me so."

Roars from the crowd and applause. Jenny laughed, breathless, striking a strong-legged raised-arm pose, while tears came to her eyes. It was so good to reach out to women like this and have them reach right back. "Well, I'll tell you, ladies. I will tell you…"

She waited. The crowd went quiet except for occasional shouts of encouragement.

"It's time to ask yourself…. What…? What…?" She held the microphone up high and gestured to the crowd to continue.

"What have I done for me lately?" The words were a blast that rocked the huge auditorium.

"Oh yeah!" She applauded for them. "I hear you, you know it! What have you done for yourselves lately? When was the last time you arranged to learn about something new that interested you? When was the last time you traveled somewhere you'd always wanted to go even if he didn't? Or stopped somewhere for dinner on the spur of the moment because you deserved not to cook that night? Bought something you didn't need but always wanted? Told your man you were going to take a spa day every other weekend just because you felt like it? Add up those golf days and football days and see if you didn't earn at least that much. More importantly, when was the last time you stood up for yourself when it was easier and more convenient to sacrifice your rights or needs or desires to someone else's?

"It's time to assign our self-worth back to ourselves, where it belongs. It's time to get angry. Not at men. At ourselves. At the way we've allowed them to run our relationships and our lives. We have the strength. We have plenty of power. It's time to use it."

The end of her sentence was barely audible over the wave of exalted sound.

"Now, ladies, answer me this. Do we love men?"

"*Yes,*" the crowd boomed.

"Hell, yes. Do we need men?"

"*No.*"

"Hell, no—do we *want* men?"

"Yes!"

"Mmm, you bet we do." She did a brief bump and grind that made hoots fill the theater. "God made those glorious naughty male parts for us and only us, and we are proud and happy to make use of them, aren't we, girls?"

If she thought the roars had been overwhelming before, they were extraordinary now, revved up with laughter and fresh applause. "We do so for our own pleasure as well as theirs. We do so because we love the men attached to those naughty male parts, yes, but also because we love ourselves first and have decided they are worthy of us."

"Amen, sister Jenny," a voice shouted. "You the woman!"

"We are *all* the woman," Jenny called back. The atmosphere in the auditorium was warm, hearty estrogen soup for the soul. "We are *all* the woman."

While the laughter and clapping died down, she wiped her forehead again and smoothed her tight black skirt, gathering her thoughts for the final section of the lecture. "Women of Wisconsin, let me give you *my* confession here tonight. Before I wrote this book, I, too, was a sinner."

Gasps from the crowd, many of whom must have read *What Have I Done for Me Lately?* so they already knew what she was going to say, but she loved them for playing along so enthusiastically. "I dressed the way my man wanted, spoke the way my man wanted, ate the things he thought I should eat. And when one day I came home and his bare ass was doing the shimmy over another woman's body, did I realize what a fool I'd been and what a fool he was and toss the baggage out?"

"Yes!" From someone who obviously hadn't read the book.

"No." She shook her head forlornly. "No, I didn't. I collapsed. I crumbled. My world caved. My life was over. This was my fault—my failing and my general repulsiveness as a human being."

"Nooo! Booo!" The crowd went nuts. Jenny grinned and let them have fun for a while.

"And then one day I lifted my blotchy face from the pillow of misery and I said, 'Wait a second. Just wait one second here. This is not my fault. My only failing was in choosing a guy who was not, as it turned out, Prince Charming, but a tyrant emperor who slaughtered my self-esteem in the name of love.' That I let him do that was my gravest sin of all, the Original Sin of womanhood.

"But I did not fail in the end. I succeeded. In getting him out of my life and getting over him and in knowing that never again…" She held up a finger and waited until the auditorium went quiet so she could lower her voice. "Never again will a man dictate anything about me or about my life. I'll make my choices and my mistakes and live my life for myself. And if I can't find a man strong enough and deep enough and smart enough to take me as I am, then I'll live it *by* myself, too."

More cheers, interminable cheers, cheers that brought more tears to her eyes and a huskiness to her voice she had to clear before she could speak again.

"'Men' is not the answer to the questions, 'Who are we? What do we need? Who can we become?' Nor does 'men' ever answer the question, 'What have I done for *me* lately?'" She backed up a few steps and lifted her face to the white, hot lights. "I wrote my book, then I started to *live* my book. Because it had been so long since I'd done anything that wasn't engineered someway, somehow, to please my man, who was never, ever pleased. The more he wasn't pleased, the harder I tried. Girlfriends, if you find yourself in that cycle, you have got to get yourselves out. Out! Or you'll get so dizzy and sick chasing the version of you that he wants, you will never have the chance to catch up to your real self. Only by becoming whole vibrant exciting women *for* ourselves will we finally get the love we're meant to have, the love we truly deserve."

She waited a few beats, skipped downstage and gave a

big cheerful wave. "Thank you very much, and a special thanks to the Women of Note lecture series for inviting me here. Good night, Milwaukee! I love you!"

She gave a quick bow, and strode off the stage, over-whelmed by the booming cheers and chants of, "Jen-ny, Jen-ny, Jen-ny."

Four more bows later, blowing kisses, opening her arms wide, then putting her hands to her heart, the crowd finally quieted, and the sound of seats flapping up, rustling programs and normal-voiced conversations replaced the applause. Backstage, Jenny gulped a glass of water prof-fered by the stage manager, who refilled it so she could gulp it again. "Whoo! Thank you. Man, it was hot out there."

"You were sensational!" Gwen, the sweet middle-aged president of Women of Note, gave her a long hug. "I haven't heard the audience that excited for a long time. You really had them."

"Hey, thanks." Jenny mopped at her forehead again, and laughed, energy still rushing so strongly through her it had to come out somehow. "The crowd was the best. I had a blast."

"It showed." Gwen smiled, looking down at the hot pink sandals on Jenny's feet. "By the way, I meant to tell you how much I love those shoes."

"Designer knockoffs. I got them at a discount outlet for thirty-nine ninety-five. No lie. Get yourself a pair."

"Oh, I couldn't."

"Why not?" Jenny looked at her, direct, challenging. "If you like them so much, why not?"

A flush of pink only slightly less loud than the sandals tinged Gwen's generally pale face. "Oh, but, I don't wear...shoes like that."

"Then start." Jenny grinned. "That's how it was for me. I just started. Felt like a complete imposter for a few weeks, and ended up growing into them. Trust me, if you love them, then you have a hot-pink-sandal-wearing person caged inside you, too. All you have to do is let her out!"

"Oh, gosh." Gwen's blush deepened. "My husband would—"

She clapped her hand over her mouth. Jenny winked. "I heard nothing. Buy the shoes and enjoy them. Next time I'm in Milwaukee I'll call you and we can go out on the town in them together. Okay?"

Gwen nodded doubtfully once, then more firmly. "Okay. Are you ready to eat? You must be hungry."

"Famished. I think I sweated off twenty pounds. Let me shower and change and I'll be right out."

Dinner was the usual loud and fun affair after one of her lectures. Great food at a place called Eagans—she'd eaten in so many places in so many cities over the past six months she could hardly keep track—with women stopping by her table to tell their stories, confess their "sins" or ask her to sign their copies of *What Have I Done for Me Lately?*

She still couldn't get over how this had all happened. One month she'd been a bank teller and Paul's fiancée. The next, she was single, living with her friend and roommate in college, Jessica, writing the book in an angry rush on nights and weekends while Jessica cheered her on. Some of the anger was directed at Paul, who had treated her so badly and cheated on her, but most of the anger she aimed at herself. How had she not seen this train wreck coming? How had she allowed herself to became so passive that Paul had cheated on her just to ease his boredom? She couldn't blame him completely. Partly, sure, she had no problem with partly. Or even mostly.

The sick irony of course was that *he'd* made her into that passive woman. Telling her what to wear, what to eat, what to say. Not outright, she wasn't that weak. But subtly. "Wow, three of those cookies has twelve grams of fat," as she was stuffing the fifth one into her mouth. "Sure, we can go to the movies tonight. Of course there's an oldie on TV I was wanting to see." "I like that dress. Or there's that red one you look so much skinnier in." Criticizing her conversation at parties, answering "no" automatically for both of them when waitstaff offered a predinner cocktail or dessert.

Through it all, she sat, bump on a log, smiling graciously, pathetically eager to please, insisting she was madly in love, letting him make her over into a spiritless, mindless Paul-reflection.

Not until she'd been without him a few weeks did it start to dawn on her how insidious their relationship had been, and how creepy that his control of her had felt so safe. And if this disaster had happened to her, a college-educated, upper middle-class woman from the liberal northeast, there must be others by the tens of thousands.

If her nearly seven-figure book sales were anything to go by, she'd vastly underestimated that number.

When the manuscript was finished, Jessica had shown it to a girlfriend who had a literary agent friend. Nothing would ever change Jenny's life so radically, she was sure, as the day that agent called saying Xantham Press wanted to buy her book. Jenny had barely even comprehended what she was saying, let alone been able to foresee the changes in store for her life and for herself.

Having her book published, having her words mean so much to so many women…it validated her existence and her worth in a way Paul could never even have begun to understand. More amazingly, she hadn't really understood how much she'd needed it, either. With that nurturing, freeing validation she had blossomed into the kind of person she'd always dreamed of being, wearing what she wanted, saying what she liked, doing what she pleased. Growing up shy and overlooked in a country club town of beautiful people, she never would have seen herself evolving this far in a hundred years.

Unfortunately, her publisher very understandably wanted a follow-up book, to keep her—and them—riding the wave. But writing a book that had poured out of her in an extended fit of passion and in a need to document her pain was very different from sitting down on purpose and conjuring something up. Her next book was tentatively titled *Jenny's Guide to Getting What You Want*.

What Jenny wanted was to be able to write the book. Three chapters lay on her desk, as they'd lain for the better part of the last year, each page practically red from all the revisions and crossouts and edits….

In short, the book wasn't happening. Her regular online advice column and the occasional pieces she wrote for women's magazines presented no problem. They were satisfying and fun even if they were only rehashes of *What Have I Done for Me Lately?* So maybe this would be it for her, a one-shot wonder. Better to have shot once than never to have shot at all was how she'd decided to look at it, though she wasn't sure her publisher agreed.

After dessert at Eagans—she always ordered dessert now, without Paul to give her The Disapproving Look—she thanked her hostesses warmly and, declining their offer of a ride, walked the few blocks down Water Street to the Wyndham Hotel, enjoying the chilly night breeze off Lake Michigan on her still-heated face.

Up in her room, she went into her antihyper routine, to calm herself down after the rush and excitement of a lecture/performance so she'd have some hope of falling asleep. First, the deep warm bath, then lavish amounts of perfumed powder and lotion so she smelled way too strong, then the bright coral silk teddy she adored, the kind Paul thought made her hips look big, and a long, leisurely emptying of a cup of herbal tea in bed reading the *New York Times*. Not that news was always restful, but fiction risked bringing on the can't-put-it-down syndrome, and she'd never had a problem dropping the paper when sleep overwhelmed her.

Halfway through a front section so full of natural and political and man-made disasters she was starting to get depressed, she rolled her eyes and picked up the Sunday Styles section. Nothing could be more soporific than that. A few pages of wedding and engagement announcements and grinning rich people at fund-raisers should put her right off to dreamland.

Tomorrow she'd be on a plane back home to New York, arriving in time for a lunch date with her agent, then she and Jessica were going to the Metropolitan Art Museum to see—

Jenny gasped, sat bolt upright and held the paper closer. Oh. My. God. Oh my god. Omigod.

Ryan Masterson.

Ryan Masterson.

Only he didn't look like Ryan Masterson. He looked like…she wrinkled her nose and peered at the awkwardly smiling tuxedoed image. Ryan Masterson's boring twin brother.

Was this what Wild Boy Masterson had turned into? Geez o Pete, was nothing sacred? The sexiest rebel alive reduced to posing at some society event with Frumpy Dame So-and-so and Squeaky Debutante This-'n'-that?

Had hell, in fact, frozen over?

She couldn't stand it. What a waste.

And yet…okay, he wasn't twenty-one anymore. Being wild and angry was hot as hell in high school and college, but she supposed it wouldn't help in the career department.

Imagine the résumé: Exceptionally skilled at sullen smoldering looks and general bad attitude. Expert in alcohol consumption and high-speed motorcycle operation. Some experience with mild street drug use. Unpredictable outbursts available upon request. Vast experience in seduction of women, including one shy straightlaced girl from Southport, Connecticut, who had never forgotten a second of their time together….

Jenny's rapturous sigh trailed off. But of course *he* had probably forgotten, most of it anyway. Before that summer when they'd both been home from college—she from Tufts and he from UC Berkeley—he'd undoubtedly thought of her only as the daughter of his widowed mom's friend from down the street. She'd thought he was way hot, like every other breathing female that saw him, and made herself sick with nerves every time their families got together—his family being a loud, out-of-control one with six kids and an always stunned-looking mother; hers consisting of her and her parents, jovial, but reservedly so, warm, loving…quiet. Jenny and Ryan had overlapped two years at Fairfield High, but they hadn't acknowledged each other as more than familiar faces passing in the hall, though once in her sophomore year he'd made a point of complimenting her performance in *Brigadoon* and she'd nearly hyperventilated. That was it.

Why he'd turned to her of all people… Maybe at such a turbulent time he'd needed someone rock-solid predictable and not at all challenging.

Jenny lay back, holding up the picture of his staid, respectable face, bland smile in place for the camera. If his name hadn't been under the photo, she wouldn't have believed…

He was extraordinarily good-looking, no question. She'd bet heads still turned. But not like before. Not like when he strode around the village of Southport, Connecticut, looking like a savage bomb that could go off any second.

Not like the night a month or so after the motorcycle accident that killed his best friend, when he came to her house while her parents were away, pale and haunted, soaked by the rainstorm he'd been walking through, dark hair hanging over his forehead, blue eyes glowing behind the clumped strands.

On her doorstep, he'd mumbled something she hadn't heard. She'd let him in anyway, and he'd stopped next to her, fixed her with an angry pleading look she'd never forget, and to her total rapturous shock, he'd kissed her. Not a sweet peck, not a gentle "may I?" kiss, not the soulless kisses Paul had given her. But a hot, hard rush of a kiss. A kiss she measured all subsequent kisses against.

That night and many nights after, in the park by Southport harbor, in cars, on the country club golf course, on the beach by Long Island Sound, she'd let him use her body to rid himself of his rage and his guilt over his friend Mitch's death. She'd never told anyone, not about the visits, not about the sex, not about the way he'd cried in her arms after.

She'd just wanted to heal him. And then, sweet, ignorant, impressionable girl that she'd been, she'd fallen in love.

Jenny tossed the paper aside. Right. Love. Who knew anything about love at age nineteen? It was a crush, that's all, born of his appeal and the thrill of being the one he'd picked out in his time of grief, the last girl anyone would have expected, least of all her. Predictably, the night she'd finally given voice to her feelings, he'd run. Far, fast and into someone else's arms. No big surprise, though it had hurt like hell anyway.

She picked up the paper again, as if he still had the ability to draw her, after all these years, even as an image on newsprint. What did Ryan Masterson now think of what he'd been?

And what would he think of what shy, sweet Jenny Hartmann had become?

3

"TELL ME ABOUT your childhood."

"Oh." Christine smiled at Ryan over the white-cloth-covered restaurant table and stalled with a sip of beer. She preferred white wine, but he'd made some comment about Thai food killing any chance a wine had, and she couldn't very well order it after that. "Charsville, Georgia. Southwest corner of the state, not far from the Alabama border. I guess you knew that already."

"I did, yes."

He looked at her expectantly and she kept smiling, searching for what to say next. He'd told her about his childhood, mostly pleasant impersonal facts, though she got the feeling all had not been rosy, even in such privileged surroundings. Maybe he'd tell her the whole truth someday, as she would tell him hers. But not today. Charsville was an entirely different world from Southport, Connecticut. You could count the number of wealthy on no fingers. People didn't live large there, they grew up, married, had kids, grew old and died. She didn't want to give Ryan any chance to think she wasn't good enough for him.

"It was a safe, quiet, wholesome place to grow up." As long as you didn't venture out when the Dargin brothers had been drinking. "People didn't lock their doors, kids hung out at the Dip-Delite ice cream and candy store, and everyone knew everyone else's business."

She gave a laugh as if the last was a quaint and lovely trait, whereas she'd found it a suffocating junior high existence.

Ryan was listening politely, but watching her with a blue-eyed intensity that unnerved and excited her at the same time. What was he thinking?

If she had her way, he'd be thinking thoughts that had nothing to do with her childhood past and everything to do with her womanhood and her future. Especially because being across the table like this for so long, she'd barely been able to keep herself from imagining their first kiss, though she doubted it would happen tonight. But maybe soon? They'd had a nice time so far, talking easily, laughing together and sharing food.

Or was he wondering why he'd asked her out in the first place, this small-town girl from nowhere with nothing of real substance to say? Should she embellish her life? Beef up her education from a two-year degree earned in four years to a four-year degree earned in two? Casually drop some mention of her mom's catering business and her dad's club? Ryan would picture elegant cocktail parties, pools and golf courses—things he could relate to. He didn't need to know Vera Bayer threw kids' birthday parties, and that the pool at Dick Bayer's men's club involved cues and drunken betting.

No. She'd keep to the bare-minimum truth. Any false picture she painted would come crashing down when he met her parents.

"What kind of girl were you?"

"Shy. Lonely. A dreamer." With iron determination driving her life. "But I knew what I wanted."

"Which was?"

"To leave Charsville, live in New York and see the world someday." *And marry someone exactly like you.*

"Why New York?"

"After small-town living?" She lifted her eyebrows, thinking no other answer was needed, but he still seemed to be waiting for an explanation. "The bigger the better as far as I was concerned. But L.A. has earthquakes, and Cairo and Tokyo were too far away and exotic for me."

"Makes sense." He nodded seriously where she expected him to laugh. Was it her imagination or did he look disappointed? What had she said? What was wrong with loving New York?

"So I came here." She forced herself to calm down. Ryan could undoubtedly live anywhere in the world he wanted, so he must love the Big Apple, too.

"I'm getting tired of the city." He picked up his beer and tipped it absently back and forth, staring at the shifting liquid. "I've been thinking it's time to move on, maybe back to Connecticut. I'm thinking of looking at houses in Southport or Fairfield."

Dang, darn, hell and damnation. How was she going to get herself out of this one? It would be so nice when her time with Ryan no longer felt like a job interview.

"Well." She gave a laugh that, thank the lord, didn't betray her dismay. "I was *just* going to say, now that I've lived here even this short while, I've been thinking I didn't know myself all that well wanting to come here. But I thought I should give Manhattan a year at least, before I did anything I'd regret."

"Very sensible." He nodded slowly, eyeing her speculatively over his glass. "Would you like to go back to a smaller town someday, to settle permanently?"

"Oh, yes." Sweet Jesus. Was she dreaming? "Definitely."

"Back to Georgia?" He seemed anxious about her response.

"Oh, no. Not Georgia." She beamed, her heart enjoying a Texas two-step. "I'd feel like I failed if I went back."

"I understand." The tension left his face; he lifted his beer across the table, eyes warm. "Here's to a new future for both of us."

"To a new future." *Together.* She clinked her glass with his, wanting to shout a few rounds of her sister Iona's favorite cheer: *"Hey, go, go, go, hey, go. Charsville Chiefs...hey go!"* Unless she was wrong, she, Teeny Bayer, was under consideration for the position of Mrs. Settle Down In Connecticut.

Please don't let me blow it.

The waiter came to clear their plates and returned with the check, which he put on the table between them. Should Christine offer to pay? Some men were insulted—as if the woman thought he wasn't capable of taking care of her. On the other hand, if she wanted to keep the "friends" pretense up, she should probably not assume Ryan had planned to take her out.

She reached for her purse at the same time he slapped a credit card on top of the bill and shook his head at her. "My treat tonight."

Tonight? As if there would be others? She withdrew her hand from her purse and beamed at him. "Thank you, Ryan. The meal was delicious."

"My pleasure."

And there they were, smiling at each other across the table, and warm joy started flooding Christine's body and her heart. His pleasure. Ohh, she'd love to show him pleasure of all kinds. Pleasure at the front door welcoming him home, pleasure in the kitchen eating the dinner she cooked and pleasure in the bedroom later that night.

One step at a time, Christine.

The waiter brought back Ryan's receipt; Ryan thanked him and shoved it into his wallet. "Ready?"

"Yes." She got to her feet, hoping her yellow linen sheath didn't have too many horizontal wrinkles across her lap, and picked up her purse, even more pleased when he waited for her to precede him out of the restaurant. The last guy she dated had been in such a New York hurry all the time, he'd rush off without even glancing to see if she'd followed. The day she met Ryan, she'd ended that relationship, which was going nowhere in that same New York hurry.

Out on the sidewalk, they strolled along 14th Street. Christine forced her feet, which wanted to skip, to keep a slow, even pace. Strolling meant Ryan intended to prolong the evening. He hadn't hustled her into a taxi, or fled down the sidewalk so she could barely keep up. Strolling was another good sign in an evening that had already been full of them.

They passed a street musician playing a saxophone, and stores with bins of perfect produce laid out on the sidewalk stands. She loved New York, especially at night. The energy, the lights, the natives out enjoying their city. She loved feeling part of something so huge and so important and so vital to the world. If she and Ryan worked out, she hoped Ryan would want to come into the city often after they left.

"I'm curious about something."

"Mmm?" She imbued her voice with a touch of sensuality and was rewarded out of the corner of her eye with the sight of him turning to look at her. She made sure she appeared calm and peaceful.

"You grew up in Georgia. What happened to your accent?"

"I lost it on the way here." She did turn then, to smile at him. "Somewhere over Virginia."

Her accent had been disposed of deliberately, starting when she was a girl, imitating TV or movie personalities, practicing over and over in her favorite spot, a copse near a stream a short way from home. A place where she could escape two brothers and three sisters and two parents and the all-too-frequent visiting aunts, uncles and cousins, and have room and quiet to think her own thoughts and dream her own dreams. She'd even taught herself rudimentary French from books and tapes she'd gotten from the library, to be ready for the trip she'd someday take to Paris.

She always knew she'd come north to live—New York or Boston or Chicago—because she didn't belong in a small Southern town and never would. And she'd wanted to fit in here from the start, not be pegged as an outsider the second she opened her mouth.

"Let me hear it."

"Hear what?"

"Your accent."

Christine rolled her eyes. "Why sugah, whatevah for?"

He laughed and swayed toward her so they bumped shoulders, which felt as intimate as a kiss on this crowded beautiful city street.

Way too soon they got back to Bank Street and inside their building, to the familiar smell of wood and carpet and a faint whiff of cleaner. Way too soon the elevator ride was over, their walk down the hall finished in front of their two doors.

"Good night, Ryan. Thank you for a really fun time." Christine smiled warmly and took a step back toward her apartment so he wouldn't think she was angling for a kiss, though frankly, she'd like nothing else right at that moment. His lips were as appealing and sexual as the rest of him. Sharply defined, slightly full, but not at all feminine. The kind of lips that would leave you no doubt whatsoever that you were being kissed.

She looked forward to experiencing that, and how. But while men might say they liked a woman who took charge of the physical pace of a relationship, and maybe they did for a time, those weren't the women they took home to meet Mom. Those weren't the women they settled with in Connecticut. Deep down in the cave-man depths of their DNA, men wanted power and control firmly on their side.

She could live with that. Even if it meant saying goodnight tonight starved for more of him.

"I enjoyed it, too." He put his hands on his hips and studied her, appearing taller and broader in the low-ceilinged narrow hallway. "Are you free Wednesday next week? My oldest sister lives in the city and can't use a pair of ballet tickets. Would you like to go? It's *Romeo and Juliet.*"

"Next Wednesday…" She frowned, trying not to show her delight. As if she would possibly say no. She'd postpone emergency surgery to spend time with him. "I *think* that would be fine. I'll run in and check and call you in a few minutes. Is that okay?"

"Sure." He smiled and lifted a hand. "Talk to you soon."

"Soon." She let herself into her apartment and gave herself an enthusiastic thumbs-up. Perfect. Not only had he asked her out for a specific day instead of the dreaded, "Let's do this again sometime" which meant never in this life, but she'd engineered it so they'd get to have a phone conversation tonight. She could speak to him in the seductive tones she'd wanted to use all evening, but where the relative anonymity and physical distance would make it safer—and more tantalizing. There was something so intimate about not being able to see—

She stopped abruptly, her dreamy mood shocked out of her.

Fred.

"Hey, Chris." He rose from his chair—*her* chair—and his short stocky frame made the admittedly cheap wood creak. "How goes it?"

"What in heaven's name are you doin' here?" Her accent came out as it always did when she got upset, which made her even more upset.

"You told me to come tonight."

"It's ten o'clock!"

"Isn't that right?" He stared at her, dark eyes curious under lashes most women would kill for. "You look beautiful in yellow. Good date, huh? You came in all misty-eyed."

"I did not. And it's none of your business how my date went."

He shrugged balefully and mumbled something that sounded like, "I wish it was," which she ignored.

"I fixed your shower. Thought you'd like to take a look at it while I was here, so if there was anything you didn't like I could change it for you."

"So you've been here in my apartment? Waiting for me?"

"Who else would I be waiting for?"

She sighed. *All right, Christine.* Fred had done her a nice favor on his own time. She'd been afraid to ask Ryan for too much help, in case he figured she was totally helpless or figured out why she was asking so often, but she'd been unable to get the old showerhead off so she could install the new one, a handheld model with a massager she'd gotten from the hardware store clearance bin. Fred, of course, had been more than happy to help. And while he was puppy-dog eager every time he was around her, he didn't strike her as creepy or dangerous, so she'd do well to be kind to him, if for no other reason than that she might need another favor someday.

"Lead the way." She followed him into her bathroom, where the gleaming new white-and-silver unit sat happily in its bracket. "It looks fine. Thank you."

"Wait, check it out." He pulled down the showerhead and turned on the water, demonstrating the five different settings.

Christine watched, barely curbing her impatience. This much she could have figured out on her own. She wanted to call Ryan. "That will be so nice. I can't wait to use it."

He turned off the water and threw her a look as if he were happily imagining that very thing. "He good to you?"

"What?"

"The guy you were with. He nice to you? Polite? Try anything you didn't like?"

"No." She shook her head rapidly. Was he going to talk all night? "Nothing like that."

"Good. You ever have trouble with any guy, you call me, understand?"

She bristled. "I appreciate the offer, but I can take care of myself."

"No." He slid the showerhead back into its bracket. "Not you."

"*Pardon me?*" She wished she had the showerhead back to brain him with.

"Not you." He had the nerve to shake his head with utter certainty, feet planted, beefy arms folded across his broad chest. "There's plenty of women in this city that can take care of themselves. You're not one of 'em."

"You…" She started breathing too fast. To hell with the showerhead, give her a crowbar. "I am not like that. How can you—"

"A woman like you…" He took a step toward her, his

voice low and gravelly. She stood her ground, itching to move back. This close his eyes were level with hers and the intense way he was staring at her made her desperate to look away. "A woman like you needs a man."

Not you. She lurched away from him and stumbled. He grabbed her arm with strength that astounded her and held tight to keep her from falling.

"I gotcha."

"Let go." He was holding her way too close. And she was registering with confusion that he smelled honest and soapy clean and comforting.

There was something obscene about this coarse man— barely taller than she was, half-bald and older by a decade at least—smelling so appealing.

Of course, Ryan wore the most amazingly sexy cologne she'd ever had the pleasure of coming into contact with. One of these days she'd still be able to smell it on her clothes and body after a date. One day soon.

"Look, Chris." Fred's voice gentled further from its usual rough heartiness. She tried to pull away, but she got the impression he wouldn't let go until it was *his* idea to, and she didn't have the strength to object. "I wasn't trying to make a move on you or do anything you don't want. I would never do that. You got nothing to be afraid of. You get me?"

She nodded, wanting him out of her apartment, and preferably out of her life as soon as possible.

"Okay." He released her arm. "I'm real sorry I scared you."

"It's fine." Her breath was dropping back to normal and she was starting to feel foolish. "I'm fine."

"Good." He indicated she should precede him out of the bathroom, but she would have had to snuggle her rear right by his groin in the narrow space, so she shook her head and gestured him out first. To her relief he went. Out of the bathroom, good. Through the living room, good. All good progress toward his exit.

Finally, she could call Ryan, who must be thinking she was—

"I brought you something."

"What? You what?" She faced him irritably in her living room, wanting to be alone with her phone call, which she now wouldn't be able to do as sexy-perfect as she wanted because this little man had gotten her all riled up.

"I brought you something." He'd retrieved a package from somewhere—she hadn't noticed it when she'd come in—crudely wrapped in a plastic shopping bag and tied with a crumpled red ribbon.

She had no clue what to say. He was bringing her *gifts* now? Where was this going to end? How many times could she clearly not be interested before he went away? If he was going to become a problem she might have to speak to Ryan.

Or, of course, she already had Fred's offer to deal with any guy who was bothering her. Maybe he could beat himself up.

The idea made her smile just as Fred was handing her the gift. Of course he thought that smile meant she was thrilled he'd gotten her something, which was the last message she wanted to send.

She glanced at her watch and sighed. Ryan would think she wasn't interested by now. She'd have to tell him she'd gotten another call, or—

"I know it's late. You can open it tomorrow. No big deal."

The look on his face said it was a huge deal, and Christine couldn't bear to be that rude. She wearily began to pick at the knots in the ribbon.

"Here." Fred's big hands came into her range of

vision, holding a knife that jerked up through the thin red line and snapped it in a way that made her have to work to control a shudder.

She slipped her hand into the bag, praying it was nothing that cost more than five dollars, and pulled the package out.

Mercy. It had cost a dollar fifty-nine when she was a girl with her own allowance, maybe double that by now. A tin of Grebner's pecan praline cookies, made in Charsville, Georgia. She hadn't had one in nearly nine years, not since she left without looking back.

Her mouth started watering and she jerked her head up to find Fred looking at her with the expression of a man terrified his beloved wouldn't like the ring he'd picked out.

"Why did you buy me these?"

"Oh, I dunno. I think maybe you mentioned where you grew up. You're pretty far from there." He hitched at his jeans, then examined his fingernails, which she'd noticed in the bathroom were clean and neatly trimmed.

"*Where* did you get them?"

"Just came across 'em." He rubbed his head, his scalp highly visible through the hair he kept nearly shaved. "Thought you'd like a taste of home."

She stared down at the familiar pink-and-gold package in her lap. He sure as heck hadn't gotten the cookies at any of the stores in this neighborhood. Grebner's wasn't exactly a household name, especially outside Georgia.

"Thank you." She nearly choked on the words. She didn't want to be touched by this man any more than she wanted to be reminded of where she came from. "This was...nice of you."

"You're welcome. I gotta go." He tugged at his ear. "Sorry if I butted in tonight."

"Oh. Well, it's…thanks. For the shower and the cookies." She got up and followed him to lock up. At the door he turned suddenly and she had to step back to keep from being too close.

He searched her face, then gave a quick shake of his head. "G'night, Chris."

"Bye." She shut and locked the door behind him, breathed a sigh of relief and rushed to the phone to dial Ryan's number. He picked up on the third ring.

"Ryan, it's Christine. I'm sorry to be calling late. I…" She was about to tell him about the fake phone call when it occurred to her if she planted the seeds of the Fred problem now, it might be easier to ask for Ryan's help later. "Fred was here."

"Tonight?" His voice sharpened and she couldn't help a little thrill. Was he jealous?

"He decided this was the perfect time to put in a new showerhead." She let her full measure of exasperation show.

Ryan chuckled. "Fred is a character. Great guy, but he plays by his own rules."

"I guess you could say that." She smiled, thinking if that definition fit anyone it was Ryan. Fred didn't have power and limitless opportunities. His life was fixed, probably had been for years. He had to play by the rules of the building. No chance for big changes in his life plan. People would move in and move out, and Fred would still be here, year after year, fixing and patching and replacing. Not so different from the people in Charsville, which she'd left for a very good reason.

"I checked my calendar and that night is free, Ryan. I would love to go to the ballet with you."

"Good." He sounded genuinely pleased. "Dinner after?"

"I'd love it. Thank you." She faked a swoon and had to

wrench the phone away from her mouth in case the giggle bubbling up spilled over. "My treat this time?"

"We'll see."

She smiled. He'd pay. He played by his own rules.

"Have you been to Café des Artistes?"

"Not yet." She bit her lip to stay cool. Café des Artistes was not the type of place you'd take someone you were only casually interested in.

"Good. We'll go there."

"I'll look forward to that."

"Same here. Good night, Christine."

"Thanks again for dinner." She hung up the phone and did three Charsville Chiefs cheers all around the apartment, cheers she'd learned by watching Iona practice, though she'd never had the slightest inclination to be on the squad herself.

She'd see Ryan again. For ballet. And dinner! If she'd stayed in Charsville, the most she could hope for on a date was chicken fried steak and a crude pass in the back of a pickup.

Things were looking really, really good for Christine "Teeny" Bayer.

She wandered around, window to window, too restless to settle into anything, until the clock reminded her she'd better get some sleeping done, if at all possible. Maybe a long shower and a few more rounds on the sweater—the one she was gambling wouldn't be too personal to give Ryan for his birthday in September—would calm her enough so she could sleep. Maybe if she was really lucky she'd dream a few sweet dreams that would come true, about a certain tall handsome neighbor and a house in Connecticut, maybe a Parisian honeymoon.

She made her way to the bathroom to start her relaxation regimen. But not before she gave into temptation and stopped by the dining table to pry open the pink-and-gold tin and stuff a pecan praline cookie into her mouth.

Fred had been right. The cookies tasted like home.

4

To: Jenny Hartmann
From: Natalie Eggers
Re: My husband

Jenny, you rock. I finished your book and had to write! Your description of that guy you were seeing was so much like my husband it made me want to scream. He never wants me to go out at night. He never wants me spending any time with my friends. He hates when I buy myself new clothes. I think if he had his way I'd dress in his old T-shirts and sweats.

But your book gave me courage. I'm starting to stand up for myself more now. It's feeling really good.

Thanks, Jenny! I love you!

Natalie

"THANK YOU." Jenny smiled at Café des Artistes' gorgeous young blond bartender, who had just delivered a bright orange passion fruit martini across the narrow shiny wood bar. "What is your name?"

"George." He glanced at her, poured three types of booze into a shaker in quick succession, then glanced again.

"Well, may I say, George, purely for the joy of spreading good feeling, no strings attached, that you are one serious treat for the eyes."

He looked taken aback, and the hawk-nosed bartender rinsing a glass next to him sniggered before moving down the bar to serve another customer.

"Uh…thanks."

"You're welcome." She lifted the drink to him and took a sip, then closed her eyes to let the sweet-sour fruity taste register. "*And* that is one hell of a martini. You're an artist, too."

"Yeah?" He put the lid on the shaker and shook, a smile trying to break through. "Thanks again."

"You're welcome again. I'm Jenny, by the way. Nice to meet you."

She winked and he managed to look friendly that time, straining the drink into a waiting glass. His co-worker, who'd moved back into hearing range, raised his nearly joined eyebrows and mouthed "go for it" not very subtly.

"No, no, no." Jenny waggled her finger at him. "I said no strings and I meant it."

He snorted and mumbled something undoubtedly snarky.

Jenny frowned. "What's your name, bartender-who-is-not-George?"

"Chaz."

"Pay attention, Chaz." She gave him her most insincere smile. "When a guy tells a woman she's beautiful, it means, 'I want to sleep with you.' Right?"

He shrugged sullenly. "Maybe."

"Get this. When a woman tells a guy he's attractive, she means, strangely enough—" she spread her hands "—that he's attractive."

Chaz shot her a dirty look and Jenny patted the bar sympathetically, unable to reach his arm. "Complicated, I know. You keep working at it, it'll come to you."

George chuckled outright. His co-worker rolled his eyes and moved to serve his next drink.

Jenny grinned and toasted George with her brilliant orange martini. Nothing in the world was more freeing and wonderful than not worrying what anyone thought, saying what you wanted to say, letting other people's uptight judgment roll off you. Especially when you'd grown up so enslaved by those very things. George didn't mind having an attractive woman tell him he was hot—why would he? His friend could go trash-diving in the East River.

Nothing could bother her tonight anyway. She was a woman on a mission—all dressed up with somewhere to go. Ryan Masterson's oldest sister, Anne, happy to hear from Jenny, had been a rich and willing source of information on her younger brother, including that Ryan would be using her ballet tickets tonight, though he would only tell his sister he was taking "a friend," which for a normal guy meant a woman he hadn't been able to get into the sack yet. In Ryan's case, however, it would mean a woman he wasn't interested in getting into the sack, because there was no way any age-of-consent female could resist him.

In Jenny's completely unbiased opinion.

Of course he could mean a male friend, but men taking men to the ballet involved a change in Ryan Masterson that would be so utterly tragic for womankind the globe over that Jenny wouldn't even consider it.

Anne had managed to worm out of him that he and this "friend" were hitting Café des Artistes for a drink and maybe a bite after. So here sat Jenny, resplendent—if she did say so herself—in her sexiest black slit-up-to-there skirt and equally sexy "is-she-naked?" black lace top, lined with flesh-colored fabric that happened to be a nearly exact match of her skin tone.

Quite a coincidence she happened to be in the same bar tonight, wasn't it? But who could resist the opportunity to peek? Of course she could have called him, or shown up at his apartment, but a supposedly chance encounter was so much more fun and risky and exciting, and it gave her the opportunity to spy on him in his natural habitat and see what vibe she got before she spoke to him, since she was positive he wouldn't recognize her at first glance.

Anne seemed pretty sure he wasn't dating anyone seriously or exclusively, so it wasn't as if Jenny was out of line. She was an old friend! And if he seemed hot and heavy with his date tonight, she'd say "Ryan is that you?" and "Gee, how long has it been?" and "Great to see you!" and go home none the worse for wear.

Okay, perhaps a micro-bit disappointed. Be serious. This was Ryan Masterson.

And if his friend did turn out to be a friend—or a colleague—then maybe the door would be wide open. She was the kind of women who walked through wide-open doors now, instead of cowering at the threshold wondering if she should knock on the jamb.

She couldn't wait to see how Ryan reacted to this new truer version of herself and she couldn't wait to satisfy her curiosity as to how much he'd really changed. Possibly no one but Ryan had ever glimpsed this long-suppressed other side of her before the book and her metamorphosis. But in all their admittedly brief time together, she hadn't sensed even the faintest hint of inner blandness in him.

She turned for the hundredth time to check the door, when a dark-suited tall man—guess who?—walked in.

Oh, my. Oh, my my my. Someone tell her heart to slow down or she'd lose at least a month off her life. He was still— He was soo—

"Need another drink?"

"No, George." She didn't take her eyes off Ryan, though she tried not to stare too openly in case he saw her before she was ready. "A drink is not what I need right at this moment."

"Him?" He made a sound of amused disgust. "Women are so fickle."

"Oh, yes." She threw an apologetic glance over her shoulder. "We are, aren't we. But he is…I mean he's…well just look."

"If you say so."

Jenny fixed George with a stare. "You're not gay, are you George."

"Nope."

"I thought not." She turned back to drink in the sight of Ryan, who was pulling out a chair for his unfortunately stunning blond companion. "You couldn't possibly understand."

"I guess not."

Ryan smiled and leaned forward, listening to his date, apparently fascinated. But…politely fascinated. His features were alert, but his eyes were neutral. He wasn't turning on…The Sex Look. Jenny had been on the receiving end of that look many times. It was unmistakable. And lethal. The places he'd gotten her to say "yes" with just that look…well it was a miracle they'd never been arrested.

"George, send Mr. Perfection a drink from me, would you?"

"While he's with someone else?"

She smiled at the distaste in his voice. "Believe it or not he's an old friend. Grew up down the street from me."

"No kidding."

"Edible, isn't he." She rested her chin on her hand and stared her fill. "The One That Got Away."

"I have one of those." George's voice sounded nearly as wistful as hers. "I'd buy her a drink even if she showed up with Russell Crowe."

"Ha!" Jenny turned to him. "She'd go for you *way* before that temperamental slab of beef."

He grinned and Jenny returned to her high-level spying. Ryan was laughing at something Ms. Blond Perfection had just said. Hmm…

"George."

"Yeah."

"Make him…a seven and seven, please. Tell the waiter to say, 'Seven and seven and seventh heaven.'" Jenny wrinkled her nose. "And whatever she orders I better pay for that, too."

"I'm on it."

She heard the drink being poured and caught peripheral flashes of George's practiced white-sleeved arms working their magic.

Two minutes later, the waiter stopped at Ryan's table and put the drink in front of him. Ryan frowned and looked questioningly at the server.

Jenny shook back her hair, about six inches longer than when he'd known her, arranged herself in a casually sexy pose and winked at George, who was smirking—not that she entirely blamed him.

"Wish me luck."

"Okay." He smirked harder. "Good luck."

"Maybe you could seduce his date away from him?"

He rolled his eyes and moved away to fill another order.

The waiter finished his spiel. Ryan looked startled, then slowly turned toward the bar.

Here it came…

Kaboom. *Houston, we have contact.*

And with contact came extreme thrills chasing each other up and down Jenny's seductively black-clad torso.

But wait, there was more. He was pushing back his chair, excusing himself and coming over to…well, a girl could always hope.

Oh, yes, indeed. Even with his savagery dumbed down to what would be tedious respectability on another man, even wearing a suit any businessman—who could afford it—would wear, his magnetism persisted, electrified him, singled him out as someone to watch, someone to follow, someone to be reckoned with…someone to beg into bed.

She'd expected to be attracted to him. What she hadn't expected was the subsequent rush of nerves, the bizarre flash of panic, similar to how she'd felt around him growing up, before their summer as lovers, whenever he'd shown up at her house with the rest of his family, scowling, mutinous, barely civil, teasing her as often as he ignored her…the way a shy, romantic teenage girl felt around her look-don't-touch dream boy.

She'd been as much of a wreck then as she was heading toward being now. A highly conditioned response: The Masterson Effect.

He was close, standing beside her so she had to tip her head up. "Well. Jenny Hartmann."

Oh and the voice was even deeper with age, as deep as…a really deep thing. His eyes were so blue, she hadn't forgotten, as blue as…something very blue, and oh God, her brain was gone.

"Well. Ryan Masterson." Somehow, through force of habit maybe, her voice emerged when she needed it to. She tried also to appear in control of her mind and body, if not her hormones. "Fancy meeting you here."

He narrowed his eyes and she had a feeling he already suspected the meeting wasn't entirely by chance. "Mom told me a while back that you were in New York."

"As are you."

"Yes." He seemed at a loss for what to say next, which made her own nerves easier to bear. Her brain cleared, and calm returned—relative calm, considering Ryan Masterson was standing next to her for the first time in thirteen years.

"Want me to keep up the small talk or can I ask what I really want to ask?" She shot him a provocative look. "Well *one* of the things I want to ask."

"Shoot."

"What's with the fancy suit? It doesn't look like you."

"Adult uniform. What's with the…" He looked her up and down leisurely—the lace top that didn't appear to cover much, the slit-to-there skirt that made no bones about not covering much. "It doesn't look like you, either."

"It's me now." She gave him a come-on-baby stare from under her lashes. "What do you think?"

His eyes returned to hers and she was suddenly back to that summer in college, to the night of the storm, when those intense blue eyes had stared at her exactly like this, as if he'd never seen her before and wanted to devour her whole, when he'd leaned in and kissed her as if there was simply nothing else he could do.

Unfortunately, history was not lucky enough to repeat itself so many years later. He glanced over his shoulder at his date and beckoned, then pointed to the empty seat next to Jenny. Blond Woman shook her head, coolly declining, and he gave a reassuring wave and turned back. "You're looking well."

Well? As in not sick? That was the best he could do? "I'm healthy as a horse, thank you so much for noticing."

He blinked, and then his old mischievous grin snuck onto his mouth, the one that used to make her want to giggle before she even knew what was amusing him. Only it looked sort of wrong and unfamiliar over a starched shirt collar and perfectly shaven chin. "I heard about your book from Mom. Congratulations."

"Thanks. Have you read it?"

"No." His expression said liberals would have to vote Republican first. "Are you writing another?"

Guilt. She kept her expression carefree. "Supposed to be."

"Then what *are* you up to?"

"Either staying out of trouble or trying to get in."

"You?" He shook his head in amusement. Or maybe amazement. "In trouble?"

She shrugged. "If the mood hits."

"What kind of trouble?"

"Hmm." She tipped her head, un- and re-crossed her legs, watching him watch her. "Maybe I'll get to show you sometime."

"Are you coming on to me five minutes into a chance meeting?"

She *tsk-tsk*ed. "What is this world coming to?"

Those killer eyes narrowed again. "Anne told you I was going to be here."

"Ooh, you're good." She sipped her drink, put it carefully back down and flashed him another me-woman-you-man glance. "But then from what I remember, you always were."

He looked at her in quizzical amusement. "Is this the new you? Or a few extra martinis?"

"Ha! No. I behave when I'm drunk. I'm bad when I'm

sober. *George.*" She lifted her arm and he came right over as if he'd been spying on them all along. "How many have I had? This gentleman would like to know."

"Still on your first." He gave a thumbs-up and went back to his duties.

"See?" She sent Ryan a sweet smile. "Why don't you introduce me to your gorgeous date? I think she's getting lonely. We could have a threesome."

His eyes popped. "It's Jenny Hartmann, right? Shy, sweet girl who lived down the street from me?"

"I meant a threesome for drinks. I haven't changed *that* much." She touched his sleeve and was rewarded with the feeling that for the instant her finger was in contact with his arm, he stopped breathing. "You still haven't told me if you like me this way."

"It doesn't fit the girl I knew."

Jenny raised her brows. "About as well as Armani fits the guy I knew."

"Touché."

"So what have you been up to, since we…knew each other?" She put a hand to the back of her neck, lifted her hair and let it cascade down. "Besides getting boring and making a lot more money than you used to doing yard work for the Baileys."

"Boring?" He gave her the look she remembered too well, the half-angry, half-aroused look he used to give her when he'd be stripping her naked within seconds.

Oh, my my *my* goodness. "Did I say that?"

He raised an eyebrow. "After college, business school, Wall Street, now I'm partner in a venture capital firm."

"Of course not boring." She clucked her tongue. "S-s-s-izzling excitement."

"Jenny…"

She smiled up at him. "Just having fun."

"Apparently."

"You don't really mind, do you?"

He held her gaze and she pretended to be interested in his answer, when all she was interested in was asking George to turn out the lights and clear the bar area so they could become immediately and passionately reacquainted.

"No. I don't mind."

"Good. Now tell me." She lifted her chin in the direction of Now Probably Impatient Blond Woman. "Are you serious about her?"

"What, Anne didn't fill you in?"

She moved her eyes back to his, not that they needed any persuasion to go. "Let's hear your version."

"Okay." His jaw tightened; she wondered if he was aware of it. "I'm planning on being serious about her, yes."

"But you're not yet?"

No answer. He just looked at her, and so help her, she felt positively dizzy with excitement. She moved her leg to touch the side of his thigh and this time she was pretty sure neither of them was breathing.

For a second he didn't move and she thought he was going to stay and let her be that close to him, and that she'd be hearing from him as soon as he could get away from the blonde. Then he broke eye contact and took an abrupt step back. "I need to get back."

"Of course." *Damn.*

"Great to see you, Jenny. Stay well."

Well? What was with this "well" stuff? "I never get sick. I told you. And it was great to see you, too, Ryan."

She kept the smile on her face while she waved to his date, who had clearly spent the last five minutes imagining Jenny being trampled by elephants.

George leaned his forearms on the bar. "So what happened? You struck out?"

"Who, me?" She made a scornful noise and took a big swallow of her drink. "Never."

"Then why is he over there and you're here by yourself?"

"Maybe because he's not enough of a pig to ditch her mid-date?"

George mumbled something, shamefaced. *Honestly. Men.* And yet…

She frowned and fingered the napkin under her drink. "Something strange about him and her. I'm not sure I know exactly what."

"But you're going to find out?"

She drained her drink and set down the glass, turned again to look at Ryan, talking politely to his date, looking as detached and calm as he'd looked engaged and intense talking to her.

"Oh, yes, George. I'm going to find out."

How she was continuing to smile and talk normally to Ryan, she had no idea. Christine took another sip of her second Baileys, more than she usually drank but she was gripping herself so tightly emotionally that the alcohol wasn't affecting her at all.

Up until an hour ago, her date with Ryan had been perfect. They'd met before the ballet near Lincoln Center for a soup-sandwich-salad kind of meal to tide them over through the performance. They'd chatted easily, and there had been moments when she'd felt their camaraderie was becoming more natural and relaxed. Or at least she hadn't felt quite so on edge over every word.

Ryan had talked again of the town he'd grown up in, and mentioned a plan to drive up and look at houses. Then he'd paused, and she'd had an eerie premonition—or maybe just another fantasy—that he was about to ask her to come with him, when the waiter interrupted with food, and the moment was lost in a change of subject. She really, really hoped the topic would come up again, but so far she hadn't managed to work it back into the conversation.

The ballet had been wonderful, even if most of its true brilliance was probably lost on her. She still couldn't get over how the dancers could make every gesture, even a simple wave of a hand, so very beautiful and graceful, how they could jump so high, and land so elegantly.

Sitting rapt in the audience, she'd managed to touch her shoulder to Ryan's now and then without making it seem on purpose, and he hadn't moved away. She had felt so happy, so secure, so sure they were heading forward together on their destined path....

And then they'd come here, to Café des Artistes, and not only their late-night tête-à-tête dinner, but the mood of the whole evening, had been ruined by what Christine's mother would have called, "a floozy." Another word had popped into Christine's mind, which began with an S and ended with an L-U-T.

It hadn't been so bad at first, when Ms. Obvious had lured Ryan over by plying him with some drink they'd shared a hundred years ago. Christine hadn't minded when Ryan had gone to speak to her, though she wouldn't have joined them for anything. He'd been sweet to invite her, but if she'd sat with that vampiress, any hope of recapturing the intimacy of her twosome with Ryan would have gone gurgling down the plumbing. Christine was attractive in her own right, but she refused to put herself in the position of being compared to...that.

So she'd waited. Watched. And seen the dark-haired

beauty inviting sex with her eyes and body, and maybe with her words, too. Even that Christine hadn't minded. Ryan was on the receiving end of that type of crude behavior all the time. Christine had gained the upper edge by being different, by offering him something other than sex: her friendship and her respect.

Far worse had been when Ryan finally extracted himself and came back to the table. Five seconds later, any idiot could tell part of him had stayed at the bar with her. Christine was no idiot.

Even now, long after this sex-starved person had finished her vile-colored drink and undulated out, smiling insincerely at Christine and meltingly at Ryan, she lingered between them.

Ryan was distracted, moody, withdrawn. Worse, he was trying not to be and failing. He wasn't the type to be hijacked by anything but the strongest emotions. Christine had had to repeat some sentences, and got responses to others that suggested he hadn't been listening. For the past ten minutes she'd been babbling like a person with half her intelligence, just to cover the silence.

She needed to implement damage control. Immediately. But how? Maybe like her Daddy always said, "You gotta tackle trouble head-on, or it'll whirl 'round and chomp on your ass."

A true poet, her father.

"The woman who was here…she looked familiar." Christine smiled blandly, her stomach in knots. "What is her name?"

"Jenny." He shifted and cleared his throat. "Jenny Hartmann. We grew up on the same street. Our parents were friends. I hadn't seen her in years."

"Oh, how fun, to run into an old friend like that." Her

smile became warmer, while the knots in her stomach turned to ice bricks. Not good. The two of them had a long history.

"Yes. Quite something." He laughed, but didn't seem amused. "She looks nothing like she used to."

"How so?" Christine leaned her chin on her hand as if this was the most fascinating topic she could imagine, and she was delighted to be discussing it, when she'd rather chew the head off a gecko.

"She was shy growing up, and…sweet. She'd walk around with this dreamy expression like she lived in some other world. I used to tease her about it. About everything."

Worse and worse. A long history and chemistry going way back.

"That's quite a change."

This was his cue to say how horrifying it had been to see his sweet little-sister friend changed into a hooker wanna-be.

He didn't.

"When did you last see her?" Her voice was light and musical by the sheer force of her will.

"We lost touch after college."

He finished abruptly and his jaw tightened. That was when Christine knew. The worst. The very worst. They'd been lovers and their relationship had ended badly.

Relationships that ended badly were seldom over. The ones that died of boredom and disconnectedness and neglect—those were over. But passion that exploded rather than fizzled…

Let's just say Christine no longer had the leisure to build their platonic friendship as slowly as she wanted before she made a move of her own.

"What does Jenny do?"

Her question startled him out of what was undoubtedly a trip down memory lane, one she hoped was more nightmare than fantasy. "She wrote a book."

"Oh. About?"

"About men, and how they're all trying to keep women down."

"Honestly." Christine made a sound of derision. "That's absurd."

"Apparently that's the new Jenny."

"Are you going to see her again?" She lifted her chin and let a tiny part of the challenge show in her expression. He was a smart man. He'd get it.

He met her gaze, then the distracted, impersonal stare focused and he really saw her again, for the first time in an hour.

"No." He shook his head grimly. "Jenny is ancient history."

The ice bricks in Christine's stomach thawed a little, and she and Ryan talked more freely again, though they never came close to the magic of the early part of the evening. By the time the check arrived, Christine was exhausted and dispirited. Maybe best to cut her losses tonight and try again later when the image of the sex goddess wasn't so fresh in his mind. If she tried anything to further their intimacy tonight, she'd suffer in comparison.

But in a few days, she should start letting Ryan catch her in her negligee more often, step up the flirtation, not that she could compete with Ms. Whoever-Sees-Me-Can-Have-Me. But he should know she was capable of more than friendship, that she'd welcome the sexual part of their relationship, as well.

She needed to keep reminding herself that this Jenny person might be hot, she might be dangerous, but she was not the kind of woman Ryan would invite to Connecticut to look at houses. Whether Christine ever got that invitation, time would tell. But Jenny never would.

At worst, Jenny and Ryan would rekindle an affair. Christine would simply wait for the explosion of passion to burn out, and be available on the other side, cool and comforting and solid and eternal. Ryan would realize his mistake, and with Jenny finally out of his system, would return to Christine.

She was a patient woman, and if she needed to change strategies to reach her goal, if it took a little longer than she'd originally hoped, fine, though her bank account might not stand the strain of waiting that long. But as long as he was hers in the end...

They left the restaurant and took a taxi to Bank Street, not talking much in the cab. When they arrived and Ryan pulled out his wallet, Christine got out without offering to pay. Ryan owed her tonight for emotional trauma.

The thought made her smile tightly, and the tight smile lingered as they entered the lobby, where, to cap off a dreadful evening in dreadful style, *Fred* stood, mopping up something that smelled unpleasantly sour and winey off the floor.

Immediately Christine brightened her smile to communicate to him that she'd had the time of her life out with someone handsome and successful whom he didn't stand a chance against, so he'd better leave her alone.

His face darkened as Ryan came into the lobby behind her.

"Fred, how's it going?" Ryan offered his hand and the two men shook. "What happened here?"

"Some delivery guy brought in a case of wine and the bottom fell out of the box. Big mess." He leaned on his mop and surveyed the two of them, his gaze lingering on

Christine's face, which she kept set on ecstatic. "Out on the town tonight?"

"We were at the ballet."

"Oh, the *ballet*." He kept his eyes on Christine.

Christine looked down at his mop, at the burgundy stain and the sparkling bits of glass between the grey rope strands. She didn't want to meet his eyes.

"Had a nice time?"

"We did." Ryan's hand touched the small of her back, and Christine moved automatically toward the elevator, grateful for the rescue, even if Ryan didn't know that's what he was doing. Maybe it would be okay after all to make herself available for a kiss when they said goodnight. That way—

"Christine."

She turned impatiently to Fred. "What?"

"Can I talk to you? Alone?"

"What, *now?*"

"Yes." He stood calmly, holding his ridiculous dirty mop as if it were a scepter.

"It can't wait?"

"No."

Her face started burning. Stupid stubborn fool. Fred knew exactly what he was doing, exactly what could happen at the end of a date, what she'd decided should happen tonight to offset the dismal end to their perfect evening, and he was trying to ruin it for her. He knew she could never be rude enough to turn him down in front of Ryan.

"I'll go up. Thanks for coming with me tonight, Christine. I had a great time." He moved in and kissed her cheek.

She smiled warmly at him, thinking she'd like to hurl another case of wine on Fred's floor. No, at his head. Bottle by bottle. "Thank you, Ryan. I had a really nice evening."

"We'll do it again." He backed toward the elevator and lifted his hand. "Soon."

"Yes. I'd like that." When the doors closed, she let her smile drop and turned to Fred, bracing herself for the irritation of triumph in his eyes.

Instead, he gazed at her with puzzled concern.

"What is it?" She folded her arms over her chest. "What did you want to talk to me about?"

"I wanted to make sure you were okay."

"*Okay?* What do you mean okay? I don't *look* okay?"

His puzzlement increased. "No."

"Well, at the moment I'm not real happy, but that's not about my evening, it's about *you* cutting it short."

"Hey, you walked in here looking like he'd been beating on you all night. I wanted to make sure he didn't upset you."

Her furious protest never made it out of her mouth, which had just dropped plenty wide enough to allow it to. She'd walked into the building outwardly bursting with happiness. How had he seen through it? Even Ryan hadn't sensed her anguish, and she'd been two feet away from him for hours.

"I had the time of my life." The words sounded lame and she hid a cringe.

"If you say so."

"I do."

He looked hurt for a second, then rubbed his balding head. "You know, Christine, you can trust me. And if you ever need to talk about—"

"Why on earth would I turn to *you?*" She hurled the sentence at him before she thought, then mumbled an apology, too late of course.

"A couple of reasons." He hitched up his pants and leaned the mop against the wall, not appearing at all insulted by her rudeness. "First, because I get the feeling you have no one else to turn to."

"That's not true." She took in a breath and lied through her teeth. "I have Ryan."

He scowled impatiently. "He's not for you."

"What?" She didn't bother to hide her scorn. "What do you know about it?"

"He's way out of your league."

"Oh, and I suppose I'm way down 'n yours."

"Yup." He nodded cheerfully. "Bang down in it."

"In your dreams." Her fists clenched and her breath whooshed in and out. Her accent was popping back onto her tongue. Damn it, she was so mad she could spit. "I'm not spending the rest of my life on the floor cleaning up other people's messes."

He shrugged, her poisonous words rolling off him again. "I'd rather clean 'em than make 'em."

"What does that mean?"

He swaggered closer and she took an instinctive step back before she reminded herself to stand her ground. Closer still, and she couldn't escape those dark-lashed eyes or the clean male smell that had been assigned to him by some weird mistake. "It means, Christine, that if you marry that guy, you'll be making such a mess, there won't be a chance in hell anyone can clean it up."

5

RYAN FINISHED WATCHING the Internet virtual tour of a property for sale in Southport and whistled. The house on Willow Street had everything: style, space, luxury, space, a view of Long Island Sound, space…

Quite different from the cramped four-bedroom next to the fire station his family of seven had lived in. And roughly fifteen times the price his parents had paid forty years ago. He closed his browser and grinned, stretched his ankles under the desk and clasped his hands behind his head, imagining himself living in a house like that. King of his castle. Lord of his manor. The prodigal black sheep returning to buy the whole farm.

Owning a house like that would feel good. Very good. Proof he'd evolved, proof he'd settled into something mature and lasting.

Just for the hell of it, he imagined Christine in the house, cooking in the remodeled state-of-the-art kitchen, helping him entertain guests in the vast living room, puttering with him in the large backyard gardens. And up in the bedroom…

A picture rose immediately, and he dropped his head back with a groan, covering his face with his still-clasped hands.

Jenny.

Someone please get her out of his daydream.

She'd picked a hell of a time to saunter back into his life…no, not into his life. He didn't want her in his life. Into his brain then, into his dreams and his thoughts—he wouldn't admit to the fantasies.

Or the memories. Seven and seven and seventh heaven. Sharing the drink and tearing each other's clothes off…

This was ludicrous. He was finally on track to the way he wanted to live the rest of his life: out of the city, doing a job that meant something and satisfied him, and committed to a wife who fit his life and supported him in what he wanted to achieve. He and Jenny had been together a mere few weeks thirteen years ago; they'd both been different people then.

That summer he'd hit bottom when the numbness had finally worn off and the fact of Mitch's death and Ryan's stupid frat boy part in it had hit him full on the face. Motorcycles and alcohol. Guess what? Adults really meant it when they said mixing the two was dangerous. Guess what? They weren't making it up to spoil the fun.

Barely functional from the pain, he'd at least had the sense to turn to Jenny for help, though he hadn't known then that's what he was doing. She'd known what he needed as if he came with a manual. Whatever he'd dished out, she'd taken, which was plenty. He'd been cruel to her often. Practically raped her more than once. Sobbed on her, shouted at her, been a general maniac. And from her he'd gotten back understanding, acceptance and rock-solid calm during the weeks he couldn't recognize much about himself.

She became an addiction. He came to her or called her to him night after night, desperate for what she gave: a shoulder, a body that drove him wild, passion he'd never experienced before or since and, eventually, what she'd called love.

Had he repaid her by promising she could lean on him whenever she needed him? Saying she meant more to him than she'd ever know? Letting her feel even a fraction of the gratitude he owed her?

Nope. She'd whispered those three powerful words in the dark and he'd bolted as soon as it got light.

Nice.

She'd scared him to death, not because she'd loved him. But because he'd been terrified he loved her, too. What the hell was a selfish, screwed-up twenty-one-year-old kid going to do with a woman who loved him? The kind of woman for whom love spelled apartments and weddings and babies and careers? She deserved ten times better than the man he was then.

But that was too noble. In the end, he hadn't run to protect her, but to protect himself from feeling too deeply again.

Seeing her last night had brought home that they still had unfinished business—though not the sexual kind Jenny was angling for so openly and that Christine feared, though he'd tried to put her at ease. Unfinished business that involved old wounds and still-sore places there was no point reexploring, even from a fresh adult perspective. And a lot of intense memories, which might cause complications when he was trying to see what could evolve between him and Christine.

Which reminded him...

He rolled himself back to his desk, pulled out his Blackberry and checked the weekend on his calendar. This Saturday he had a soccer game with his over-thirty team, the East Side Bombers. But he could drive to Southport Sunday to look at the house. And he could bring Christine, see how it felt to be there with her, see if the property and town suited her taste.

He grinned through a wave of affection. The more time he spent with her, the more he liked her, and the more he thought their temperaments would suit. If all went as planned, he could be engaged by Christmas, married next summer. The house was big enough for the wedding and reception, or they could get married at Trinity Church and have the reception at the Fairfield Country Club, maybe down by the—

His phone's ring jolted him out of his bridegroom fantasies. Maybe he could stand to do a little work. He'd been distracted today, unable to focus on much. Big decisions ahead.

He picked up the receiver. "Ryan Masterson."

"Ryan…" The low throaty voice could only belong to one woman. He closed his eyes, body tensing.

"Who's calling?" As if he didn't know.

She laughed. "As if you didn't know."

"Okay." He smiled, in spite of himself. "What's up, Jenny?"

"Ohh, nuthin'. Whatcha doing?"

"Working." He kept his voice brisk.

She tsk-tsked. "All work and no play makes Johnny dull."

"All play and no work gets Johnny in trouble."

"But it's much more fun. Come play with me, Ryan."

He closed his eyes, trying not to picture her the way she'd looked last night. Trying not to picture her the way she'd looked a decade-plus ago. "I don't think that's a good idea."

"Why not?" Her voice was still low, seductive, unconcerned, as if she didn't care if he agreed or not—or as if she was so sure he would agree she wasn't bothering to worry. "We always played well together."

"That was a long time ago, Jenny."

"I know."

"A lot has changed." He grimaced. He sounded like someone's father. Maybe his own had sounded like that; he'd died too young for Ryan to know him.

"Is it the woman you were with the other night?"

"Christine? Partly."

"Only partly, Ryan? That doesn't sound like enough."

"Enough to what?"

"Stop me."

"Look, I know you're—"

"Remember the night you got me off in your car parked right in Southport village?"

He drew a sharp breath he hoped she hadn't heard. Her voice. He'd forgotten she could use it like that on the phone, breathless and low, the way she'd sounded underneath him. "That was crazy kid stuff."

"Mmm. Out of control. Anyone could have walked by and seen me spread out in the back seat, remember?"

He remembered. Every second. "We could have been arrested."

"But we weren't," she whispered. "I was so scared at first, then you made me so wild I came under your fingers. Do you remember?"

He shoved his chair back and strode to the window, looked out, seeing Connecticut instead of Manhattan, the inside of the Volvo her parents had handed down to her, heard his own voice urging her on, her whimpers of fear turning to whimpers of arousal as he'd pressed her mercilessly to do what she'd feared. He'd been possessed. Possessed by guilt and grief and by Jenny Hartmann, stripping in the back of a car in Southport Center just because he'd wanted her to.

She'd come intensely, quickly, much sooner than he'd expected, and he'd realized he'd been pushing her to do something that had excited her all along. He hadn't been dominating her, but freeing her to act out one of her own fantasies. That knowledge had made him crazy; he'd been inside her so fast and hard he'd barely lasted forty-five seconds.

And then…

That was the first night tenderness had sliced through his infatuation with his own misery, the first sign of his return to realizing there were other people in the world besides him.

She'd been good for him that summer. Maybe in some way he'd been good for her, too. But that was past. Their futures had led them to places as different as those they'd started from. "What do you want from me?"

"Isn't it obvious?"

"Just sex?"

"It's as good a place to start as any. Actually, better than most."

"Why do you want this?"

She laughed, a low musical chuckle. "Why not, Ryan?"

"It's not that simple."

"Sure it is."

"There's Christine…"

"Ah, Christine." A short silence made him hope his point had gotten through. "Have you kissed her yet?"

He didn't answer.

"I didn't think so. Why haven't you?"

"None of your business what I've done." Why hadn't he? Because it hadn't ever felt like the right thing to do.

"You're right. It's not my business." She took in a long breath, let it out, and even managed to make that sound sexy. "Ryan…"

He should hang up the phone now. Right now. "Yes?"

"I'll be at the corner of Fifth Avenue and East 96th at exactly two a.m. in a white Volkswagen Passat. And I'll be—"

"No." He was already shaking his head. "I'm not going to—"

"Ryan," she whispered.

"What?" He braced himself for her reply.

"I'll be wearing a black lace bra, a low-cut red top and high-heeled sandals." She exhaled on a low *mmm* that made it all the way to his cock. "And that's all."

A click and the line went dead.

Ryan punched off his phone and banged it back into its cradle. This was insane. She was insane. There was no way he could do anything that crazy. No way. He was too old and had too much at stake to be risking arrest making out in public.

A knock sounded on his door, and he had to unlock his jaw to speak. *"Yes."*

"It's Christine."

"Christine." Thank God. "Come in."

She came through the door holding a small paper bag. She was impeccably dressed in a rose-colored suit with a short skirt that showed off her long beautiful legs, bringing a waft of floral perfume with her. Her presence was like a cool, soothing bath, easing him down from his agitation into the reality of who he was and what he wanted. "I'm glad you came by."

"Really?" She gave him the special sweet smile he'd come to look forward to.

"I was thinking of driving to Connecticut on Sunday to look at houses."

"Oh, nice." She regarded him calmly, but he thought he saw a sparkle of excitement in her eyes.

"I could use a female opinion. Would you like to come along?"

Again the flash in her eyes, though her face stayed

serene. "I'd love to, Ryan. It'll be nice to get out of the city."

"Good." He grinned, as happy she was coming as he was relieved she'd turned his world right side up again. "I'll knock around nine a.m.?"

"I'll be ready." Her smile shone, teeth white and straight, eyes blue and turned down at the corners, lips delicate, a perfect Cupid's bow.

Why hadn't he ever kissed her?

"I brought you some pecan rolls." She lifted the bag toward him. "I made them last night."

"How do you have time to do all this?"

She winked and put a finger to her pretty lips. "Shh, I'm the perfect woman."

"I'm starting to think you're right."

"Oh." She blushed and put a hand to her throat, looking so flustered and pleased and sweet he nearly couldn't stop himself from reaching for her. But his office had glass panes next to each door anyone could look through….

"Thanks for these." He took the bag of rolls. "I'll see you Sunday."

"You're welcome. And yes, see you then." She left his office, throwing him a surprise sexy look over her shoulder that made him think he'd be kissing her very soon.

He couldn't let his past get in the way of the promising start he'd made with Christine.

The unfinished business with Jenny would just have to stay unfinished.

To: Natalie Eggers
From: Jenny Hartmann
Re: Your husband

Hey, girlfriend, you hang tough. Tell that man he doesn't own you or your time. You and I know, men come and go, but girlfriends are forever. Buy those clothes! Take those chances! Go out and party! Be yourself! If he loves you he'll stand by you as you really are.

Thanks for writing!

Jenny

JENNY CLIMBED into the stands at the East River Park soccer field in Lower Manhattan, wearing low-slung jeans cuffed midcalf over spike-heeled boots, and a zipped-low hoodie that didn't quite meet the waistband of her jeans. On her head sat a Yankees baseball cap, her hair in a ponytail sticking out the back.

She smiled at a couple halfway up the bleachers and thanked them when they stood to let her pass into their row. The air was chilly in spite of the sun, the trees' first attempts at leaves promising that summer was, however, still intending to arrive. Two groups of men were warming up on the field, one in red shirts and black shorts, the other all in blue.

"Excuse me."

The man next to her turned.

"Which team is the Bombers?"

"Red." He gestured to the right side of the field.

Jenny thanked him and peered at the red-shirted men, thinking if she got to heaven she'd like hers to be populated with lots and lots and lots of soccer players.

Mmm, *that* one in particular. The tall one. The one tapping the ball up in the air with his feet, graceful and athletic and yes indeed, time had only improved Ryan's shape. He'd always been lean, but now he was broader, with a mature man's body, a stupendous pair of muscled legs and a butt that made her sigh. Someday soon she hoped to see his chest again.

In fact, she'd been hoping to see it Friday on 96th Street at two in the morning, but he hadn't shown. After he'd sounded so negative about the whole idea, she hadn't really expected him to, not that it had stopped her from sitting in the back of her car, blanket over her naked lap, wildly turned on even at the thought that he might have changed his mind, peering as unobtrusively as possible out the tinted windows to see if he was sauntering toward her on the sidewalk. She'd almost been able to sense him out there….

But after twenty minutes of gradually feeling less and less aroused and more and more ridiculous—not to mention disappointed—she'd put her clothes on again and driven back to her apartment in Brooklyn's Park Slope neighborhood to admit to her roommate Jessica she'd scored a big fat nothing.

So Ryan wasn't going to fall into her lap after a few heavy breathing sessions on the phone, huh? Maybe she'd been a fool even to try. Maybe he *had* changed and she was wasting her time. Maybe he really was into this Christine woman, though why a man as passionate as she knew Ryan could be would choose a woman who didn't inspire him to out-of-control kisses way before it was sensible to be exchanging them, she hadn't any idea.

Why did he want that now? His sister Anne said the motorcycle accident that killed Mitch and miraculously threw Ryan to safety had scared him straight. He'd stopped drinking and whatever other substances he was doing, got a job, put himself through business school, and did the stint on Wall Street that had set him in clover for life, then he'd joined the investment company he was still with. Anne sounded proud of him, pleased he'd found his way.

Jenny watched the teams take the field, her eyes on Ryan and the look of intense concentration on his face as he waited for the game-starting whistle. Had he really found his way? Or was this another, safer path he'd chosen out of fear or guilt? The fear that had made him bolt when she'd told him she loved him? The guilt that had made him bury his wild side along with his friend? She didn't know. She wasn't even sure it was healthy for her to spend this much time and effort trying to find out.

Yes, she wanted him in the sack. Yes, she was out for herself these days and whatever Lola wanted Lola could get if she tried hard enough. But even though she hated to admit it, a deep part of her also still cared enough about Ryan—bless her sappy schoolgirl soul—and cared enough about their history and his friendship, to want to know who he was now and want him to be happy.

Hmm…given that he'd fried her heart so many years ago, maybe she'd be smarter and safer to keep this about sex.

The whistle blew and oh, yippee, testosterone erupted into motion on the field.

She couldn't claim to be an expert on soccer, but the minutes flew by in a breathless rush of momentum. She couldn't take her eyes off Ryan. He flew down the field and back, passing with perfect aim, dodging, shooting, setting up his teammates to take shots on goal. As far as she was concerned he owned the field. His power, his intensity, even his sweat was sexy. Controlled perfection got replaced with the passionate man she still wanted him to be.

Why?

She snorted at the question that popped into her head. Because she wanted in his pants. Right? More of the best sex she'd ever had. She was Jenny Hartmann, and she was out to please herself and she wanted to have done Ryan lately.

The half ended with Ryan's team ahead by one. On the sidelines for the break, he gulped water, talked to his teammates, moving with restless energy, unable to sit for more than a minute or two before he pushed up from the bench and paced in a familiar loose stride.

The players retook the field, the whistle blew. Early in the second half the other team scored, and the resulting tie revved the action to a frenzy. Ryan set up two shots that failed to score. His face grew grim; he bore down on players and went after the ball like a man possessed, using his legs, his head, his chest, being tripped by a player once, bounding up a second later.

Three minutes to go. Jenny found herself standing, breathing hard, watching him. A red player stole the ball in front of their goal and passed it to Ryan, who had the field clear in front of him.

The crowd went wild. Blue players in hot pursuit, he passed close to the stands, moving with impossible speed, ball perfectly controlled at his toes, thigh muscles bunching and loosening as he ran, teeth bared in concentration.

Oh. Yes.

He approached the goal, feinted to his left, kicked right. The goalkeeper dove, too late, and the ball nailed the top right corner of the net. Score!

Ryan pumped his fist. Jenny cheered and whistled with the rest of the Bomber supporters.

Then Ryan turned toward his teammates and she could see his face clearly. He shouted, raised his arm, fist clenched, face savage with triumph, and started a slow run toward the center of the field.

Jenny stopped cheering, stopped whistling, battling emotion that felt like desperate homesickness.

Ryan.

Not the venture capitalist, not the man who waited before kissing a woman he planned to become serious about.

Ryan. Her Ryan. And she wanted him back the way they used to be so badly it hurt.

The crowd's cheers faded, the applause weakened and died, and the teams lined up to shake hands.

Her phone rang and she sat back down with a thump on the bleachers, which were starting to empty around her.

"H'lo?"

"So, is he there? Have you seen him? I couldn't wait to find out. Just say 'wrong number' if you're with him." Her roommate's voice was over-the-top eager.

"Jessica, yeah, um, yeah." She put the phone to her other ear and glanced on the field again. "He's here."

"And, and, and? Didja talk to him yet?"

"No."

"Game's still on, huh?"

"No, it's done. Just finished."

"Well what are you waiting for, girl, an engraved invitation?"

Jenny forced a laugh. "'Course not. Just…waiting for the crowd to thin."

"Uh. Are you stoned or something? You sound weird."

"No, geez, Jessica, I'm just…distracted." She roused herself. *Get a grip, woman.* "Overcome by lust."

"Ha! Now *that* I understand. Well, okay, call and let me know. I'm home being seduced by a box of Nutter Butters for the rest of the day. Oh, and Lori and Sharon want to go clubbing with us again tonight unless you're…otherwise occupied."

"Okay. I'll let you know what happens." She clicked the phone off, wishing she hadn't told Jessica about Ryan. Not in quite so much detail. Maybe not at all.

Right now she wanted to go home and eat Nutter Butters, too, and that freaked her out. Almost as much as seeing Ryan transform back into the man she'd been young and foolish enough to imagine herself in love with.

And? So? What was the problem? Where was her inner diva? C'mon, she'd written an entire book about women going after what they wanted, no apologies necessary....

She searched and found Ryan talking to a member of the crowd whose head was provocatively tipped to one side, her auburn hair hanging sexily over one shoulder.

Uh...no. Move on over, babycakes.

Jenny stood, and the movement must have caught his eye, because he glanced at her, smiled down at something the woman said, then did a classic double take.

And unless she was experiencing this all on her very own, fireworks had just started going off in the airspace between them.

She climbed down the bleachers toward him, a slow saunter as sexy as possible, while making sure her heels didn't get caught and throw her off. The auburn-haired groupie turned to see what Ryan was watching, turned back, saw he was *still* watching, and beat a disappointed retreat.

Sensible girl.

Jenny stopped a few feet away, on the last rung of the bleachers so she was his height. "Nice game."

"Thanks." He poured some bottled water onto a towel and mopped his face and neck, then, oh be still her heart, he took off his shirt and did the same to his torso. "Anne tell you about this, too?"

Jenny nodded, trying to tear her eyes away from his chest and the undulating muscles in his arms and failing. "You starting to feel like you're being stalked?"

"A little." He poured the last of the water over his head, toweled himself, then pulled a clean shirt out of his bag and put it on, which made Jenny want to weep as his six-pack abs disappeared.

"Hey, good game, man." The last of his teammates came by lugging his bag. He slapped Ryan on the back. "You meeting us at Pete's?"

"Thanks, Scott. I'll be there, yeah."

"See ya." The guy nodded to Jenny and walked off.

Which left Jenny and Ryan alone. Or at least not the center of anyone's attention but their own.

She hadn't even planned it this way. Was she good or what?

"So what did you think?" He put his hands on his hips, face still flushed from the exercise, making her think of other times she'd seen his color high like that.

"I enjoyed watching you."

He nodded, blue eyes glowing under the dark hair that curled over his forehead in water-clumped strands. "Thanks."

Now what? The silence lengthened. She couldn't take her eyes from his, and he didn't seem to be looking away, either.

Screw it.

She got down from the bleachers, walked up to him, grabbed his clean shirt in two fistfuls and walked backward, leading him with her.

"Jenny?"

"Mmm?" The bleacher hit the back of her knees and she stepped up so she was on his level again.

"What are you doing?"

"You're too tall."

"For what?" He started to move back; she grabbed and pulled him forward.

"This." She slid her hands together across the back of his wide shoulders and locked them at the base of his neck, then looked straight into his hot blue eyes, her heart hammering so hard her body shook from the impact.

His mouth went still when she touched hers to it. Stayed still when she pulled back and moved forward again, tasting his top lip, his bottom, lightly tracing the line between them with her tongue.

His hands moved to rest on her hips, thumbs grazing the bare skin below her waist, but he didn't pull her closer. Nor did he return her kisses. She stopped, but didn't move back, not wanting to meet his eyes, feeling suddenly raw and scared, like there was something vital at stake that she hadn't anticipated when she'd started this.

Crap.

"Sorry." She unclasped her hands and sent him a cool glance so she wouldn't have to expose anything real and feel even stupider. "My mistake."

She turned and walked away, stumbling on the bleacher and, thank God, righting herself in time to be spared injury on top of insult.

Ryan strode past, startling her, and stopped at the end of the bleacher, cutting off her intended route down. "*What* was that?"

"What…? I wasn't…" She stopped walking. What *was* it? "You didn't—"

"Is this a game? Kiss me, oops, my mistake, sorry, goodbye? Chapter two of your next book? Men, the toy of new millennium?"

She almost folded her arms over her chest but forced

them not to move. She wasn't going to act the petulant teenager. "You acted as if you'd forgotten how to kiss. Not great incentive to keep going."

"That's not what I meant."

"Well?" She raised an eyebrow. "What *did* you mean?"

He made a sound of exasperation. "What the hell made you do it in the first place?"

"I wanted to."

"So now you're prey to every impulse?"

"Around you I always have been."

His eyes darkened. "Don't fuck with me, Jenny."

"As long as you've gone apparently impotent there's no fear of that."

"Damn it." He fisted his hands on his hips as if he'd much rather be putting them to good use on her face.

"You want me to leave you alone?" She took a step forward. "Is that it?"

"That's it."

"Why?"

He opened his right hand and brought it down on the bleacher with force that must have hurt. "Because you drive me crazy."

True confession? She was glad she could rattle him now as thoroughly as he could rattle her. It was power, and she felt badly in need of some. "I always have."

"Yes." He spoke through tight lips. "You always have, one way or another."

Closer still, only a foot away now. She was playing in gasoline with matches, and she knew it. But she wanted to provoke him, she wanted to feel his anger, his passion, some sense of the vibrancy she'd glimpsed again on the field. If not for his sake, then for hers. "Does *she* drive you crazy, Ryan?"

He grabbed her shoulders. "Don't. Talk. About. Christine. That. Way."

"Or?" She'd seen his anger before, but she'd never crossed him like this; she'd always absorbed his rage until he'd spent it.

Another true confession? God this was exciting. She felt wildly, electrically alive—and crazily aroused.

"Or what?" she whispered.

His grip on her shoulders tightened, then he let go, closed his eyes and put his hand up to his forehead as if she were giving him a headache, which she undoubtedly was. "Or nothing. Never mind."

"Aww, c'mon. No threats? No promise to tear me limb from limb? Maim my lovely face? At least rip my clothes off and take me hard up against the bleachers."

He laughed unwillingly and opened his eyes. "You are a piece of work."

"And you love to work. We're a perfect match."

"Look, what's between us is ancient history. We can't go back to that summer. I'm not the same guy you—" He broke off, totally exasperated. "Listen to me. Now I'm a bad movie script."

Jenny laughed and took another step, wanting to touch him again, but not daring rejection twice in one hour. "Because you're not saying what you really want to say."

"I'm not even going to ask what that's supposed to be."

"I want you, Jenny." She was whispering into the inches that still separated them. "I want what we had. I want to feel that alive again, feel your body in my hands, be on top of you and the whole world. I've got nothing to lose but the Washington Monument growing in my soccer shorts."

He sighed and glanced down. Guilty as charged.

"Why would we have to go back to ancient history?"
She reached and brushed the wavy strands off his forehead,
knowing they'd fall immediately back down. "Who says
we can't go forward?"

"I do."

"Why?" She let her hand trail over his jaw, down the
side of his neck and to his shoulder, expecting him to
back away.

He didn't.

"You're not—" his voice dropped "—what I want
right now."

"No?" Her hand slid from his shoulder and started its
way down the solid breadth of his chest. "In spite of the
Washington Monument?"

"I do want you." He barely got the words out; his hand
stopped hers. "Physically, I'll probably always want you.
But physical isn't enough for me anymore, not at this stage
in my life. I want a wife, and a big house in Connecticut
and a bunch of kids to raise."

She stepped back to see his face better. He appeared
deadly serious. "Oh, my God. *That's* what you want now?
To become our parents?"

His eyes held hers. "I take it that doesn't appeal to you."

"Not the wife part."

He smiled grimly. "Or the rest."

"No." She kept her voice light while tears burned the
back of her eyes. "To me it sounds like a high-security
prison sentence."

"I thought so."

She stared at him helplessly. Her Ryan was gone after
all. "I take it Christine does want that."

"Yes." He cleared his throat and took a step back.
"Christine does."

"Okay, then." She put on her most carefree expression, bludgeoning back her misery. "It was great to see you again. I wish you the best."

She snapped her mouth shut before her voice broke, sure she was wearing an over-earnest expression that didn't fool him for a second.

"Thanks, Jenny." His voice was gruff. "Good luck to you. Your book and tours and…all that."

"I don't need luck. I make my own." She stuck a grin on her face, jumped off the bleachers and walked to her car, not moving to wipe the tears rolling down her cheeks in case he saw.

Somehow this playful attempt to tease him back into bed with her had backfired in a big way. And it hurt.

She sniffed and fumbled for her car keys in her jeans pocket. Christine the Ice Princess wins the Prince. Jenny the Slut Handmaiden goes back to the village of Brooklyn.

Which was fine. All good in fact. She unlocked the car, got in and slammed the door, jammed her key in the ignition and twisted.

A house in Connecticut? She'd go nuts. She needed the city, the noise, the energy, the 24/7 possibilities waiting outside her door. Parties, shopping, all-night dance clubs…

The engine sprang to life and she put the car in gear and checked for traffic. This was the best possible way it could have happened. Any less contact with him and she'd always wonder if they could have picked up where they'd left off. Any more and she might have ended up in too deep again. Like Goldilocks in the cabin in the woods, this one was ju-u-u-ust right.

She pulled away, and a glance in her rearview mirror showed Ryan trudging toward his car, gym bag slung over his shoulder. *Ju-u-u-st right*. Except for one little itty bitty thing.

Giving up on him felt totally and absolutely wrong.

6

RYAN STEERED his hardtop convertible Lexus off Route 95 north onto Exit 19 heading toward Southport. Traffic had been horrible due to an accident outside Bridgeport, and as if that wasn't bad enough, half an hour ago it had started to rain, which made the idiots around him drive as if they were in a dangerous ice storm. Beside him, relaxing on the car's grey leather seat, sat Christine, looking very pretty in black form-fitting pants and a soft grey-and-pink top. She'd been doing her best to keep conversation going for the past two hours, and she didn't deserve his mood today.

Jenny did.

He'd skipped drinking with the team at Pete's after the game yesterday because he knew himself, and knew he wouldn't stop at two as he'd trained himself always to do now. He would have gotten roaring drunk, his mood would have only gotten fouler, and he probably would have done something stupid, like picked a fight or shown up at Jenny's door. He hadn't been like this for over a decade—and last time he'd had Jenny to ease the way back to peace.

Nice little irony.

"What a lovely town." Christine's polite tone broke the silence.

He felt a prickle of irritation he couldn't help. Not Christine's fault she'd been reduced to artificial pleasantries.

He'd done what he could, but conversation had been strained at best, and he sure as hell couldn't discuss what was really bothering him. Thank God she was too polite to ask.

"Southport is beautiful, yes. Wait 'til you see the harbor."

He turned onto Harbor Road and she let out a soft "oh" of appreciation, though he couldn't tell whether it was directed at the finger of water pointing inland from the sound, the country club golf course rolling green on the other side, or the line of elegant yachts moored close to shore. Or simply because he'd prompted her that it would be beautiful and she wanted to please him. He had a feeling she'd always try to please him.

"Look at these *houses*."

"Yup." A while back they'd passed the one he'd grown up in, next to the fire station, painted yellow now. His mom had moved to a condo in Fairfield, though she was currently at a Florida time-share with friends. He hadn't bothered pointing out his old house to Christine, though he should have. Eventually he would; they had plenty of time to get to know each other.

They passed the house Jenny had grown up in, and his mood went further south. Her parents still lived there, retired, her father from medicine and her mother from interior decorating. For the first time he wondered if it was a mistake to want to come back to live in Southport. Bad enough he'd have to deal with Mitch's house, though Mitch's parents had long ago moved to upstate New York rather than stay where their son had lived and died.

Maybe it would be better to start over somewhere new, without the memories. If one touch of Jenny's lips could turn back the clock so many years, what would it be like to see the places they'd been together every day? Living here could eventually exorcize the demons, or it could give them continuing opportunities to torment him.

Jenny Hartmann was everywhere in this town. Even here, overlooking the harbor, on that bench one night…

How could he have been so wrong in thinking he'd thoroughly turned her off all those years ago? Friday night at two in the damn morning, he'd even gone to the corner of Fifth and 96th where she'd waited for him, not to take advantage of her offer—he had good reasons not to and was sticking to them—but because he couldn't bear to think of her sitting half-naked in Manhattan in the middle of the night. Who knew what kind of weirdos were around? Bad things happened. Quite often in New York.

He'd stood in the damp dark chill watching her car, feeling alternately ridiculous, angry and tempted, occasionally catching a glimpse of her at the window, looking for him, he supposed, then retreating to the car's dark center.

If a policeman had wandered by and found him pressed back against a building, watching nothing in particular with a massive hard-on, he would have had a lot of explaining to do.

He turned onto Willow Street and drove nearly to the end where the line of houses on the east side of the street stopped and the unobstructed view of the harbor and sound began for properties on the west.

"Here we are." He pulled into the driveway of the massive Greek revival he'd coveted online, and parked behind what must be the realtor's car.

"Oh, my lord." Christine's voice was hushed and awed and Ryan hoped that was a good sign. The house was beautiful. No question. He blamed his reluctance to get out of the car on the rain, which had suddenly worsened, wipers barely making a clear space before the downpour obscured the windshield again.

He and Jenny had gone at it in her car during a storm like this, parked in the high school parking lot....

He turned to Christine. "Want to wait it out?"

"Sure." She smiled sweetly and he tried to imagine pulling her into his lap and having her come apart on top of him while the rain thundered all around.

He couldn't.

So he'd settle for more chitchat. That kind of easy familiarity between them would come later, from knowing and trusting each other more. "The house was built in the mid-nineteenth century by a retired ship captain."

"Tired of wandering, but still wanting to be close to the sea?"

"That would be my guess." He managed a grin, feeling guilty as hell obsessing over another woman while he'd brought Christine here so they could consider sharing this house for the rest of their lives.

He was too old to be obsessed like this, and too sensible. No longer the type to risk everything for the promise of hot sex. He'd read Jenny's book, or as much as he could stomach. How had the most generous woman he'd ever known turned to such a me-first extreme? He understood what she wanted from him. God knew he wanted it, too, in the short term. But Christine represented the long term, and he wasn't going to screw up a chance with her for instant gratification.

"I think it's stopping."

"Yes." He peered up through the windshield, unsettled that he hadn't noticed. "Want to risk it?"

"Sure." She grinned and grabbed her door handle. "One...two...*three*."

They erupted out of their doors, slammed them shut and raced for the front door. They arrived together, Christine flushed, breathless, laughing and radiant, rain on her face like beautiful tears.

Ryan grinned and wiped a drop under her cheek with his thumb, a deliberately intimate gesture. She caught her breath and stopped laughing. He cupped the back of her head and kissed her gently since it was high time he did, willing himself not to compare. He didn't have wild sexual memories with this woman to fuel the kiss, and this wasn't a wild sexual time right now.

The kiss was fine. It was all going to be okay. He was doing the right thing with the right woman.

The realtor, a thin bleached blonde with a large mouth and dark eyes, opened the door wearing a pink pantsuit and an extrawide fake smile he wished all salespeople would realize was more irritating than ingratiating. "Hi, I'm Sally Granger. You must be Mr. Masterson. You two staying dry today?"

"Sure. Nice to meet you." He and Christine entered the house and Ryan did a three-sixty of the foyer after introducing Christine to Super Smily Sally, whose chin-length streaky hair didn't seem able to move independently of her head.

The foyer and glimpses of the rooms off it looked exactly as they had on the Internet tour, only grander…and less inviting. The fact that the previous owners had a passionate love affair with the color white hadn't escaped his notice online, but while the rooms had looked elegant and pristine on his monitor, standing here the space felt antiseptic and cold.

Sally began the tour, talking nonstop, pointing out the amenities of each room, pouncing on any appreciative murmurs they made and insisting whatever they liked was her favorite, too. She made the place sound like God's house in heaven…which could explain the white.

Christine, clearly agog, murmured, "Oh, sweet mercy, look at that" over and over until it became nearly comical. Maybe he was wrong, but he'd guess her parents hadn't owned a house like this in Charsville, Georgia.

White carpets, white walls, a wild splash of color in the form of…wait for it…beige curtains. White porcelain and tile in the bathrooms—the gold taps seemed gaudy and loud in comparison. The kitchen was the same—white counters, white cabinets, hardwood floor washed lightly over in white.

In welcome contrast, the gardens out back were brilliant green, floral and expertly maintained. Every plant in its place, every color, every shape having the sole purpose of looking perfect next to its neighbor.

Beside him Christine heaved a huge sigh looking out at the yard. "Isn't that glorious?"

"It is. Yes."

He couldn't live here.

As soon as he had the thought he cut it right off. The house was magnificent, everything he wanted. It only felt strange because it wasn't his yet, because it had been fancied up and over-perfected to impress prospective buyers. Add in color and plants and bookshelves and kids and toys and it would turn into a beautiful, warm place to live.

He touched Christine's arm. "You like the house?"

She turned glowing eyes up to his and at that moment he knew that she knew why she was here, and he felt a brief irrational kick of panic.

"I love it, Ryan. I think you'd be really happy here."

"Is it the kind of house you'd be happy in, too?"

"Oh, yes." She whispered the words gazing up at him, and what should have been a blissful moment of shared understanding dissolved into a jolt of worse panic and a bizarre upwelling of rage.

He told himself to calm the hell down. He'd signed nothing, promised no one anything. No reason to freak out. Once he got used to the idea, he'd be fine. Too many changes to contemplate at once.

"I have one other house I'd like to show you today. Just down the street." Sally's smile stretched wider, which didn't seem possible. "A very special house."

Ryan nodded politely. "Special" meaning no one else would buy it and she was determined to unload it onto some sucker. "Would you like to see it, Christine?"

"Sure." She caressed the white counter and stepped back, letting her hand linger as if she were saying, *Goodbye, I love you, I'll be back soon*. "That sounds like fun."

The rain had retreated to a drizzle as they walked the short distance to the north end of Willow Street, Sally pointing out houses along the way to Christine, the two chattering like old friends. Ryan tuned them out, breathing in the cool humid air as if he'd been denied any in the house they'd just left.

What the hell was wrong with him? He'd been on a slow sure road to this point since he turned his life around. Now that he was about to get everything he wanted, he was starting to have doubts? It made no sense.

"Here we are." Sally stopped walking, Christine beside her. Ryan had to veer to one side to avoid bumping into them.

Forty-Six Willow Street was a rambling jumble of a Victorian, long open porch on two sides, enclosed porch on another, three stories poking up in seemingly random stages. They mounted the creaky steps and entered the front door—which was actually on the side—into a foyer that led to a dining room painted bright red. To the right was a jaggedy dark wood staircase; to the left, a tiny cozy sitting room. Beyond the dining room lay another small living room, and the door leading to the covered porch, which was stuffed with junk and obviously not used. Colorful modern rugs cheered and warmed the hardwood floors. Paintings and other objets d'art hung everywhere, sometimes three or four high, each with its own dark-green hooded light.

"The owner is an art collector and professor of art history at Fairfield University." Sally dropped that fact on her way into the sunny-yellow kitchen which was narrow with odd angles the owners had made the best of with a counter and stools for eating. The appliances were good quality, comfortably used. A door in the side of the kitchen led to the yard, another in back led down to the basement, which Sally didn't seem anxious to show them.

Upstairs, bedrooms sprouted off a long narrow hallway, a bathroom at one end with an ancient clawfoot tub and exposed pipes. A third floor with slanted-ceiling attic rooms was jammed with possessions, old furniture, luggage, clothes and kids' old toys.

The layout was odd, the plumbing ancient, it would undoubtedly be a heating nightmare, but—

He turned for Christine's reaction. She was as cool-eyed and closed as she'd been open and glowing before. The anger and panic came flooding back.

"What do you think of this place?"

"Oh." She raised her eyebrows. "Well. It has lots of personality."

"True." He made himself chuckle.

"But—" she gestured aimlessly around her "—it's not like the other one."

"Nope." He couldn't argue with that.

Sally finished the tour in the small not-like-Versailles backyard and forgot herself enough to let her fake smile turn slightly dim. "It's a lovely property."

It was. But that's all it was. Property. He'd undoubtedly felt drawn to it only because it looked like humans actually lived there.

Back outside the all-white mansion, which looked even more pompous and unwelcoming in comparison, he thanked Sally and got into the car with Christine, who leaned forward in her seat, gazing up at the Greek revival with love in her eyes.

"It's such a beautiful house. And the view. The gardens." She gestured and let her hands fall helplessly into her lap, clearly overcome.

"Yep. Gorgeous." He backed the car out of the driveway, tamping down an urge to punch something, and headed back toward Westway Road, not bothering to glance at number forty-six on the way.

The location was unsurpassed. The house was perfect. The view sublime. And Christine loved it. What other reasons did he need?

He turned left onto Westway on the pretext of showing Christine more of Southport. This road took him past the houses where the Johnstons and the Lanes, the Thompsons and the Balingers lived, on toward the beautiful Pequot library.

And on this road he didn't have to drive past the house that used to belong to Jenny Hartmann.

THE SECOND THE DOOR to her apartment swung shut, the pasted-on smile dropped off of Christine's face.

What had gone wrong? What could possibly have gone

wrong? How could *anything* have gone wrong after he
practically asked her to marry him right there in the house?

Something had.

On the way up, she'd been anxious, nervous. He was in
a bad mood or distracted or annoyed with her. He'd regret-
ted having asked her along to look at his house, she was
sure of it. Maybe this Jenny person had come back into his
life in a sexual way in spite of his having assured Christine he'd have nothing to do with her. He'd believed the
words while he was saying them, she was sure. But men
had a way of saying what they wanted to be true rather than
what was, and didn't seem to be able to tell the difference
until it was too late.

So sitting for hours in the luxurious interior of his car
in the ghastly traffic, she'd done the best she could, been
as pleasant as possible, covered her frustration and worry
so he'd have no clue he was upsetting her.

At the house, parked in the driveway, when he was still
a thousand miles away and hadn't even noticed the brief
downpour was over and it was dry enough to walk, she'd
been about to give up hope entirely. Then they'd jumped
out of the car and run to the house and it was as if something had clicked into place after being dislocated, and they
were back to the way they were before Jenny.

Only better. Much better. Because he'd looked at her in
the doorway and she'd read the intention in his eyes as if
it had been written there in ink. He wanted to kiss her. Even
more amazing, he did. Not much of a kiss, not a passionate be-mine kiss, but a kiss of promise, of what might be
someday.

On top of that…the house. Dear lord what a house. Never
in her wildest, most outrageous princess fantasies as a girl
would she have imagined herself living in such a place. Cin-

derella, eat your heart out. And at the height of her enchantment, Prince Charming had said those magical, wonderful words— Is it the kind of house you'd be happy in, too?

What could be more perfect? It was everything to her, finding out that what she wanted, he wanted, too.

So what had happened?

On the way home they should have been bubbling over with excitement, making plans, talking about the house, the rooms, the furniture, what they thought would go where and how it would look, even if they still had to pretend they weren't planning to live there together. If he wasn't ready to bring his feelings that far into the open yet, fine; she was fine with that. But their unspoken commitment should have been the thrilling undercurrent to the whole drive back to the city.

It wasn't.

Ryan had relapsed into his sour mood and Christine had been stuck babbling about nothing like a fool all over again, feeling as disconnected as she had listening to Sally the Realtor go on and on about her trip to Nepal and her golf game and her flower-arranging classes. Christine planned to look up Nepal sometime today, since she knew next to nothing about it. She'd have to get used to a whole new class of people, a whole new outlook on life.

A little intimidating. She didn't want to let Ryan down. She never wanted him to regret marrying her.

Her phone rang and she rushed to answer it, as usual hoping it was Ryan.

As usual, it wasn't.

"Hi, Mom."

"Hey, there, Teeny. How goes it?"

She winced at the use of her nickname. "Fine."

"You always say that. Give me details."

"Well…" She shrugged. "I was in Connecticut today, looking at houses with…a friend."

"Oh?" Her mom's voice rose with excitement. "And what kind of a *friend* is this?"

"A man I—"

Her mom gave a delighted shout. "Have you been holdin' out on me, Christine?"

"Nothing's been said yet, but—"

"He rich?"

"Well, yes." Christine rolled her eyes but couldn't help the pride in her voice. "You should see this house."

"He buyin' it for both of you?"

"I think so, yes."

"Well, well." Her mom gave one of her great long laughs and Christine pictured her, head back, mouth wide open, a few molars short of a full grin. "It's about time you got yourself settled. Connecticut, huh? Awful far from Georgia."

No kidding. "I know, but it's beautiful. I hope you'll get to see it someday."

"I can hardly wait."

The picture of Vera Bayer, plump and worn, inside that house made Christine wince. Her mother talking to Sally or another woman like her, her mother in that kitchen…she'd be bewildered. Lost. Who the hell was she to be in a kitchen like that? She'd prefer her own warm cheerful cozy kitchen back home in Georgia. With jars and jars of homemade jams and put-up vegetables from their own garden. With a sampler on the wall she'd stitched herself and another their neighbor had done to thank them for help after a fire in their garage. With pots and pans her own mother had used before her in the full-to-bursting cupboards. With the chunky wooden countertops scratched and scarred and burned from years of use. With the table barely big enough for all of them, loaded with food, even more when the neighbors stopped by with pies or cakes, coarse laughter caroming off the ugly harvest gold walls.

Christine's insides started to feel hollow and sickly. Her mother was still talking, catching Christine up on all the doings of her party business, on people she no longer knew and family she hadn't seen in years. She sank into a material-swathed folding chair and listened, or tried to.

Finally Mom ran out of news, or maybe time, or maybe breath, and Christine ended the call, still slightly queasy, promising to keep her mother up on what happened with Ryan and the house.

She turned and stared at the Chagall print on her wall. *Lovers Over the City.*

A burst of restless energy hit her and she stood, grabbed her keys off the tiny table in her entranceway and went back out into the hall. She needed to walk. She didn't much care where.

Too impatient for the elevator, she clattered downstairs in her black flats, through the door into the lobby and banged out onto the street. A second later, she heard her name called and her already weighted stomach sank further. Just what her day needed. Fred.

"Hey." He ran up beside her, pulling a thick shirt on over his white T-shirt, stretched as usual over his belly, but at least unfailingly tucked in. "You look like you could use some company."

"How do you figure?"

"You seem upset."

"I'm in a hurry."

He took hold of her arm, stopping her and turned her toward him. "I'm not stupid, okay?"

She met his eyes, startled out of any idea of what to
say, and wished they weren't so deep and intense and
long-lashed.

"I know the difference between in-a-hurry and upset.
You don't want to tell me? You just say, 'Fred, I don't want
to tell you.' I can handle that. Okay? Try it with me." He
gestured at her to speak. "'Fred, I don't want to tell you.'"

She scowled, beginning to get annoyed, then he winked
and a surprised giggle burst from her instead, made louder
when he started chuckling along.

It was odd how natural and sweet it felt to be laughing
in the street with Fred Farbinger. Of all people. Especially
after such a tense, complicated day. She found herself
wanting to tell him. Maybe he'd even understand.

"I... This morning..." She threw her hands up, feeling
stranger when she recognized the gesture as one of her
mother's. How could she even begin? Why bother? "I had
a bad day."

"Yeah? Tell me." He started walking and she hesitated
only a second before she fell into step beside him. He
seemed taller, or broader, or just...bigger all of a sudden,
and it was an admitted relief to be around someone she
didn't feel she had to walk on eggshells with.

Of course, her and Ryan's relationship was much more
intricate, with more at stake, so it was naturally tenser at
the beginning while they got to know each other.

"I was in...Connecticut. With Ryan. House-hunting."

"Really."

He was looking at her and she didn't want him to see
her face. She'd heard the pain in his voice and was shocked
at how much she didn't want to be the cause of it. "We saw
a beautiful one. I think he's going to buy it."

He stopped walking. "For you?"

"I don't know." To her horror the words came out as a wail and tears started springing up. "I don't know. I think so. But then everything seemed so wrong after that and I don't know what I did or what I could have done to fix it or what I even *want*…"

"Shh." He guided her gently out of the pedestrian path, away from the street, next to a grey building.

She couldn't stop crying, face covered with her hands, beyond mortified at her public loss of control.

Then arms came around her, and she was enveloped in a strong solid embrace and a wide shoulder presented itself at a perfect height for her to lay her head on, so she closed her eyes and did just that, working to bring her sobs under control, though she felt she could have taken all afternoon to do it and he wouldn't have minded.

And then she felt a hand at the back of her neck where Ryan's had been only hours earlier and she felt her face lifted, and for the second time that day, Christine was kissed by a man.

Only…this was different.

Where Ryan's kiss had been tentative and sweet, this one was I-own-you deep, and to her profound shock, with his clean scent surrounding her and his strong male arms surrounding her, Christine found herself kissing him back, in full view of anyone passing by…so help her, please not Ryan.

Then Fred kissed her again, and something animal and wild that hadn't stirred when Ryan kissed her started growling to be set free. And with a shock she realized that even if Ryan did come by, if he walked right up to her and tapped her on the shoulder and demanded to know what she was doing…

She wasn't sure she could have stopped.

Ryan opened his refrigerator and stared at the bottles of Beck's lined up in the door, scowling at the voice in his head saying, *Don't do it. Just don't do it.*

Yeah? Got a better idea?

He grabbed a beer, yanked open the drawer in front of him and rummaged for the opener. His finger caught on something sharp and he shouted a word his mother wouldn't have appreciated, shoved the drawer savagely shut with his hip and jammed the bottle back where he'd got it from.

Okay. Drinking was a stupid idea. He knew that.

He examined his finger, found no blood and shook it to ease the pain from whatever had stabbed him.

Now what?

He strode into his living room, threw himself on the couch, grabbed the remote and clicked on his big-screen TV. Commercial. He changed the channel. Feel-good family movie. Change. Another commercial. Change. Not-funny sitcom. Change. Unreal reality show. Change.

Ten minutes later, he turned the set off and prowled around his room. Too restless to read. Maybe he should go to the gym and blow off steam.

Whatever crap-assed mood he'd been in before, it was worse now. Twice he'd picked up the phone to call Sally and make an offer on the house, twice the panicky rage had risen in his system and he'd banged the phone down.

Once he'd picked up the phone to call Christine, to apologize for his behavior. That got nowhere even faster.

She was the woman he intended to spend the rest of his life with and he didn't even want to talk to her? Something was wrong with this life plan. Possibly fatally wrong. And if his entire life plan was about to die, what the hell was he left with?

He went into his room, grabbed his gym bag, stuffed it

with shorts, T-shirt and a change of underwear, and slung it over his shoulder. With all this angry energy he'd probably run twenty miles on the treadmill. Or maybe he should go right to the punching bag.

Back in his living room, he couldn't find his keys. Damn it. He'd flung them somewhere when he got home, after he couldn't bring himself to kiss Christine again out in the hall, which pissed him off even more.

Of all the stupid situations to be in. A woman he thought he'd like to marry whom he didn't want, a woman he couldn't imagine marrying whom he couldn't stop wanting.

He brushed aside some newspaper on his coffee table and exposed a book with a hot pink cover showing a cartoonish drawing of a stylishly dressed woman grinning at the viewer.

Jenny's book.

Immediate flashback to the night thirteen years ago when he'd first gone to her, feeling helpless, furious, terrified, though all he'd registered at that age was anger. He'd been walking through a storm, wallowing in the misery of getting soaked, and had seen the light on in her house, remembered at the same second his mom mentioning her parents were away in Maine and that Jenny was home. He should take her out, Mom had said. Have some fun to get him out of his funk and keep his mind off of what had happened a month and a half earlier.

As if.

He'd gone to the front door, half of him feeling an inevitable pull, the other half unsure what the hell he thought he was doing.

But the second she'd opened the door, the second her dark eyes met his and he saw her expression, he'd known he'd come to the right place. No fear, no sympathy, just understanding and the promise of forgiveness he hadn't yet been able to give himself.

He'd kissed her because he had nothing to say, no way to express what he was feeling. Once he'd kissed her, nature took over and he'd gone with its instructions, expecting her resistance. When she gave none, he'd let the demons out, barely aware of what he was doing, restraining himself only from outright violence, instinctively searching for a release other than the physical though he hadn't understood that then.

Ryan picked up the book. *What Have I Done for Me Lately?*

What kind of crap was that? He slammed the book on the table, picked it up and slammed it down again.

His phone rang. He stared at it, breathing hard. It rang again.

Jenny.

Ring. Ring. He couldn't make himself move. He heard the machine pick up, then the female voice over the answering machine. "Hello. This is Joanne Argyle from Hartley and Benson opinion research. We're calling to—"

He lunged for the phone, picked it up and let it drop back into the cradle, cutting her off.

Damn it. *Damn it.*

It wasn't Jenny. He wanted Jenny.

He picked up the receiver again, dialed information, asked for her number. Unlisted.

Her parents. He dialed the number he still remembered by heart and waited. Their machine picked up. No one home. Shit.

Anne. He called her, misdialed, tried again.

"Hello?"

"It's Ryan. I need Jenny's number. Did she give it to you?"

"Sure did. Hang on, I'll get it. You okay? You don't sound good."

"I'm fine."

"Right." Anne blew out a breath of exasperation. "Mr. Communication strikes again. Okay, here it is."

She read the number and he scrawled it on the corner of a gas bill. "Thanks, Anne."

"Sure. If you need someone to talk to, I can—"

"I'm fine. Thanks. Bye."

He hung up, feeling guilty for cutting her off, and dialed Jenny, knowing he should stop, that he needed to sit and think this over, wait until he was calm. The phone rang. Rang again. He closed his eyes and put his hand to his forehead. What was he doing? This was crazy. He couldn't—

"Hello there." A cheery unfamiliar voice came on the line. "You've reached Jessica and Jenny. Leave us a message. You know how!"

The beep sounded. He choked. Christ, she had a roommate. What the hell message was he supposed to leave?

"Jenny." His voice came out thin and desperate, and he laughed harshly. This was ludicrous. Fucking ludicrous.

He hung up the phone and squeezed hard at his temples. Stupid move. No point. He'd be much better off working out.

He found his keys under the corner of *Forbes* magazine's April issue, slung his gym bag over his shoulder and headed for the door.

The phone rang. He stopped. Waited while the machine picked up and his message played silently.

Beep. "Ryan. It's Jenny."

His adrenaline surged.

"Pick up. You sounded horrible."

He swallowed, staring at the machine.

"*Pick up.*" Two beats of silence, then a sigh. "Okay, don't. I know you're there. I'm at Ninety-seven Second Place in Brooklyn. Anytime."

He stared at the machine, stared at the keys in his hand, stared at the door. Then he dropped the bag from his shoulder, zipped up his sweatshirt, and went out.

7

From: Natalie Eggers
To: Jenny Hartmann
Re: I did it!
I did it, Jenny! I went out with my girlfriends even though he didn't want me to. It was so amazing. I felt so free and had a totally amazing time! Today I'm going on a shopping blitz. I earn a decent salary, and I deserve not to look like a bag lady.
Woo-hoo! Thank you, thank you, thank you!
Natalie

"HE'S COMING *HERE?*" Jessica stared at Jenny over the tops of her funky green half-glasses, spoon poised over a pint of Ben & Jerry's Butter Pecan ice cream.

"I…don't know. I gave him our address. He might have gone out and missed the message." Though she doubted it. Jenny put her spoon in the sink, stomach unable to handle the concept of ice cream. Or the concept of what she'd done.

"Well, I say take no chances." Jessica slapped the top onto the half-eaten carton of ice cream and launched her spoon into the sink. "Code purple."

"Jessica, I don't think—"

"Uh-uh-uh." Jessica regarded her sternly, hand raised to silence objections. "We agreed."

Jenny watched her call their friend Sharon to ask to spend the night, feeling as if she'd gotten on the wrong train and it was picking up speed, carrying her out of the safety of the station to who knew where.

Reaching out to Ryan had been instinctive. After a week of clubbing and parties, she and Jessica had been having a girls' night in, celebrating Jenny's having written another half chapter for her next book—though she was still staggeringly behind her deadline—by eating ice cream and gossiping, and hadn't bothered to answer the phone. When the machine had picked up, Ryan's despondent voice saying her name had frozen her colder than the ice cream.

Without stopping to think or to consider the consequences, she'd lunged for the phone and gotten a dial tone. Had that given her the respite she'd needed to gather her thoughts and make a sensible plan of action?

No. She couldn't call back fast enough—star-sixty-nine since she didn't know his number. He needed her, she was here.

Ten seconds after she'd left the message and hung up—and where had her common sense been hiding before that?—it had hit her. A man she knew a long time ago who'd made it clear she wasn't what he wanted anymore had called, communicated the sum total of "Jenny," and she was prepared to rearrange her evening, make herself available, do whatever it took to help fix whatever was wrong, no matter the cost to herself.

Hello? *Had she read her own book?* Her articles? Her advice columns? Anything?

Jessica hung up the phone. "Green light on code purple.

I'll pack my bag and be on my way. Sharon's home watching a movie tonight, something with Pierce Brosnan. I don't even care what, if he's in it."

Jenny took a panicked step toward her roommate who was already heading for her bedroom. Great. Now what display of amazing inner strength was Jenny planning? Begging Jessica not to leave?

Regroup, darling. Remind yourself that you are a fabulous, hot, independent strong woman, and whatever happens tonight or any other night—even with Ryan—you can handle it. And him.

Though she was going to change out of sweats.

In fact she was going to follow her own advice to a teenage girl today and dress how she wanted to feel instead of how she did. She strode toward her bedroom, throwing open the door to her microscopic closet. Off came the oversized T-shirt with her own book cover silkscreened on it, made for her by a fan. Off came the fabulously comfortable navy sweats. Fine for a girls-in evening, not for an encounter with…what? Her past? Her nemesis? Serious testosterone?

Instead…she pulled out a hot pink cami top with a shelf bra that did impressive and uplifting things to her cleavage, and a multitiered pleated black midthigh skirt.

This was how she wanted to feel, and how she would feel when the clothes were on. *This* was how she wanted Ryan to see her if he actually showed. The New Jenny. Confident. Sexual. Secure. A woman to be reckoned with. A woman whose sympathy and trust and support and time he had to earn. They would not be given freely anymore, not until he'd proven himself worthy.

"Bye, doll." Jessica came to the door and caught sight of the clothes Jenny had picked out. "Oooh! This man is going to get his eyeballs burned tonight!"

Jenny laughed. "Bye, Jess. Have fun with Pierce."

"Not as much as you'll be having. Make sure you don't behave! And videotape the whole event so I can watch later." She slapped a hand to her cheek, mouth and eyes wide in did-I-say-that? shock, winked and banged out of the apartment.

Jenny's chuckles died; she started to dress. Then frowned. Could it be *any* quieter in here? The silence was getting on her nerves, though New York was never truly silent.

She put on an Annie Lennox CD, volume loud. Much better. The clothes made her feel better, too—stand straighter, taller, move with more purpose. She put on makeup, then caught herself adopting the more natural style Ryan preferred, and slathered it on with a vengeance, swinging her hips to the music. *Men were not the answer to who she was or what she needed.*

Jewelry next, bracelets piled on, jangling as she clapped her hands over her head in time to the beat, multiple earrings in her many-pierced ears, a ring on every finger. And finally, zebra-striped high-heeled pumps slipped onto feet covered in black thigh-high stockings—in case he behaved appropriately lewdly and she needed to get naked fast.

A look in the full-length mirror behind her door and...*ta-daa*.

Her triumphant smile drooped.

She looked overdressed, overdecorated, obviously armored. Might as well pick up the eyeliner and write "Compensating for Insecurity" on her forehead.

Okay, then. Tonight her strength would come from within.

To the bathroom she marched to wash off the makeup and reapply it more subtly. She removed the jewelry and covered the cami with a sheer loose white top, though she left it unbuttoned. Finally, she took off the heels and replaced them with black flats.

Back to the mirror. She took a series of centering breaths to take the anxious worry out of her eyes, opened them and checked again.

Good. She looked good, and still like herself. She knew who she was, way more than when he'd known her before, and that would shine through the simpler outfit and make a stronger effect than overkill.

So. After all that…would he come?

She laughed at the irony. Wouldn't *that* be pathetic? But her reaction to his call had been an effective lesson. Probably good for her to be put to the test once in a while in her personal life. Just because she'd written the book and understood the concepts, didn't mean she'd been able to transform herself completely. Not yet. And maybe not ever completely. Maybe hers would be a lifelong fight against the weakness she'd cultivated for so many—

The buzzer rang. Her heart leapt.

He was here. He'd come.

Okay. She could do this. She was strong. She was woman. Head lifted, shoulders squared, she marched to the intercom and jabbed it as if she were squashing an intruding bug. "Ye-e-es?"

"It's Ryan."

His hoarse voice nearly undid her. Damn it. She needed to stay in control. "Come on up."

She pressed the button to unlock the downstairs door, fighting to keep her composure, reminding herself of all she'd learned. She sauntered to the front door, opened it and positioned herself against the jamb, languid and loose-limbed. Her apartment was on the second floor; she had about thirty seconds…

He appeared through the stairwell door in fifteen. One glance said she had her work cut out for her. He must have charged the stairs, now he was striding down the hall with a look on his face she knew too well.

Steady, girl.

She put out her hand and stopped him, laying it flat against his chest. "What's your hurry, soldier?"

"I need to talk to you."

"Talk?" She lifted her eyebrows. "That's funny. I'm not getting a *talk* kind of vibe from you."

His jaw was tight; his eyes had that don't-mess-with-me warning that used to get her juices flowing.

Some things never changed.

"Let me in, Jenny."

She tipped her head. *Sorry, not going to be that easy anymore.* "Did I hear *please*?"

A door opened down the hall, Jack and Terry's place. Ryan glanced, then picked her up by the waist and forced her into her apartment, slammed the door shut behind them.

"My, my." She smiled sweetly, every atom in her body charged and ready for the encounter. "We are still quite the caveman after all. What happened? Christine didn't like the hair-drag maneuver so you ran to me instead?"

Bang. Direct hit. His hands tightened on her. "This isn't about Christine."

"No?" She ignored a traitorous stab of joy. "You mean she's not everything you want?"

"Not everything. No." The words seemed dragged out of him; his grip became painful.

"Then what *is* this about?"

"You. And me. And whatever is still between us."

"Hmm. At the moment, that would be…" She glanced down. "Clothes."

No smile, not a glimmer of one.

O-kay. "So you came to talk? Start talking."

He opened his mouth, drew in a breath, then let her go and gave a bitter laugh, shaking his head. "I shouldn't have come."

"No?" She smiled, trying to stay as detached as possible, her only weapon. "But you did. Why?"

He stared steadily as if he could see inside her; she had to work not to fidget. "I was looking for someone I used to know."

"Ohh, don't tell me, I know this one. Your ex-doormat. Jenny Stepford-Girlfriend. I remember her. So young and lovely, all give and no take. Every man's dream." She dropped the pretense at sweetness. "My nightmare."

"So now you have an entirely new personality," he said with clear skepticism.

"Yup." She lit her expression as if a fabulous thought had just occurred to her. "Hey, whadya know, just like you do!"

He stepped close, not touching her anywhere, but he might as well have been naked against her for the way it affected her. "Obviously the old me is still lurking under the surface."

She hung on to her bravado. "Obviously."

"Where's the old Jenny?"

"Dead and buried, thank God. What did you want her for?"

He caught her face in his hands and held it an inch from his. "Guess."

Oh, my— "Sorry, she's gone."

"I can find her."

"*Gone,* I said. So you can leave without seeing her…" She cemented her gaze on his blue one, and felt the familiar jolt of their sexual connection. Her voice dropped to a sultry whisper. "Or you can take me."

He froze for a beat, then pulled her sharply forward and kissed her savagely.

She had to fight to keep from clutching him to her, backing away instead, pushing at his iron shoulders.

He followed for a few steps, then grabbed her wrists, forced her arms behind her so her pelvis came into way-too-exciting contact with his. "Where's your bedroom?"

"Gee, I forget." Somehow she managed to make her voice come out strong and calm. *Go, Jenny.*

He started walking her backward, making her stumble a few times, tightening his grip before she fell. The living room couch hit the back of her knees and she tumbled onto it, then sat looking at him, brow raised in "what now?" challenge, heart sledgehammering in her chest.

He smiled under narrowed eyes and lunged forward. She rolled to the side, too late.

"Going somewhere?" His padlock arm pinned her against him.

She closed her eyes, feeling him strong and solid behind her. He liked it rough when he was in a mood like this. But she wouldn't submit, not the way she used to.

His hand traveled over her abdomen and came to rest between her legs, a possessive pressure that gradually warmed the material of her skirt and transferred that warmth to her sex. She fought not to gasp at the pleasure of it.

"You like that?" His voice was low and sexy at her ear.

Don't answer. She held herself still, the only sound her high shallow breathing.

"Mine." He yanked up her skirt and put his hand over her again, this time even warmer through her panties. "Still mine."

She tried to turn from his hand, hating the thrill running through her. "I don't *think* so."

He ducked down and lifted her leg, flipped her onto the cushions on her back and grabbed her hands, keeping his shoulder shoved against her thigh so her sex was open to him through smooth black cotton.

She stared at him, mutinous, sullen, trying to control her raging arousal. Damn it. Damn him. She was hanging on by a thread, and he could undoubtedly tell.

He smiled an I've-got-you-now smile and lowered his mouth to the crotch of her panties. This would be her test.

Slow, steady, openmouthed, he began to blow. The heat of his breath came through the thin material first, then the dampness. She closed her eyes, forcing herself still. The outcome was inevitable; they both wanted it too badly. But in the meantime she'd prove he could no longer automatically get his way.

"You like that?"

"Sure. Very pleasant."

He grinned; she wasn't fooling him. He let her go suddenly, rose from the couch with his trademark masculine grace, unsnapped and unzipped his jeans and then dropped them along with his navy boxers. He was hugely erect.

She saw her chance and took it, grabbing him and taking him ravenously into her mouth, something she hadn't done in college.

At least not like this.

He went rigid—the rest of him, too—and she had to fight not to smile, since smiling and sucking didn't mix. Who was in charge now?

Up and down, up and down, swirling her tongue over the tip, cupping his tight balls in her hand, stroking them, letting their weight caress her palm.

He let out the tiniest groan and she did smile then, at the look of closed-eyes bliss on his face, and backed her mouth off him, took his erection in her hand and squeezed firmly.

"Mine." She spoke clearly, forcefully, daring him to contradict her, loving this new twist to their game. "Still mine."

His eyes opened. He pushed her back onto the couch with his body, settling between her legs, pinning her arms, powerful, absolute. "As if."

He started thrusting, his erection working the material of her panties inside her. Her desire climbed. She tried to twist away, making him work for every ounce of his pleasure and hers.

"There's no escape." He flipped up her skirt and had her panties down so fast she barely had time to drag herself halfway up in protest before he was on top of her again, cock straining against her sex.

"Condom, Ryan." Her voice was breathless; her body ached for him.

He held still, mouth next to her ear. "Every woman I've been with since you, I've used one."

She shook her head. "Condom."

He teased her opening with the head of his penis. "You don't trust me?"

"What about me?"

"What about you? You have something I can catch?"

She clamped her mouth shut. She'd been tested for everything after she found out Paul had cheated, then again six months later and had come up negative.

He grinned, reading her like a book. "You're clean."

"There's stuff you can't test for. And what if I got pregnant?"

He raised himself over her, solid and muscular and huge. "You'd have to marry me."

"Condom." She nearly shouted the word as another

thrill washed over her, and then realized he was holding one, already unwrapping it.

"You bastard. Get off me." She took advantage of the time he spent sheathing himself, and wriggled toward the arm of the couch before he caught her, pulled her back and spread her legs, the old Ryan, staking his claim, asserting his dominance.

Not this time. She struggled in earnest, pretending distress. "Stop. Please."

Ryan froze, searching her face, then rolled off her to the floor, onto his knees. "What the—"

He only got the two words said before she surprised him with a shove that landed him on his back on her thick Oriental. Before he could move or recover, she sprang off the couch and straddled him, bronc rider victorious in the saddle.

He stared, astonished, and she smiled pure evil enjoyment. "Ryan, I'd like you to meet New Jenny. New Jenny, this is Ryan."

She lifted and positioned herself over his still hard cock, let it sink slowly inside her, fighting against the depth of her reaction to Ryan filling her again. "Mmm, *very* nice to meet you."

"You are so—" He broke off when she started to move; his eyes closed, his mouth half-opened in ecstasy. She rode him, keeping her own arousal under control, needing to be in charge, to prove to herself that she could do it, that she could conquer her weakness. *Men are not the answer to the question "What do we need?"*

His eyes opened as if he heard her thoughts. He took hold of her hips, supporting her rhythm, then slid his thumb to her clitoris, watching her face.

She inhaled sharply, and her rhythm faltered. A whimpering sound left her lips.

"Yes, Jenny," he whispered. "Let it go."

She moved more frantically, her breathing erratic. Steady. *Steady.*

His thumb rubbed harder and she gave a cry, then focused every effort on his pleasure, trying desperately to ignore hers.

His face flushed; his circling thumb paused. He jerked up his hips, then grabbed hers with both hands again and whispered her name, pumped savagely into her and gave a low hoarse moan.

Done.

Her triumph never materialized. Watching him climax unleashed emotion far more powerful than triumph.

Would this man never leave her alone?

He opened his eyes and met hers, and for a long moment something unbearably sweet threatened her strength and her control. Then he pulled her down and turned her carefully under him so they stayed joined, circled his pelvis over hers, digging his hands under her to cushion her hips from the rug, an embrace that surrounded her and made her feel protected.

Ironic, since the only protection she could possibly need was against him.

"Your turn," he whispered.

It was. She closed her eyes and concentrated on the sensations in her body so she could ignore the sensations in her heart.

"Come for me, Jenny."

Her orgasm started to build as if she were obeying his words, slowly approaching until she was panting and tense anticipating its arrival. The feel of him inside her was too intense, too much; she wanted to come soon and be able to separate herself from him again, back into safety.

He murmured her name and the sensations burst; she wrapped her arms around his neck and he kissed her with passion that would have scared her if she wasn't feeling it in equal amounts. Her climax didn't release her quickly, but went on and on, fueled by his movements and his kiss.

Then finally, the inevitable comedown, contractions lowering her gradually until she was back in herself.

Except his body felt solid, warm and familiar on top of hers. Like coming back to a place she'd missed desperately, without realizing it until she was there again.

He lifted his head and she found herself wanting to avoid his eyes. Every time they'd made love thirteen years ago, when this moment came, Ryan had looked at her with something between amusement and awe, then he'd opened his young mouth and whispered an earnest, if crude, compliment about her performance. She found herself getting stupidly nostalgic, though if he told her she was totally hot in the sack she'd probably sock him.

His eyes danced. "I think this is where I say, 'Baby, you're the best lay a guy could ever hope for.'"

She cringed. "I was almost hoping you'd forgotten about that."

"Almost?"

"Almost." She fought to keep tenderness from her eyes. "It was sweet. Back then. Now, however..."

"Yeah, some things are best left in the past." He kissed her. "You okay?"

"Sure." She pretended to concentrate on the smooth curve of his shoulder. "Never better. A killer orgasm is one of my favorite ways to spend time."

He didn't respond, didn't chuckle or tease her. She glanced up and found him gazing at her thoughtfully, a slight line between his brows.

"Are *you* okay?"

"A hell of a lot better than when I came in here, why?"

"You look…pensive."

"I guess I am. I want you to do something for me."

"Oh?" She traced his collarbone intently, not sure she wanted to hear this. "Besides coming?"

"Yes, though you still do that damn well. Something else."

She rolled her eyes. "One good lay and he thinks he owns me."

"Can we stop the comedy show now?"

This time she met his eyes for real, and her heart punished her with a violent thud of longing. "Sorry."

"Come to Southport."

Huh? "Why would I—"

"I'll skip work. Come with me…." He frowned, concentrating. "Wednesday. Afternoon."

"Why?"

"For old times' sake."

"That's all?"

"That's not enough?" He was watching her apparently calmly, but she sensed the tension in him.

Before that intense blue gaze melted her onto her rug, she looked away toward the living room window, gray sky visible in a geometric stripe between black buildings. She didn't go back to Southport often, hadn't been back since…well, Christmas her family had spent in Utah with her uncle, then last summer she'd been touring…

If she said yes, she'd have to be saying yes because she wanted to go, because it had been a while since she'd been home and because it would be fun to be back there with him. Not because she was dutifully trying to please him.

She pictured the harbor, the beach, the village, all the

things she'd done there with Ryan…and all the things she'd done there without him.

It would be fun. She'd like to go.

"Okay."

"Good." He grinned and kissed her nose. "I'll pick you up at three?"

"Sure." She smiled, relaxed and happy, and watched him get up, dispose of the condom and start dressing.

She'd done it. She'd spent time with him, argued and held her own, gotten him to admit Christine wasn't perfect for him, brought out the wild side she knew he still harbored. She'd even had sex with him, and hadn't betrayed who she'd become. She was, in fact, entirely intact. Maybe a little bruised here and there, slightly shaken. But intact.

And if she could stay intact around Ryan Masterson, then no man alive could break her.

8

RYAN THUMBED THROUGH the last few pages of Carden Blank, Inc.'s annual report. The CFO had a daughter who'd started a successful business selling hand-knit sweaters a few years back. The father might be a good bet for investing in Gilbert Capital's latest fund.

He closed the report, turned off the green-shaded reading lamp to give his eyes a rest and stretched in the wooden chair of his firm's library where he'd been since five-thirty researching prospects—and hiding from phones and drop-by visitors. His muscles felt tight and restless. A trip to the gym before dinner would help blow off residual stress, though not all of it was work-related. Very little in fact.

Thoughts of Jenny had been dominating every waking moment since he'd left her last night. She'd even starred in a dream that could have made a nice triple-X feature. Had he thought going to see her would exorcise her from his brain? Stupid logic…except he hadn't been operating under even the pretense of logic.

One taste of her and he wanted more. And more and more. In her powerful presence, life with Christine had seemed distant and surreal, like something he'd wanted as a child.

But in the cold light of reality today, the inevitable question had raised its ugly head. More and more and…then what? Now that he'd gotten over the commitment phobia that haunted his youth, where would their affair lead them?

He needed to call the Baxters, ask if they had questions on the fund's prospectus, invite them to dinner and make another attempt to win them over. Having Christine beside him would charm and soften them, smooth the way, as she'd charm and soften and smooth the way for the rest of his life. Having Jenny there in a sexed-up outfit, making sarcastic or outrageous remarks or trying to turn him on under the table would be...

Fun. Really fun. But a disaster. And after a taste of her book, he didn't think she'd welcome any suggestion she tone down her act for the sake of his career.

So what now? What did he owe Christine? What did he owe Jenny? Technically he owed neither of them anything. But he wasn't the kind of a guy who slimed by on technicalities. Sooner or later he'd get busted...by his own conscience if nothing else.

He shoved his chair from the table and dropped his head back on clasped hands. After the passion, the fury, the sexual connection he'd had with Jenny, the life he'd been imagining with Christine seemed bland and colorless.

But who could build a life on sex? Passion faded; everyone said so. When his passion with Jenny faded, he'd be left with a woman who equated the life he wanted in Connecticut with a high-security prison sentence. Maybe his ploy to get her up there looking at houses would soften her stance, but he'd be stupid to count on it. Jenny knew what Jenny wanted and what Jenny didn't.

So did Ryan. Aside from where to live, he didn't want a relationship with a woman who insisted on putting herself first at all times. Their sex life would be a metaphor for the rest of their struggles. Instead of compromise, one of them would always have to win by sheer force. Exciting yes, but exhausting, at a time he wanted life to be calm and predictable.

How ironic. Their positions were nearly exactly reversed from thirteen years ago. He wanted stability, peace and commitment. She wanted to let the good times roll, now and retroactively, for all the years she missed.

The door to the library squeaked opened and clunked closed. A few seconds later Christine came around the bookcase at the end of the row with her usual graceful stride and sat next to him at the big wooden table, holding a plastic shopping bag. "Hey there, overtime guy."

He smiled warmly, expecting the nasty kick his conscience gave him. She was her usual beautiful self in a turquoise suit, her hair in a fancy braid past her shoulders, though maybe she looked a little tired. His protective side revved up. Was she upset about something?

She smiled into his eyes as she always did—except today hers looked wary. Or was it his own guilt reflected? Hours after he'd implied he and Christine could have a future, he'd been writhing in bed with another woman.

He'd be lucky merely to burn in hell.

"Working hard?"

"Trying to." He scrubbed his fingers through his hair. "After this many hours my brain cells get used up."

She laughed. Christine would always laugh at his jokes, even the stupid ones. He loved that about her, a sign of her generous and sweet spirit. Though today it also struck him as a little…spineless.

"I bought you a book I saw at Barnes and Noble last night, when I was looking for history books on Connecticut. It's about Southport. Maybe you already have it?"

"Wow. No, I don't, thank you." Now he felt like an even bigger jerk. While he'd been all over Jenny, Christine had been out buying something she thought he'd like.

"Did you put an offer on the house?" Her face was smooth, peaceful, but her eyes darted to the side and back twice.

"Not yet. I'm going back up on Wednesday." *With another woman. Better and better, Ryan.*

"Oh?" She smiled, but her smile was strained. Upset that he hadn't offered for the house yet? Or that he hadn't offered to bring her with him again?

"I thought I'd take another look."

"Okay." She stared at him, gripping the book in front of her like a shield. He felt a rush of concern.

"Hey." He touched her shoulder. "Are you okay?"

She started, laughed nervously and lowered the book. "Of course. I'm fine."

"You're sure?"

"Positive."

Except that she obviously wasn't fine. The situation was crazy. Nothing had been promised in words. Nothing had moved beyond one chaste kiss on a Greek Revival doorstep. How could he talk to her about something that ostensibly didn't exist? More to the point, how could he help if she didn't tell him what was bothering her? Would they ever break through to the intimacy he assumed would come with time?

"Well, I'll let you get back to work." She laid the book next to him on the table and got up from her chair.

"Thanks, Christine." He stood to see her off, aware he should be wanting her to stay longer. "For the book and the visit."

"You're welcome." She turned to go and he took her elbow to stop her. Something had to be said.

"Yes?" She looked up expectantly.

He couldn't say it. Not here and not now, with the better part of his thoughts still in confusion. "I'll…call you tonight."

She turned back and nodded. Then with a determined look she stepped forward and raised her face.

Kiss. Kiss her.

He did, twice, trying to find something more than affection in his reaction and failing.

Passion didn't last. What could fade if you never had it? Life with Christine would hold no unpleasant surprises.

No surprises at all.

She stepped back, expression flat. Had she also hoped for more? "I'll talk to you soon."

"Right. Tonight."

"Bye." She turned, smiling her trademark smile without seeming happy.

He watched her until she disappeared around the shelves of reference books. Seconds later he heard the door, *squeak…clunk*.

Damn it. He couldn't string Christine along unless he was at least close to a hundred percent sure he wanted to marry her. And let's face it. He wasn't. Not since Jenny had shown up. He could call Jenny his last wild oats, but he didn't want to be that kind of man. It was disrespectful to her, to Christine and to himself.

Unfortunately, there was no clear sign, no perfect road map. Christine was right for him in many ways; they could build a good life. Even if it wasn't the most thrilling he could imagine, at least it would be stable and affectionate and successful. Many people didn't even have that.

His desire for Jenny was extreme, powerful, exciting, especially by contrast. But that didn't mean Jenny was

OFFICIAL OPINION POLL

ANSWER 3 QUESTIONS AND WE'LL SEND YOU
2 FREE BOOKS AND A FREE GIFT!

0074823 ‖‖‖‖‖‖‖‖‖ ‖‖‖‖‖‖ ‖‖‖‖‖‖   FREE GIFT CLAIM # 3953

YOUR OPINION COUNTS!

Please tick TRUE or FALSE below to express your opinion about the following statements:

Q1 Do you believe in "true love"?

"TRUE LOVE HAPPENS ONLY ONCE IN A LIFETIME."
○ TRUE
○ FALSE

Q2 Do you think marriage has any value in today's world?

"YOU CAN BE TOTALLY COMMITTED TO SOMEONE WITHOUT BEING MARRIED."
○ TRUE
○ FALSE

Q3 What kind of books do you enjoy?

"A GREAT NOVEL MUST HAVE A HAPPY ENDING."
○ TRUE
○ FALSE

YES, I have scratched the area below.

Please send me the 2 FREE BOOKS and FREE GIFT for which I qualify. I understand I am under no obligation to purchase any books, as explained on the back of this card.

2 FREE BOOKS AND A FREE GIFT!

K7II

Mrs/Miss/Ms/Mr _____ Initials _____

BLOCK CAPITALS PLEASE

Surname _____

Address _____

_____

_____

Postcode

Offer valid in the U.K. only and is not available to current Reader Service subscribers to this series. Overseas and Eire please write for details. We reserve the right to refuse an application and applicants must be aged 18 years or over. Offer expires 30th November 2007. Terms and prices subject to change without notice. As a result of this application you may receive further offers from carefully selected companies. If you do not wish to share in this opportunity, please write to the Data Manager at PO Box 676, Richmond, TW9 1WU. Only one application per household.

Mills & Boon® is a registered trademark owned by Harlequin Mills & Boon Limited.

Reader Service™ is being used as a trademark.

Visit us online at www.millsandboon.co.uk

The Reader Service™ — Here's how it works:

THE READER SERVICE™
FREE BOOK OFFER
FREEPOST CN81
CROYDON
CR9 3WZ

NO STAMP
NECESSARY
IF POSTED IN
THE U.K. OR N.I.

right for him or that Christine was any less so because of her.

The door to the library opened and closed again. He turned distractedly back to his work.

He could go over this and over this until he was dizzy chasing logic in circles. The bottom line was that he wanted Jenny more than he wanted Christine, and it wasn't fair to Christine to pretend they had a future when he was obsessed with someone else. In the meantime, he'd back off the physical with Jenny before he got in too deep, take her to Southport on Wednesday, and gauge her reaction to—

"Working late, cowboy?"

He turned his head slowly. Jenny, long dark hair tousled, a flush on her cheeks, dressed like a sexual invitation. Spike-heeled black boots rode up to her ankles, then let her perfect calves take over. A red clinging miniskirt bared the rest of her endless strong legs nearly all the way to heaven. Above the skirt, a bulky leather jacket, her hands stuffed in the pockets as if she were cold.

She wasn't cold. Not by any stretch of the imagination.

"I'm going over some reports." He sounded like an automaton.

"Ooh, reports." She took two steps closer. Her thigh touched his knee. "That sounds so interesting."

He swallowed, feeling his brain run out of blood and common sense. Her scent enveloped him; she was a grab away, and he was figuratively sitting on his hands to keep from giving in.

"What are you doing here, Jenny?"

"Looking for you."

"And." He lifted his brows. "You found me."

"I want to give you something."

He guessed it wasn't a book on Southport. "Yeah? What's that?"

She took her hands out of her pockets, tossed her hair and unzipped the jacket. "This."

Her breasts hung naked, full and free between the panels of black leather. His cock hardened. She wasn't playing fair. His conscience wasn't strong enough to overcome a sight like that.

"Jenny…"

"Ye-e-es?"

"We shouldn't—"

"Why not?"

"Someone could come—"

"I'm hoping we both do."

He forced himself to think of Christine, who still thought they had a future together, to think of how he'd told himself to back away from Jenny. That this thrill couldn't last. That he had bigger things to worry about.

Unfortunately the big thing between his legs had a way of making itself seem most important. Sometimes being a guy was pathetic.

"It can't happen here, Jenny." His voice came out halting and uncertain. Who was he kidding? If he really wanted her gone, all he had to do was stand up, grab her jacket, zip it up and escort her out.

He wanted her like hell.

"No? I think it's a great idea."

"And you get everything you want." He stared up, challenging her.

"I don't want that much, Ryan." She ran a hand between her breasts, then down over her firm stomach, slid her fingers under the waistband of her skirt, making him want to cry like a baby. "Right now I only want you."

"For sex."

"Here and now."

"And later?"

"Later…" She gave a sultry siren's wink. "We can do it again."

"That's all you're offering me?"

"No, there's something else." She lifted the hem of her skirt, and when he saw what she didn't have on underneath, he wanted to cry harder.

"You can't resist me, Ryan," she whispered. "Admit it."

He groaned, deep in his throat. There might be a million reasons not to, but he couldn't think of a single one that made more sense than easing the agonizing ache this woman brought him.

"Admit it." She moved closer, touching herself between her legs, sliding her finger up and down her sex. "Say it, 'I can't resist you, Jenny.'"

He broke, let out a rush of breath and a hoarse whisper. "I can't."

One step and she was on his lap straddling him. She knew how to move and her hips were doing it all the right ways.

"This is crazy." He ran his hands over her beautiful firm ass. "I could lose my job."

"That's the fun of it," she murmured. "That's always been the fun of it."

She shrugged her black jacket halfway off her shoulders, brought her hands up to her breasts and cupped them, lifting them toward him. "Taste."

He closed his eyes and dropped his head back in frustration. What the hell was he going to do with this woman?

"Taste me." Her whisper came out as an absurd answer to his question. He lifted his head and found a cinnamon-scented breast in front of his mouth.

He tasted. Cinnamon, vanilla, some edible lotion she'd found; he couldn't get enough.

His cock was hard, painful. He fumbled to release it, kissing her body, unable to stop. Her hands took over, she unzipped him, freed him, sheathed him with a condom from her pocket and sank onto him with a moan of pleasure that nearly made him come right then. He clutched her hips, moved her up and down, listening for the door, dread fueling his excitement. Her vaginal muscles gripped his cock, latex doing nothing to slow down his desire. Sweat dampened his undershirt; he wasn't sure he could stop even if someone came in and found him pumping this sexual fantasy of a woman.

She nipped his ear, breathing hard, then whispered to him, telling him how she'd get him the next time and the next, what she'd do to him, how he'd feel, using words he'd never heard her say except in his fantasies, words that had exactly the effect she wanted.

He clutched her harder, his breath coming out in short jets through clenched teeth.

"Give in to it, Ryan," she whispered.

And he was over the edge, straining into her, pouring himself into a condom in the hottest woman he'd ever known, in a hard chair in the silent library of a straitlaced firm he couldn't afford to be fired from.

He threaded his fingers into the thick mass of dark soft hair at the back of her head, and brought her lips to his, kissed her over and over, dazed, satiated, tender, humble and pissed as hell that she'd driven him to take a risk like this. His other hand stroked down between her breasts, over the bunched stripe of her skirt and found her clit, rubbed until she arched and writhed, coming the way he loved to watch.

He saw her down from her climax, gradually slowing

his finger. Then he put his forehead against hers. "Oh, momma. You're the hottest trick in the universe."

She giggled and he laughed, then they breathed together, laughing again occasionally, until emotion he refused to name got too strong and he pulled her close, laid his cheek against hers, closed his eyes and drank in every part of her that he could.

This was insanity. Sheer insanity.

And he was desperately afraid he'd never find the means or will to recover.

CHRISTINE STOOD outside Fred's apartment, fist raised, knuckles incapable of making final contact with the wood.

Maybe coming down here had been a mistake. She'd drummed up a lame excuse that her bathroom sink caulking had come loose, but the truth was, she desperately needed someone to talk to, and Fred had seemed so adamant that she could talk to him about anything. Not that she'd talk to him about what was really bothering her—how could she confide in him about another man when Fred was so obviously smitten with her? But just to have a friendly receptive face to chat to about her day, to get her grounded back into normalcy.

She'd kissed Ryan earlier this evening to reassure herself that the kiss with Fred was a fluke. That she really loved Ryan—or would come to love him—and that their dream life in that perfect house would really happen exactly as it seemed to be happening.

But the kiss was the same as the kiss on the steps of the house. No spark. Practically…boring.

How could kissing a man like Ryan be boring? More to the point, as she steeled herself to knock on his door, how could kissing a man like Fred be so…not?

She'd come out of the library at Ryan's firm, upset and confused, and gone down the hallway to the elevator. As the doors closed, the elevator next to hers unloaded, and guess who came strutting out, looking wild and sexual and on the prowl. No question what Jenny was after. His name was Ryan, and the sooner she got him naked the better, if she hadn't already.

Christine wasn't sure what was worse, that she couldn't compete with Jenny or the panicky fear she wasn't sure anymore that she wanted to try.

"Hey, my favorite visitor."

Christine spun around, mortified that Fred had seen her standing there, fist raised, not knocking yet.

"Hi." She felt herself blushing, wanting to look away. She had no trouble meeting Ryan's eyes, and had always thought that was because she felt more comfortable around him. Which she did, but maybe not for the reason she wanted to.

"You need something?" He hauled out his huge set of keys and thrust one into the lock on his door. "Or to talk?"

She started to bring up loose caulking, then stopped. Yes, she did need to talk. Why come down here for that and then lie to him? "Are you busy?"

"I'm never busy for you, Chris."

"Christine." Immediately she felt stupid. He'd said something incredibly sweet and she'd corrected him. "I'm sorry. You can call me Chris if you want."

He turned in the act of pushing open his door and grinned, and she got a fizzy feeling in her body. The one she was supposed to get when Ryan kissed her.

"You know why I call you Chris?"

"To drive me crazy?"

"That, and…" He leaned closer, which made the softly

lit hallway feel twilight-dim and narrow. "Because no one else does. That way you'll always know it's me."

The blush started again and she scoffed so his words wouldn't hang in the air with such oddly possessive intimacy. "That's for sure."

"And because it suits you." He straightened, but didn't take his eyes off her. "Christine is perfectly controlled and wears perfect suits and perfect pumps. Chris is the woman inside you're pretending not to be."

The fizzy feeling turned instantly prickly. "Well, I guess you know everything about me."

He winked and pushed the door the rest of the way open. "Not nearly enough. But I hope to change that."

She followed him into his place, feeling as if she should be marching back upstairs again. What did she hope to accomplish here? At best she was leading him on unfairly. He wasn't the kind of man she wanted, no matter what her body kept telling her.

"Welcome to my home sweet home."

She looked slowly around her, admittedly astonished. The place was nothing like what she expected. Not even close. Oriental rugs in rich shades of burgundy and black, blue and cream, green and gold. A wall of books and CDs. Plants in baskets and in pots near the window, cyclamen and paperwhites and crocuses. Tasteful furniture in blues and greens and golds. The kind of apartment she'd expect from a professor or a symphony musician or a doctor. Not a superintendent.

"Want a drink? Coffee? Tea? Juice? Soda? Something stronger? I've got wine, beer and pretty much anything else you might want."

"Wine would be nice. Maybe red?" She found herself hoping he wouldn't ask about what type of red, and couldn't believe she was worrying about impressing Fred. Except that here, he was in a place that made hers look like a hillbilly had moved into Buckingham Palace. "Your apartment is beautiful."

"Thanks." His voice came from the kitchen; Christine stepped over to see and fell prey to another wave of astonishment. The tiny spotless room was painted a dark rich blue, neatly organized, with pots hanging from a series of iron hooks arranged like a chandelier. A microwave was tucked up under the cupboards, espresso machine gleaming in a corner, fruit hanging in copper mesh baskets, more plants thriving by the window. Magnets of different kinds of sushi held laminated children's drawings on the stainless refrigerator door.

Her heart skipped a beat. Did Fred have children? Had he been married at one time? The thought bothered her. It bothered her more when she realized she'd shown up at his door intending to ease her own pain, and she'd never wondered about who he was and what kind of pain he might have suffered.

"My nieces. Back when they were kids. They're both in high school now." He'd seen her looking at the drawings and, as usual, read her mind. "Here you go."

She took the wine he handed her, relieved he hadn't turned out to be one of those people who couldn't open a bottle without discussing vineyard locations and grape varieties and cherry-leather-burned-toast bouquets. None of which she'd have expected of Fred until she'd seen his place.

Back in the living room, he put his own glass on the dark wood coffee table, on which lay picture books of southern France and Lebanon and Ireland.

"Have a seat." He paused at the CD player and a few

seconds later, a classical orchestra piece filled the room, making it feel as classy as it looked. "Like that?"

She nodded, still bewildered by this other side of him and curious to know more. "It's lovely."

"I'm gonna shower off the day's work." He ran his hand over what was left of his hair in back. "That okay? You have somewhere else you gotta be?"

"No. No, it's fine." Where else would she go?

"Okay. Back soon."

Ten minutes later she was halfway through the wine—which tasted really good to her, but what did she know?—and he was back, wearing a black turtleneck and grey pants that made him look as distinguished as his apartment, and made her feel at home and out of place at the same time.

"So." He picked up his glass and sat at the other end of the sofa. "What's on your mind?"

"I…I don't…" She laughed and shook her head. "Just wanted to talk."

"Yeah? What about?"

"I don't know. Just a neighborly visit."

"Uh-huh." He tucked an arm across his broad chest and sipped wine, clearly not buying it.

She gestured toward him. "Why don't you tell me about you?"

"To change the subject? Or because you really want to know?"

"Because…" She looked down at her hand in her lap. "I really want to know."

"Yeah?" His voice dropped. "How come?"

"Geez, I just do, okay?"

"Okay." He beamed as if she'd told him he'd won the lottery. "Let's see. Capsule version of the life of Fred Farbington. I'm forty-three years old. I grew up in Brooklyn, two parents, two brothers older than me, and a dog. Education was real important to dad. I studied hard to please him, ended up going to Boston College, and I'd just been accepted to a Masters program in economics at Rutgers when…I guess fate intervened."

He paused for a sip of wine and something about the way his face looked gave Christine a bad feeling in her stomach. "What happened?"

"Nothing unusual. I got mugged. But I tried to fight and the guy took on the side of my head with a baseball bat."

She couldn't stop her gasp and he grinned. "Hey, do I look dead to you?"

"No." She put her glass down, uncomfortable with how strongly she was reacting to his story. "Go on."

"I woke up in a hospital a week later and couldn't move. Months of rehab, and I was pronounced recovered and released. Only I couldn't think as well anymore. I had trouble with basic math, reading took effort and often didn't make sense. I had headaches, big mood swings. I moved back with Mom and Dad, went through bad stuff for about a year." He looked over for her reaction and nodded at what must have been shock on her face. "It wasn't fun. I took a job here just to get myself out of the house again, and ended up liking it. I help people and I make a nice living. I'm not exactly who I was, but I'm still me and in a lot of ways I'm better. I don't sweat the small stuff anymore for one thing."

She stared, trying to imagine even a fraction of what he must have gone through, and how could she possibly say the right thing? "That's so…horrible."

"It is what it is."

"It must have been so hard for you, to be all that, college and the other degree ahead of you, and then…"

His eyebrow lifted and she realized what she was saying. That he had less to be proud of now because of his job? Up until this moment, sitting in his rich colorful living room, finally choosing to accept the gentleness and empathy he offered, she'd believed that.

Which didn't show her up to be a very good person. *Not the girl your Mama raised,* as her mom would have said.

"I'm…sorry. I…" The words jammed in her throat. "That wasn't nice of me."

"So who needs nice all the time? I finally got to make peace with the fact that advanced degrees and a big career never had been what I wanted, and eventually so did my dad. I don't know if I coulda done that without the sense the bat knocked into me."

"I shouldn't have assumed…"

"Hell, everybody has prejudices, everybody screws up. I'm too quick to judge sometimes. I have a temper. I'm intolerant of laziness and people who waste money on status. I'm suspicious of strangers and not kind enough." He put his wine down and turned to her. "Now, I want to hear yours."

"My what?"

"Flaws. Tell me what you hate about yourself."

She stared at him, bewildered. He wanted to see her that ugly? "I don't…think I can list them like that."

"Why not?"

"Because, I…because I can't."

"Why?"

She started to get angry. For heaven's sake, hadn't anyone taught this man manners? "Because I don't care to be…to seem…"

"Human?"

"That's ridiculous." She started to stand, but he pulled her back, and she realized with a start that she'd expected him to and would have been disappointed if he hadn't. "I just don't know you that well."

"How else will you *get* to know me that well?"

She turned on him. "Who says I want to?"

"What the hell else are you here for?"

She opened her mouth before she realized she had absolutely nothing to say back to that. She hadn't even meant her outburst. She'd been acting like the kid she was back in Georgia, desperate not to lose an argument with her brothers, saying anything that would hurt them enough to get them to leave her safe and alone.

She took in Fred's blazing dark eyes and the frustrated set to his jaw. She owed this man the truth. "I came here to make myself feel better. It was…selfish of me."

"Is that still why you're here?" His voice was quieter, but she could hear his tension.

"Not entire—" She sighed. *Let it out, Christine.* "No."

"Then I don't care why you came down. As long as you're here now for the right reason."

Tears gathered and she blinked hard and willed them to go away. "Thank you."

"We're all selfish at times. We all have evolving to do. If you stop, what's the point of life?" He picked up his wine and toasted her. "Here's to growing older and smarter and knowing what you want."

"What do you want?" She was surprised how much she wanted to know, even enough to hold his eyes without flinching.

"There's only one thing missing from my life right now, and I'm working on it."

"What's that?" The second she said the words, she realized she'd walked right into it.

His gaze softened into gentle amusement as she got

more and more flustered. "What's really bothering you, Chris? Still Ryan?"

She stared at the burgundy liquid in her glass, looking like a still life on the dark wood coffee table with the same shades of red in the rug below it. If she told him she was having doubts about Ryan, he'd take it as an invitation, and that wasn't fair to him.

At the same time, he really wanted to know what was wrong, and she owed him that much after coming in here and drinking his wine and insulting him and lying and being judgmental and generally awful. "I went to see him tonight. He was working late."

"Yeah?" His voice grew tight and hard and she had to close her eyes to continue.

"He…said he was going to put in an offer on the house in Connecticut. I actually thought he already had, but then when he said he hadn't yet…and then he's going back up there on Wednesday, but not with me."

The jumbled mess of words rushed out. She wasn't even exactly sure what she was trying to tell him.

"Ah, the perfect house. You still think you want to live there?"

She bristled. "I *do* want to live there."

"Okay, so you want to live there." The exasperation was clear in his voice. "Why?"

She pictured the massive white space and tried to articulate why it had been so wonderful. Except bringing up the picture of it, she could only remember feeling awed and a little frightened and a little greedy. Like meeting a movie star you'd had a crush on forever, and even in the middle of your bliss, understanding he was way out of reach, but wanting to land him for the rush of the impossible.

"You said you liked my place. How come?" He shifted

to sit closer on the couch, and put his arm along the back behind her. She didn't move away. His shoulders looked powerful under the black soft material and she found herself having to force her attention to what he was saying.

"Because it's beautiful."

"Why? Specifics?"

She gave him a look. "Is this multiple choice or an essay question?"

He laughed and she felt smart and funny and tried not to think about how he also made her feel sexy and accepted, while Ryan made her feel…awed and a little frightened, and a little greedy.

"Your place is colorful. And warm, and full of life and personality."

"But you could make the other place like that. Paint away all that white you told me about and fill it with books and plants and CDs. Ryan's got plenty of money for that. What else is it about my place you like?"

"It's cozier." She frowned, staring around the room, trying to figure out exactly what it was. "Less…intimidating."

"You forgot the most important thing."

"What?" She looked warily at him while his eyes sparked with mischief.

"*I'm* in it." He spread his arms wide. "The most obvious, and she leaves it out."

She burst out laughing, real belly laughter that lightened her heart. "How stupid of me."

"This place fits you, Chris." He touched the back of her neck, lightly, but her skin shivered as if he'd caressed her. "Not too shabby, not too fine. I fit you the same way. I hope you come to realize that someday, though I know Ryan makes me look like a big nothing."

"No." Her protest was automatic.

"Ah-ah-ah." He held up a finger. "Being polite or do you really mean it?"

She really meant it. But she ducked her head, unable to give him that much yet.

"Chris." He slid closer on the sofa and took her hands in his large ones, where they felt warm and secure. "Here's what's pathetic about me."

She smiled, unable to imagine Ryan using that kind of disarming charm. "I doubt there's anything truly pathetic about you."

"There's plenty. For a start, I'm crazy about you, and open to getting a whole lot crazier."

She gave him a pretend-hurt glance. "And that's pathetic?"

He chuckled and squeezed her hands. "No. The pathetic thing is, I want you to be happy. If I thought Ryan and his Connecticut castle would do that, I'd say go for it, I'll suck it up and find someone else. Because I wouldn't want you if you weren't going to be happy with me."

She swallowed, swallowed again, but couldn't stop a tear from spilling over. No one had ever treated her with this kind of…reverence before.

"Don't cry. You tear me up when you cry. I want to kiss you more than I want to go on living when you cry."

Her heart jumped. She waited, breathless. Would he?

"But I'm not going to."

She jerked her eyes to his, conveying a startled "Why not?" in spite of herself.

"Because…" He tried to smile, but it fell flat. "I'm not going to try to seduce you into seeing this my way. You've got to figure it out on your own. When you do, if it's Ryan you want and he'll have you, then you've got my blessing. If it's me…"

She listened while he took in a breath and blew it out.

"If it's me, then you need to let me know. Understand?"

She nodded slowly, tears making him look like underwater modern art.

"Of course…" He sighed in despair. "If it's neither of us, I'll call Ryan and we'll jump off the Empire State together."

She giggled, loving that he'd eased the emotional moment for her with a joke. "You're a good person, Fred."

"Damn right I am." He puffed himself up but his eyes were still serious. "Don't forget it."

She shook her head.

"I have something for you." He sprang up from the couch with a grace that surprised her. She must have looked wary because he rolled his eyes. "Not a ring, calm down."

More laughter. Laughter that emerged because she thought he was funny, not because she wanted to be polite and make him feel good.

"My niece, Linda, asked for this for her birthday. I got you one, too. I hope you're not offended." He handed her a thin book with a hot pink cover, and her warm insides chilled and shriveled. It couldn't be. First Ryan trotting her out in Christine's face, now Fred, too? The coincidence was too cruel.

She turned the volume over and the unmistakable dark-haired brown-eyed woman grinned smugly at her from the back cover. *What Have I Done for Me Lately?*

By Ryan's Jenny Hartmann.

9

To: Natalie Eggers
From: Jenny Hartmann
Re: Your adventure
I am sooo proud of you! Going out and having fun *and*
buying clothes! You are terrific. Doesn't it feel fabulous?
Keep it up girl, you're breaking out of man-jail.
Jenny

SOUTHPORT DIDN'T LOOK much different than it had two
years ago, not that Jenny had really expected it to. Since
her childhood, the highway had gotten a lot busier—and
louder—and real estate prices had taken off for distant
planets. But the sleepy village with Fairfield Women's
Exchange and Switzer's Pharmacy—the kind of store that
sold everything from aspirin and postcards to wheelchairs
and wine—hadn't changed, and she hoped it never would.

She had changed, however, and it was fun to come back
to such familiar surroundings feeling entirely reborn. She
was very glad she'd stayed up to finish an article on being
in control of your dating life for *Self* magazine so she
could feel free and at ease today.

They passed the spot on Pequot Avenue where she and

Ryan had steamed up car windows, past the beautiful homes on Rose Hill Road decorated with newly leafing or blossoming trees and early spring floral displays, down to the harbor, where they'd once sat on a bench overlooking the water and the Country Club golf course and found still other ways to send each other into orbit. She smiled now at the bench and laughed softly, not entirely surprised when Ryan squeezed her hand. That kind of memory never faded—the smell of the water, the warm summer evening breeze, the chirp of crickets and the mingled cries of their wild simultaneous orgasms.

Damned if she wasn't getting sentimental and soppy.

"Wanna park?" She let her hand wander over to visit his inner thigh.

"Soon." He turned right on Westway, left on Willow.

"Are we going on a tour?"

"Nope."

He was acting odd. A little tense, unresponsive, not even interested in high-speed oral sex on the way up. Whereas she hadn't felt this good in years. Not only was she back in the saddle with Ryan Masterson, this time she was in control of herself and her feelings. A girl could only take so much heaven or the real thing would turn out to be an anticlimax.

Near the dead end of Willow, he pulled into the driveway of a preposterous Greek revival mansion. She hated those houses, always had. Why not hang a sign outside that said More Money Than You?

"You know these people?"

He gave her a look she couldn't decipher and unbuckled his seat belt. "Come on."

"How can I refuse such a seductive invitation?"

"Come on—*please.*"

"O-kay." She stepped out of the car into the cool after-noon air, a clumsy step on high-heeled coral-colored shoes. Her ankle turned and she staggered, wishing for a brief second that she'd worn sneakers. But what fun would it be to seduce the hottest man in the country wearing sneakers? Maybe he was impervious to her charms at the moment, but she had plans to change that soon.

Nothing could have been more fun than getting him to lose control in his stuffy proper office back in New York. She didn't even tell him until she was leaving that she'd locked the door to the library on her way in, so no one could really have surprised them. The sex had been incred-ibly hot; she'd felt powerful and female and in charge....

Jenny wrinkled her nose. Okay, well things had gotten dangerously emotional at the end, when they'd been laughing together over his typically frat boy line and he'd suddenly pulled her close, as if he couldn't stand even an inch separating them. She'd rested her head in the solid curve of his neck, eyes closed, savoring the strong feel of his arms around her, and remembered too many other times when she'd been way too vulnerable to him. Luckily she'd managed to drag herself away and make light of their escapade before her girly feelings had left any permanent mark.

Lesson learned. This new way of being with Ryan was perfect.

She shut her door behind her, and surreptitiously tugged the neckline of her orange-red sweater lower, and the slanted hemline of her black skirt higher. She had no idea why they were stopping here, but she might as well play her new role to the max. *Hello, Southport, Jenny is back. Long live Jenny.*

By the time she'd arranged herself adequately sexily and had closed the Lexus's door, Ryan was already waiting for her on the house's front step, looking more formal than she'd expected him to look today, in a green-and-white striped dress shirt and nice pants.

Why the hurry? Had he arranged to meet someone here and they were late?

The door opened and a blond woman, the kind who hadn't had a face-lift only because she was still too young, welcomed him with a smile that made the term artificial whitener spring to mind.

Who was plastic woman and what was she to Ryan? More to the point, what did a stranger have to do with the "for old times' sake" excuse he'd used to get Jenny to Southport? And why was she looking at Jenny as if Jenny were the last person she expected to see? And *why*, as Jenny approached, could she have sworn she heard the woman say something about Christine?

"So you want to show the house to…" She flicked another glance at Jenny as if she wanted to say, "this trash." "Your…friend?"

Show the house. Christine. He'd been here with Christine and now it was Jenny's turn? Was this a tryout for the Wife of Ryan Masterson contest?

"I'm his mistress." Jenny gazed faux-adoringly at Ryan and put her hand into his back pocket, squeezing much harder than if she was feeling affection. "Christine is his fiancée, but he said he won't give me up even after they're married. Don't you think that's sweet?"

Ryan yanked her hand out of his pocket and smiled at the agent. "Sally Granger, this is Jenny Hartmann, old friend and lousy comedienne."

"Would you excuse us for a second?" Jenny kept the smile on her face until Sally had backed her chilly way into the house again and closed the door.

Jenny dropped the smile. "We're *house*-hunting?"

"I saw it with Christine and I wanted you to—"

"You brought me here to look at a house for you and *Christine?*"

"No. I want *you* to look at the house because I want your opinion."

She swallowed abruptly. For a second she'd thought he was going to say "because I want to live here with you" and her system had started producing spectacular fireworks which she'd had to douse immediately with the water of sanity. Hello? She'd rather eat worms than live in a house like this. Living with Ryan, regardless of the house, was a subject she didn't care to touch. They were all about fun right now, and it was working just fine.

"I can give you my opinion of this house from right here."

"Come inside."

She started to argue, and he lifted one dark eyebrow and said, "Please," in a quiet calm voice, and she shut up and gave in like the wimp she used to be.

"Okay. Lead me to torture."

Ryan pushed open the front door and nodded to Sally. "We're ready. Thanks."

"No problem." She turned, and her heels made click-click noises almost as disapproving as the expression on her face.

"I guess she likes your fiancée better," whispered Jenny.

He slid his hand down over her rear and just when she thought things were about to get a lot more fun, he gave her a playful smack, which made her sly smile turn into a glare.

Of course he knew this meant war.

She stepped away and gazed around her. The interior was just as horrible as she expected, maybe worse. Cold, white, pretentious without a single welcoming or redeeming feature. Unrelieved luxury minus the charm. "White.

My God, it's white. You can't seriously be thinking of living here."

Sally whirled around stiffly, clearly sensing her six percent of a gazillion dollars to be in mortal peril. "Of course it can all be painted to Mr. Masterson's taste."

She tappity-tapped her way into the living room, a massive museum horror.

Jenny grimaced. "I don't like this house. You'll buy a different house for *me,* won't you, Ryan?"

He frowned at her and she blinked beseechingly. *Come on, Ryan, loosen up.*

Sally pointed out a few of the room's more horrible features with forced enthusiasm: overblown marble fireplace, ridiculous decorative columns, parquet floors you'd walk on only in stockinged feet and still feel guilty.

"Yeah, okay, but I mean could you see making whoopee in a place like this? The house should be on the market for birth control."

Behind her Ryan cleared his throat. Hiding laughter? Or annoyed with her? She hated to think he'd even considered buying this house, with Christine or without her. The man she'd known so long ago would have laughed himself sick even at the thought.

"What about the bedroom?" She caressed Ryan's broad chest with her hands and smoldered intimately up at his growly face. "Any chance of going up there?"

"The *kitchen* is right this way," Freezy Face put in immediately.

"I don't know, I'm kind of in the mood for the bedroom." She let her hand linger just over Ryan's fly, watching for his reaction.

He removed her hand, his mouth twisting into the tiny beginnings of amusement. "Kitchen's fine, Sally. Thanks."

"Bedroom later?" Jenny gave him a doelike gaze and he rolled his eyes.

"You're a piece of work."

"So's this house."

"This way." Sally's command came through loud and clear and off they went, tappity-tappity, into the kitchen.

"Ah, the kitchen is *white!* Something new." Jenny shuddered. "I'd be scared to cook anything but cauliflower and Cream of Wheat."

"Maybe you'd enjoy looking at the grounds." Sally's teeth were all but clenched.

"Maybe…" She doubted it. And she was right. Lovely as they were, with every possible spring flower blooming, and the foliage of many more plants that promised displays all summer long, not a leaf or a blade of grass had been allowed to grow out of place. They even had statues, for God's sake, and fountains and a little pond with a bridge over it.

"And what's the verdict on the grounds? They're not white." Ryan came up close behind her, and she leaned back against him, ignoring the sniff from Sally, and reached to turn his face down toward her. The sight of his dark serious eyes so close made her next snotty remark disappear, and another thought take its place.

"Remember when we'd get the kids on the block together and play kick the can? Capture the flag? Hide and seek?"

"Sure."

She gestured out toward Versailles. "Would you want your kids playing out there?"

"Of course the gardens can be altered to suit your taste." This from Ms. I-Want-My-Six-Percent.

"Yeah." She didn't stop gazing at Ryan. "But what a shame, when the way they are could make some incredibly uptight couple so happy."

He almost smiled. "Good point."

"What were you smoking when you looked at this place before?"

He looked so uncharacteristically perplexed she wanted to kiss away the line between his brows. "I don't know. But it's clear now. You helped, thank you."

Yess. She was getting through to his real self, and the thought was thrilling and humbling. "That's why you wanted me here?"

"One reason."

She went up on tiptoe to bring her lips within his reach. "And for old times' sake?"

"That, too." He leaned in and kissed her—not that she'd given him a lot of choice in the matter—a long, thorough kiss that had her doing some serious heating up, and had Sally making cutesy fake coughing noises behind them.

Jenny twisted around to wink at her. "You think *I'm* bad, wait until you meet his *other* mistress."

Ryan squeezed her hard, but she had a feeling he wanted to laugh. She wished he would.

"Sally, we're ready go see the other house."

Other house? Jenny glowered at Ryan. Now that she'd done her part rescuing him from a multimillion-dollar mistake, she was ready to have some fun. "Another one?"

"The second one I saw."

"With Christine."

"Yes."

She squinted mischievously. "Will we be able to get naked in that one?"

He grinned, the first real smile she'd seen that day. "We'll see."

"Forty-six Willow?" Sally was already heading for the front door, obviously brightening at the chance to salvage a commission. "Of course."

Outside, the sun was still bright, but the air had started to chill toward evening. They walked past a few houses, toward wherever this other overpriced overfussied monstrosity was—would she and Ryan get to have *any* fun?—when an old woman sweeping her apparently clean driveway turned out to be Mrs. Cornstone, Jenny's seventh-grade English teacher, loved and feared throughout Fairfield county.

"Good afternoon. Lovely day." Mrs. Cornstone paused in her sweeping to greet them, then her clear blue eyes lit on Jenny and widened. "Why Jenny Hartmann, dear, how good to see you."

Sally said something to Ryan, and the two of them withdrew to have a conversation, probably about how to make sure Jenny stayed outside the next house.

"Hi, Mrs. Cornstone." Jenny gave her a hug and stepped back, thinking how large and impressive she'd looked through a student's eyes and how brittle and tiny and grey she appeared now.

"How have you been? It's been years since I've seen you. You look…" Her eyes flicked down over Jenny's outfit, then back up to her face in dismay.

Jenny regressed immediately to nine years old, guiltily clutching an illegal chocolate bar Mary Flaherty had ditched on Jenny's desk as Mrs. Cornstone bore down on her. Through Mrs. Cornstone's eyes, Jenny saw herself as she had been then, and as she was now.

It wasn't an improvement.

"*What* have you been doing?" The question was usual except for the slight emphasis on "what" that left the impression she was picturing Jenny selling her body in Times

Square to the lowest bidder. "I heard about your book, of course everyone has. You were always a gifted writer. I don't read books like that, but my sister read it."

"Oh. Well. That's nice." She didn't want to know what Mrs. Cornstone's sister had thought of—

"She didn't like it."

—but apparently she was doomed to find out. "I'm sorry to hear that."

"She said the world would be a self-centered greedy place if everyone followed your advice. Of course she didn't *know* you."

No. She didn't. And she was probably one of the women who closed their ears and went lalalala so as not to have to look at their own submissive self-punishing behavior. "The book was really for…a different kind of reader."

"I see." Mrs. Cornstone leaned thoughtfully on her broom. "What are you working on now?"

"I have a regular online advice column and I just finished another magazine article. And I'm working on a second book." Kind of.

Her eyes lit hopefully. "A novel?"

About a woman on top of the world who meets up with her seventh-grade teacher and feels like a tawdry disappointment? "No."

"Oh. What's *this* one called?" Said as if she fully expected Jenny to have stooped even lower.

Well, in her eyes, of course, Jenny had. *"Jenny's Guide to Getting What You Want."*

"Really." She went back to her sweeping. "Great to see you, dear. I'm sure your parents are very proud of you."

Jenny sighed. They were. Sort of. When they weren't wishing she'd written a "real book" instead. "Take care, Mrs. Cornstone."

"Lovely to see you." Mrs. Cornstone looked up, blue eyes warm again. "Please say hello to your mother for me."

"I will." Jenny groaned silently. She hadn't been planning to go see her parents. Why enjoy more censure in one day? Spread the pain around, make it last longer. But now Mrs. Cornstone would tattle that she'd been here.

And Ryan wanted to live in a small town again, why?

She caught up with Ryan and Sally. They walked past a few more houses in silence, behind Sally's tiny swiveling rear.

"Nice chat?" Ryan asked.

"Sure. If you like having your success sneered at."

"Ooh." He sucked in a breath as if he'd been hurt. "My brother Steve had Cornstone in seventh grade. Said she was a killer. She didn't like the book?"

"She's not the only one who feels that way."

He took a step away and looked at her until she gave in and met his eyes. "Why do you care? It's Jenny Hartmann ahead full power, torpedoes be damned. Right?"

"Right." She couldn't tell if he was being sarcastic or not and was suddenly too tired to ask. Her heel sank in the soft spring ground and stuck; she staggered and recovered by grabbing Ryan's bicep.

"Why do you wear those things?"

She pulled the shoes off and blew at strands of hair that had flopped onto her forehead. "To be wildly alluring."

"You're wildly alluring to me no matter what."

"Yeah?" She tried to smile through the unexpected dead weight of Mrs. Cornstone's judgment.

"Are you kidding? Bare feet?" He gave a growl deep in his throat and she laughed, flashing him a grateful glance. Maybe he hated her book, too, but at least he'd sprung to her defense, and that counted for a lot.

"Here we are." Sally stood at the end of the short

driveway and gestured up at the house, a quirky beige Victorian that looked as if someone had put it together from a kit and done it slightly wrong.

Jenny stood staring, shoes clutched in her hand, a funny feeling in her stomach, as if she'd seen this house before, which she undoubtedly had at least in passing. But…it was more than that. Did she know someone who lived here or used to? "Who owns this house?"

"The Trebles. They've lived here forty years. Moving to Florida."

Jenny bent down and wiped her shoes clean, then put them back on. She didn't know any Trebles and that was strangely disturbing.

"Come on." Ryan's hand landed at the small of her back and urged her forward, up the creaky stairs to the door on the side.

Sally unlocked it and ushered them through.

"This house has been—" Her cell rang and she peered at the number. "Oh gosh, I have to take this call. Go ahead, look around. I'll be a while."

"Okay." Ryan winked at Jenny and gave her a surreptitious thumbs-up.

She nodded, aware she should be planning to try and get into his pants immediately, but not feeling it in her at the moment.

Instead she took a long, slow look around the first floor, at a warm red dining room, two cozy sitting rooms, one with a beautiful brick fireplace. She walked toward that one, imagining snow outside, fire lighting and warming the room, mugs of coffee or hot cider or cocoa, a bowl of popcorn or brownies or apples…

Whoa. Down, girl.

Next, the back enclosed porch, cluttered with what

looked like a lifetime of discarded or unused items. She imagined it cleared, cleaned, the many windows washed, the room filled with comfortable cheerful patio furniture, plants and flowers blooming year-round in the sunny space.

Uh-oh.

The kitchen, a bright welcoming yellow, she imagined full of casual dinner guests, seated on the stools at the counter, drinking wine, sharing hors d'oeuvres. Or just Ryan, having a drink or a morning cup of coffee while she took hot cinnamon rolls from—

Aaaaaaah!

Wait a second. Just hold absolutely everything.

She was fantasizing about *baking?* For a *man?*

Oh no. *Oh* no-no-no-no. Women who fantasized about baking were…well they weren't her. Her fantasies ran more to serve-me-thou-knave-and-when-you're-done-do-it-again.

Not to mention this was *his* house. *He* was the one looking. This had nothing to do with her.

"Someone's in love." The voice came from over her shoulder, and large strong arms circled her.

"What? What do you mean?" Her heart jumped. Was he in love? Was she? What was he saying?

"You have that dreamy-eyed look, Jenny." He kissed her neck and she tried to relax, but it wasn't working. "Over this place."

"No." She twisted free and retreated to the counter. "It's a nice house, that's it."

"Well, well." He came toward her, one step after another. "Look who's panicking. You're in love, at least admit it."

"Okay, it's a *really* nice house."

"It's more than that." He was entirely too happy, entirely

too sure of himself, and getting entirely too close. "I think someone is getting back in touch with her inner house-wife."

"You...pig." She glanced around for something to brandish, but realized it wasn't her house and she better not touch anything.

"Admit it." He stopped when they were toe to toe, wearing a look of devilish smugness which made her want to sock him. "This is love. The real thing."

"Okay. I love the house. For you. Happy?"

He grinned wider, Satan himself. "Delirious."

Without warning he stooped and lifted her onto the kitchen counter, a feat requiring so much strength that she stared anxiously to see if he were about to double over clutching his back.

He wasn't. He was untucking her shirt from her skirt and kissing her bare stomach, his hands making tantaliz-ing circles on her thighs.

Or they would be tantalizing except she was confused and anxious and not in the mood. "Ryan, stop it."

"Why?" He lowered her waistband and kissed her abdomen.

This was where she was supposed to arch back and invite him to go lower. This was what she'd planned to happen on this trip. This kind of impetuous indulgence was what she stood for.

It wasn't happening. Being sexual here, right now, felt wrong, threatening, out of place. "She might come back in."

"I thought you said that was the fun of it."

"Ryan, don't." She gripped her legs together, trapping his hand between her thighs. "Don't."

He straightened slowly, adjusted her skirt back to

normal and leaned forward, hands on either side of her hips. She didn't get the feeling he was surprised she'd stopped him, and it bothered her that he'd read her that well. "You want to tell me what's going on?"

"No."

"I knew you'd say that." He smoothed her hair back from her face, a gesture so tender and sweet she felt a little misty. Was she on hormone overload? She'd lost track of her cycle. "Tell me anyway."

"I'm just…it doesn't feel right."

"What doesn't?"

"To do…*that*…here." *That?* What, she'd suddenly lost her vocabulary skills?

"But *that* felt right in the other house?" He was watching her so closely he could probably see her hair growing.

"The place was a joke."

"And this one?"

Feels like home. She shrugged, afraid her voice would crack.

He leaned forward to kiss her, and a few kisses later she felt something was different, but it wasn't until ten or eleven kisses had come and gone that she realized he wasn't turning the kisses sexual. And neither was she.

There was only one reason a man kissed a woman or a woman kissed a man when foreplay wasn't the issue, and she started to get really scared and really happy all at the same time.

Only she wasn't sure which side would win.

A tap-tap-tapping came closer and into the kitchen. Sally smiled grimly at Ryan standing between Jenny's legs.

"And what do we think?" She spoke briskly and looked at her watch.

"We think we like it." Ryan lifted Jenny down. "I'll take this house for Jenny, and the other for my fiancée."

Sally's mouth opened and a little squeak came out. From Jenny's mouth, too, only she squeaked because in spite of her freak-out, she was so delighted he'd said something outrageous, she couldn't stop her laughter.

"I'm joking, Sally."

"Of…course."

"I'd like to put an offer on this house. Can you give us a second? I want to show Jenny the upstairs."

"Sure." She flicked a distasteful glance at Jenny and probably had to fight not to say, "Don't leave stains on the beds."

They toured the upstairs, Jenny more and more enchanted with the house and more and more alarmed by her need to move in and start redecorating.

What was happening?

The town was evil, that was it. First Sally, then Mrs. Cornstone, then this place. She needed to get out of here, back to New York, back to the crowds, the noise, the chaos, back in front of cheering women reminding her what she was put on earth to do. She couldn't give in to this weakness or she'd lose everything she'd worked so hard and so long to accomplish for herself.

Give her a relationship, and it was too hard not to go back to her old tricks. Maybe she needed to swear off men for a while, stay single until the need to serve was so long buried it couldn't pull a *Night of the Living Dead* and revisit her.

"That was great." She grinned hugely at Ryan as they stood at the front door again, wanting to add, "Now can we please go?" but thinking her rush might be too obvious.

If he could sense her panic in the kitchen, this one would be setting off his internal Richter scale at level seven magnitude. "Really great. Really."

"I'm so glad you enjoyed yourself, Ms. Hartmann." His overly polite sarcasm confirmed her fears.

Okay, so much for fooling him. But no way could she talk about this. Absolutely no way. She needed to get home away from him and regroup with Jessica over a package of Oreos. Then she needed her head examined for thinking getting back in touch with Ryan had been a good idea. Like a recovering alcoholic she might be doing fine sober, but that didn't mean going back to drinking was a good idea.

"So. Home now?" She flashed a sparkly smile and opened her eyes wide.

His grin came on slowly and with obviously evil intentions. "We're not going home."

"What?" Her sparkly smile turned off as if someone had flicked a switch. "What do you mean we're not—"

"I have paperwork to do with Sally and then I want to have dinner, and then I want to have you. At the Seagrape Inn in Fairfield. We're staying. Overnight."

10

JENNY STRETCHED COMFORTABLY in Ryan's Lexus, unable to remove the blissful smile from her lips. Dinner had been sublime. They'd eaten at a French bistro in Fairfield called St. Tropez. You couldn't beat New York for restaurants, but something about this meal had been magical. Everything was perfect, from steamed mussels, to pork tenderloin with mushrooms, to die-of-happiness pastry puffs filled with ice cream and drowned in chocolate sauce.

Of course maybe the company had added a little to the pleasure of the meal. Or a lot.

She reclined her seat a few degrees and turned to watch Ryan drive, his strong profile lit by streetlights, then softened into shadow as they passed. There was nowhere she'd rather be right now—a beautiful spring night, a quiet lovely town, aglow and happy from good wine and good food. The perfect date.

A thought smacked her. "Hey."

"Hey what?"

She hitched herself higher in the seat. "I just thought of something."

"Yeah?"

She gave a short laugh. "You won't believe it."

"Especially if you don't ever tell me."

"That was our first real date." She slapped her thigh. "I

have never gone to a restaurant with you or sat across from you at a table and had a normal discussion."

He glanced at her, frowning. "That can't be right."

"It is." She started counting on her fingers. "We either met somewhere for sex or you came over and had sex or you called me to come over and have—"

"Uh-huh, sex."

"And recently there was Café des Artistes, where you were on a real date with someone else, my house where we had sex, the library where we had sex, and today, when we haven't."

"Yet." He gave her a lazy smile that made her insides turn over. "Well, welcome to our first date. About time I made an honest woman of you."

"Seriously."

They reached the end of Reef Road, Long Island Sound spread out in front of them, its blackness looking like the edge of the world. Ryan turned right on Fairfield Beach Road. "Have you thought about doing a lot more of this?"

Jenny stifled a delicious yawn, peering over at the beach. There was even a huge moon out tonight. How perfect. "More of what?"

"Real dates. With me. An exclusive relationship with the potential to get serious."

"What?" Her delicious sleepies fled the car. "You're asking me to—"

"I'm asking if you ever thought about it. Pictured it. Considered the concept in even its vaguest form."

"No." She slumped in her seat, guiltily remembering her visions in the house today.

"Do me a favor."

"What?" She sounded so wary she wanted to laugh at herself.

"Think about it."

"Uh…okay." She screwed up her face, then relaxed. "There. I did."

He shook his head and pulled the car to a stop by the deserted beach. "Flattery will get you tossed in the ocean."

"You wouldn't dare."

"No?"

He turned to stare at her in the dim light and a shiver of excitement ran over her. Oh, my lord, she was putty in his hands when he went primal like that. She pictured herself, sodden clothes clinging to her wet skin, being undressed and warmed and sent into supreme ecstasy on the beach. "Okay, maybe you would."

"Not tonight."

She was shocked at her disappointment. "Too cold?"

"Tonight I want to sit on the beach and talk to you."

"What does that have to do with sex?"

He grinned. "That comes later. Back at the hotel, in a bed, which is also something we've never done."

"Sex in a *bed?*" She gave him a look of alarm. "What's next, a minivan full of kids?"

"You never know."

Her stomach took another nervous dive and she stayed where she was while he got out of the car. Did he mean this?

He strode around to her side and opened her door, letting in chilly ocean-scented breezes. "Staying in?"

"If you don't stop talking about us getting serious."

"Why?" He pulled her up out of the car and close to him. "I want a real answer, not sarcasm."

She frowned at his white and green striped shirt, which caught the moonlight and made him glow in the darkness. What could she say to that?

"You're chicken, Jenny."

She scowled, but the chilly breeze messed up his hair and made him look so rumpled and sexy she softened. "Am not."

He did a credible chicken imitation, *bawk bawk bawk,* which was decidedly unsexy, but it did a good job of dissolving the rest of her irritation.

"Evil man." She giggled and tried to push him away. He grabbed her wrists and pinned them to her sides.

"What's scaring you?" His voice was low and intense, his body warm and very very close.

"Nothing's scaring me. I'm just not into playing house at the moment."

"Too busy indulging yourself?"

She gave him a sultry smile, which was probably wasted since the moon was rising behind her. "What's wrong with that?"

"Where's it going to take you?"

She sighed. He was determined to be serious, and in this mood he wouldn't give up until she was too. "Where I want to be. Where I am. A thousand times happier than when I was pining after more than I could get from Paul and when I was pining after more than I could get from you."

"I'm not that person anymore."

"So you've said. And here's where I say, 'Guess what? I'm not, either.'"

He frowned at her, features pale in the moonlight. "You've just stuffed the old Jenny down where no one can reach her."

"Oh, I see." She yanked her wrists out of his grasp, aware that if he'd wanted to keep holding them she'd have better luck struggling against handcuffs. "So you *evolved,* but I'm just suppressing my true self?"

"Part of your true self."

"Let me guess, the part that longs to be mistress of your house and baker of your cookies and ironer of your tighty whities?"

"Boxers."

She sent him the glare of instant death and he chuckled. "If you're fighting those impulses it's not because I'm asking you to play that role, nor would I ever. Any longing to be ironing my underwear is coming from you."

Ouch. That struck way too close to home. "Oh, yes, my deeply hidden need to be dominated."

A slow smile curled one half of his mouth. "I think we've explored your need to be dominated. Several times."

She started heating; she couldn't help it. This man made her nuts. He was Tarzan she was Jane; he was caveman, she was...cavewoman. When he got gravelly voiced and he-manlike she started a descent into weak-kneed arousal that no man had ever been able to bring on the way he could.

Damn it.

But it didn't mean she wanted to bake cookies for him for the rest of her life. Whether he'd ask her to or not didn't matter, he'd hit on a sick truth, which was that she'd probably do it anyway and wake up two or three decades from now realizing she'd forgotten who she was.

Well she knew who she was now. And looking at her he-man in the silvery near-darkness she also knew what she wanted. Hint: It had nothing to do with baking, and came more naturally to them than talking about relationships. "I know about your deep impulses, too."

"I'm sure you think you do, but—"

"The ones you've supposedly evolved beyond." She brought her pelvis forward into contact with his, holding it there in a motionless standoff. "Feel them now?"

"Not a thing."

"Even if I tell you how much I want you to take me, right here up against your car?"

His swallow was audible. "Nope. Nothing."

"How about I tell you I can feel your deep impulse getting harder?"

Even in the dark she saw him shrug.

"And that I want to unzip you and get my hot wet mouth around you and make you—"

He made a sound of frustration and grabbed her hips, pressing himself tighter against her. "No fair."

"So you haven't evolved?"

"Maybe not entirely."

She pulsed forward and back, and he closed his eyes and drew breath between his teeth. "Okay, not at all, where you're concerned."

"Give in to the da-a-ark side, Lu-uke," she whispered.

"I have given in. At your place. In the library." He backed her against the car, dipping her over the roof so she had to look up at him. "When will you give in to yours and admit how you feel about me?"

"How I feel about you is hot, ready and waiting."

He started thrusting against her, making her breath catch and her charge of the situation dwindle. "Give in, Jenny. Say you're crazy about me."

"I'm crazy about…the way you make me feel."

He reached down, lifted her skirt out of the way and hoisted her up slightly, resumed his rhythm, the rough heat of his erection pressing against her panties. "Tell me a fantasy crossed your mind about living with me in that house."

"No." How the hell did he know? She shook her head, lifted one leg to get him closer. "Not for a second."

He fumbled with his fly, unzipped and pushed her leg up higher on the car, pulled her panties aside. "Admit it."

"Condom."

"Admit you thought about living with me while we were in that house."

She stared up at him, the car's metal cooling her back, Ryan's body heating her front. And she almost said it. *I wanted to live with you. I could see it as plainly as I can see myself in a mirror.*

Almost.

"Condom," she whispered.

He let go, stepped away, breathing hard, then zipped himself back up. "Not here, not like this. I promised myself I'd do this right, back at the hotel. You just make me…"

"The wild man you still are?"

He lifted his head, hair dropping forward nearly to his eyes, which glinted in the moonlight and he looked about as wild as anyone could, and probably sexier. "Yeah. You do that. No one else."

Instead of triumph, she felt a wave of tenderness so strong she almost said it right there. *I love you, Ryan.*

Steady, Jenny. She was caught up in his maleness and the memories and the moonlight.

Perspective would be a darned good idea before she got too carried away. They'd be together tonight, she'd relax and enjoy it. In New York she'd get back on track. She was leaving the next day for Atlanta to do another lecture and she had a signing scheduled at a Barnes and Noble in New York next week. Seconds after she got on stage or sat at the table signing for fans, she'd remember where she belonged, and all this house-hunting and who-bakes-for-whom talk would seem like a distant dream.

They got back in the car, his taste for talking on the

beach apparently gone, which was fine with her. Sex was what she needed, and then some more, and after that…yup. More.

Ryan pulled a U-turn and headed toward the Seagrape, which she'd passed numerous times growing up, but had never been into.

Apparently she was going in now.

Their room was large, nicely laid out and decorated more like a studio apartment than a hotel: a living room area with a green-blue plaid sofa and wingback chairs arranged around a coffee table, a galley kitchen with table and wooden chairs set opposite. The queen-size maple sleigh bed was tucked cozily away in an alcove. French Impressionist paintings and a large mirror provided color and depth.

Lovely. Elegant. Charming. It all added up to making her unexpectedly nervous. The place felt so homey and being here with him felt so…husband-wifey. All their trysts so far had been safely risky, if such a paradox were possible.

"Home sweet home." Ryan walked into the middle of the room and surveyed it, overnight bag slung over his shoulder, hands on his hips, then turned to where she was standing next to the kitchenette as if she were afraid to walk in any further.

"Do you want some coffee? Decaf?" He gestured toward the coffeemaker perched on the edge of the white counter behind her.

"No, thanks." God, no. She was anxious enough as it was. Sitting having a leisurely hot beverage with him would make her a jittery mess, even if it was decaf. Bed was a better plan. "Bathroom would work, though."

"After you. Oh, here." He plunked his bag down on the coffee table, dug out a zippered pouch and handed it to her.

"Toiletries. Compliments of the last airline that misplaced my luggage."

"Thank you." She was impressed. The old Ryan could barely remember to show up when he said he would. This was thoughtful and sweet. And maybe a glimpse into how she'd be treated if—

Stop right there, Miss Jenny.

She took her time in the bathroom, brushed her teeth, smoothed her hair from the mess the beach breeze had made of it, wiped clean a smudge of mascara under her eye, and examined her reflection. Her makeup was spotty at best and would be gone by morning; the little bag held none for a retouch. Ryan had never seen her without any.

More nerves. She told herself to calm the heck down. Just because he'd see her without makeup didn't mean she had to move in with him. She'd get through tonight. Tomorrow she'd make a quick getaway and restore her sanity. Then she could get herself together, away from his compelling and oh-so-erotic presence.

Back in the room she waited while he took his turn in the bathroom. She briefly considered getting into bed, but since she'd never been in a bed with him before, that felt more domestic than seductive. She'd arrange herself alluringly on the couch instead.

Except seconds later, she couldn't bear sitting still and jumped back up to her feet.

Basket case.

He emerged from the bathroom to find her standing exactly where she was when he went in, and started taking off his shirt—one button undone, two, three…

She'd watched him take off his shirt plenty of times. Everything from a quick yank over his head, to slow unbuttoned seduction, hot blue eyes promising that in a very short while she'd be underneath him, close to screaming.

This was the calm, comfortable done-it-a-million-times expression of a man taking his shirt off, the way he probably would if he were alone. Or they were married.

Now she was even more nervous.

"You planning to sleep dressed?"

"No." She gave a laugh. More like a giggle. Or, God forbid, a silly titter. *Get a grip.*

"I brought you a shirt to sleep in." He pulled it from his bag and passed it over, a soft cotton tee that would probably cover her to midthigh.

"Thank you." She resisted the urge to change in the bathroom—how ridiculous would that be?—and clumsily got herself undressed and into the shirt.

She had never been even half-naked in front of Ryan without his hands all over her. Except the time she'd done a strip routine for him in her parents' house. Her flung-off bra had come blood-freezingly close to knocking over her mom's favorite glass ornament, a hand-blown perfume bottle she'd bought in Paris.

Talk about killing the mood. But not for long. When her heart had started beating again, they'd had no trouble picking up where they'd left off. Seconds after she'd worked out of her panties, he'd lunged up from the floor and toppled her onto the sofa. The mood had never been dead for long with Ryan.

Until tonight.

Wearing his T-shirt, she stood awkwardly, waiting for her next cue, then realized what she was doing. Waiting for *his* cue? *Excuse* me?

Except it felt wrong to do otherwise. It felt wrong to go over to him, kneel as his pants came down and start sending him to heaven. It felt wrong to violate whatever scene he'd decided to set in this room for the two of them.

She didn't know what to do. And she hadn't felt that way in a long time. Not since she'd packed her bags and moved out of Paul's life without a backward glance.

Not that she'd been anxious to see the look of relief on his face.

"Ready?" Ryan's grin was a tad smug, and she had a feeling he was tuning into her discomfort and enjoying the upper hand.

"For what?"

"Bed." He turned the main light out in the room, strolled to the alcove in his navy boxers and sleeveless undershirt and turned down the covers, tested the mattress by pushing it. "Seems very comfortable."

"Good." She was being chirpy again, a regular bird-woman. A slow breath, and she made her voice came out naturally. "Here I come."

They got in from opposite sides like Mr. and Mrs. Married-Forever, arranged themselves and pulled up the covers. Ryan turned out the light. Darkness took over their little space.

Uh…

Were they supposed to go to sleep? Should she offer to tuck him in and fetch him a drink of water? What happened to sex all night? She didn't think they'd ever done it without a light on unless they were outside, where they embraced the darkness as cover.

"I've had fun with you today, Jenny."

"Is it over?"

His deep chuckle echoed off the walls of the half room. "No, ma'am. Not by a long shot."

"Good." She sighed in relief. The fun stuff would start

soon. Maybe he was just trying to torture her by making her wait. "I had fun, too."

"How long since you've been to a Yankees game?"

"Um…" They were going to talk *sports?* "Too long."

"I have tickets Sunday. You want to go?"

She knew what he was asking. The same question he'd asked earlier: did she want to get serious? There was no way even they could have sex at a baseball game. Yankee Stadium had just become a metaphor for a relationship, a real one, boyfriend and girlfriend doing something they both enjoyed, together.

They'd drink a beer or two, eat stadium food, cheer on the team, chat with other fans. The worst she could do in terms of slavish behavior was offer to go buy him a hot dog, and she could just promise herself beforehand that she wouldn't.

It sounded fun. "Sure."

"Good."

She heard the swish of movement and wasn't surprised when he turned her onto her side so he could spoon behind her. She smiled and waited for the stroke of his hand across her breasts, or the push of his erection against her bottom.

And waited…

"I'm having dinner next week, Monday, with a couple I'm trying to interest in the fund. Our last dinner was a disaster and I think the female touch would help. Would you like to come?"

To a *business dinner?* What was next, deodorant shopping? "Are you trying to seduce me with the promise of attending a work event?"

"Um…no." He found her shoulders and began working them with his strong, talented fingers, which happened to know the ins, outs, oohs and aahs of her body extremely well. "I'm asking for your help."

"Mmm." Her muscles loosened under his touch. "That's nice."

"That I need your help?"

"That your fingers are a gift from the gods."

"So will you—" He sighed. "I was going to say 'come' but I know what that will get me."

She half lifted her head off the pillow. "Am I that bad?"

"You're that good."

Her head settled back down and tilted blissfully when he started in on her neck. A business dinner sounded stuffy. "Nice people?"

"Boring."

"Hmm. So you think I could liven things up?"

"That's not why I'm inviting you, but undoubtedly you would."

She caught his wry tone and smiled. "Well, then I'd be delighted."

"Good." He worked his fingers up her scalp, slow heavenly circles that released tension she didn't even know she was carrying.

"Tell me something, Jenny."

"Mmm?" She wished he wouldn't talk. Just let her keep feeling his fabulous touch until she drifted off to sleep.

"Just tell me something. Anything. About yourself, that I don't know yet."

"Like?" She barely got the word out. Ohh, he was making her feel so heavenly. Not that he ever did otherwise, but this was exceptional.

"Tell me about lecturing."

"It's a rush." She didn't sound very convincing. In fact, the idea of getting up tomorrow and going home and having to pack and get to the airport and zoom off some-where didn't appeal to her at all right now. Not with his hands making her feel like a stick of melting butter. "It's great helping women find strength and courage and the will to be themselves. They get so excited. It's like the whole theater bonds over what we need to do for our-selves."

"Estrogen cult."

"Hardly, you threatened male person."

He moved from her shoulders to the muscled path along her spine, between her shoulder blades, where she carried way too much of her day.

"It's been nice getting back to Southport."

"It has been." She was surprised to find she meant it.

"Tell me what keeps you in Manhattan."

"Ohh, what keeps me?" She breathed deeply, her lung capacity seeming to have tripled. "It's big. It's exciting. Ev-erything you could want is right outside your door. You can be with friends, you can be anonymous, you can be whoever and whatever you feel like on any particular day and no one will bat an eyelash."

"It doesn't bother you that you're competing with millions of people for the same square foot of pavement and the same breath of air?"

"Part of the territory." She yawned and moved to a more comfortable spot on the pillow. "What about you? Why don't you want to stay?"

"Remember my motorcycle?"

"Sure. The one you bought secondhand with money from working for the Baileys."

"When things at home got tense or crowded or noisy, or when school seemed more like jail, I'd get on it and ride wherever, just to feel the space around me. The rest of my life is calling me right now, and it feels the same way. I want to get on a figurative motorcycle and ride where there's more room."

"Why figurative? You don't own one?"

"Those days are over."

She frowned and turned onto her back, the subject compelling enough to give up even her brief stay in massage heaven. "You don't have to go back to acting irresponsibly just because you get another motorcycle."

"True." He leaned in close to her ear. "And you don't have to go back to being a servant just because you get involved with another man."

Ka-boom. Forget touché. He'd run her straight through. Tension drifted back into her body. "Walked into that one, didn't I."

"Bang into it. Think about it, that's all I ask."

"Okay." She would. But he'd turned tail once when she'd been slavishly willing to get serious. Now that she was strong and free, he was pursuing her. If he'd really changed that much…

"Why did you want to marry Christine?"

He sighed. "Do we have to keep—"

"Yes. Why?"

"Besides that I hadn't seen you again yet?"

She smiled. Flatterer. "Sure. Let's say besides that."

"She's beautiful. Sexy, in a quiet way. Polite. Charming. She wanted what I wanted out of life. She would have been able to discuss knitting with the Baxters."

"And that was enough?" She tried very hard to keep from sounding incredulous.

"It seemed enough then, yes."

She couldn't imagine him satisfied with that much—or rather that little, no offense to Christine. "I can't knit."

"You could learn."

"What?" She gaped at him in horror. One hour after he proposed a relationship he was already trying to change her?

"Knitting lessons. You know, to—" He burst out laughing and held her arms to the bed until she stopped trying to slug him. "I'm kidding. Lighten up."

"Geez." She laughed, too, and waited for him to release her arms.

He didn't. *Oh goody, playtime.*

"Jenny?"

"Mmm?"

"Were you thinking about living with me in that house?"

Whoa. She opened her mouth to deny it, then lay staring at a ceiling she couldn't see. She had been. And had denied it once already. Obviously he'd guessed the truth or he wouldn't keep asking. And honestly...she didn't feel like lying again. Not here, not now, when they were so peaceful together.

"Yes. For a minute." Her voice came out thin and anxious, like a child confessing to stolen candy. "Then I scared myself to death and stopped."

For a few beats there was silence and she got nervous and wanted to make a smart-assed remark, but amazingly her instinct told her it was a bad idea. Even more amazingly, she listened.

"I was thinking about it, too."

A thrill shot through her, and another when he lowered himself and kissed her, soft lingering kisses that, were they to continue, would spell serious trouble for her heart.

They did. And they did. She fought for a while and then gave herself over to his lips in the darkness and let herself feel whatever her heart wanted to feel.

It wanted to feel a lot. And just at the point when panic tinged the edges of her consciousness, his hand slid under her T-shirt and began a slow tantalizing ascent over skin that knew that hand very well. She tuned into the physical, which was so much easier to translate and comprehend than the emotional, and when his warm palm finally passed over her breasts, then came back to them, again and again, she moaned, letting him know how much more she wanted of him, without having to use words that might trap her.

He helped her out of the T-shirt and returned to her breasts, using his mouth this time, warm circles that chilled when he lifted away, and warmed double when he returned.

She shifted her hips up toward pressure that wasn't there yet, and made a whimpering noise he'd understand. They operated so perfectly together in this realm.

He ignored her plea for release, but she understood this, too, and when he kissed her neck and painted leisurely tiny circles with his tongue she allowed herself to love the torturous delay until her body stood up and shouted, *now*. She whimpered again, reached for him and found him hard and ready.

"Shh." He moved out of reach. "We have all night."

"But I want—"

"Shh." He went on exploring: the soft skin of her upper arms, her stomach, her abdomen, her thighs, the backs of her knees. And curiously, as her arousal increased, her impatience dwindled. She came to a place new to her, a quiet level of desire where time slowed down and Ryan's touch was all the world had to offer.

Then finally he put on a condom—without her insistence—and he was ready, on top of her, and then inside her, moving gently and slowly. She wrapped her arms around his strong shoulders and responded to his movements in a slower, gentler way than she ever had, able to feel him inside her more acutely than she could remember.

His lips met hers again, a kiss that went on and on, and that same wave of emotion that had threatened to carry her away at the beach was back now, knocking at her consciousness, requesting permission to enter and be identified once more.

There was no escaping the truth. Everything from this moment forward that had to be decided would be decided on the foundation of understanding that she loved him, still and again.

As if he'd tuned into the swell of her emotion, he increased his speed gradually, shifting positions, varying his rhythm and intensity, and as always she responded to him, excitement kicking up a notch every time he changed his pattern. Her breath became more audible; moans rose in her throat without being summoned. The desire focused into one need pinpointed at the place they joined.

He lifted his torso a few inches, and shortened his strokes, bringing her up to the peak but not quite over yet, not quite…not quite…

Then he drove back in, out and in. She gathered force, shot up and over, and came pulsing down the other side, aware he was making the same leap at the same time she was.

Then they sweetly settled, full-to-the-brim bliss almost bringing tears.

"Jenny."

She swallowed. For the first time, she didn't want to be called hot between the sheets or a fabulous lay. Not tonight. But she couldn't bring herself to let on, so she forced a smile, waiting. "You have something to say?"

"Yes." He lifted his head and gazed down, a darkshape against the black space behind him. "I love you."

11

RYAN DRIBBLED the ball toward the goal where Scott stood, his weight balanced, knees bent, arms swinging slightly, waiting for Ryan's approach. Ryan aimed for the top left corner of the net, took the shot—too weak—and watched as his friend leaped and intercepted the ball easily. *Nice one.* Might as well play catch.

"Hey, dude, make me work next time." Scott threw the ball back to Ryan, who knocked it down with his knee.

"Right." He dribbled slowly toward the center line, made a circle and came back around, wanting time to refocus.

Nothing felt right today.

Last night, when he and Jenny had been making love, slow and sweet, his feelings had grown so huge they'd burst out of his mouth, a humbling and terrifying moment. He hadn't told her he loved her expecting, "I love you, too." He'd simply been unable to keep the words back.

However, a response other than frozen panic and tears would have gone a long way toward making him feel more secure. And this morning when she'd opened her eyes, he'd gotten one sleepy smile before she'd withdrawn as fast and far as possible. After the long strained drive back to the city, he'd admittedly been relieved to drop her at the subway— she wouldn't even let him drive her home to Brooklyn.

Now he knew how she'd felt thirteen years ago when she'd said she loved him and he'd done the frozen panic thing himself. Only he'd panicked from feeling too much. He wasn't sure about Jenny, though he'd like to think it was for the same reason. Just a damn shame that on the heels of her panic, she'd be leaving for Atlanta. Tonight she'd be back on stage with a huge audience of women to validate her belief that men were poison for the independent female spirit.

Ryan was sure of his feelings, knew they'd merely gone dormant in the years he and Jenny had been apart. Like seeds in Death Valley that lay suspended for years and sprang back into flower when the rare rains came, his feeling had blossomed back into existence.

He gave the ball a too-savage kick and had to run after it. *Flower imagery?* He was a guy for God's sake. He should be thinking about sports and big tits. Look what she'd done to him. Maybe *he* should write a book.

He dribbled the ball again toward Scott, dodging imaginary opponents with quick feints and bursts to the right, to the left, then took a shot across the goal…to Scott's waiting feet.

"Whoa, taxed me with that one."

Ryan cheerfully extended an impolite finger and trapped the ball again on its return. The problem came when you had to fit those wonderful feelings into something as complicated as a relationship. Nice if love existed in a vacuum to be experienced always in its purest and most fulfilling form. Like last night, at the inn.

Morning brought the who-knews and the what-ifs? Who knew if they could make a life together? What if she didn't even give them the chance to try, given her skittish behavior? Who knew if she'd fit into his life the way he wanted to live it now, or if he'd fit into hers? What if she'd insist on being so abominably outrageous, that he'd end up wishing he'd married Christine?

When God invented love, he should have written a tech manual.

He dribbled back to the middle of the field and turned again, drove toward Scott with more speed, faked to his right, faked left and pounded the ball to the upper right corner...where Scott caught it.

"Old man, old man, how about a challenge?"

"Not my day I guess." He stood, breathing steadily and let the ball drop to the top of his foot, where he bobbled it back and forth, foot to foot. He didn't have concerns or questions when he'd been planning life with Christine. He'd been sure they'd have a strong and contented marriage. So why the hell couldn't he have fallen in love with *her?*

He was supposed to have dinner with Christine in two hours. He should have broken up with her—he'd intended to—when he'd called the night after their talk in the library, but he'd held off. For one thing, he owed it to her to have the dreaded talk in person. For another, deep down he probably still hadn't been sure. Not until he'd seen the Greek revival through Jenny's eyes. Not until she'd seen Willow Street through his. Not until he'd admitted how strong his feelings really were.

But he dreaded hurting Christine, even knowing for certain it was the right thing to do. She'd been his focus for so long—weeks before he'd even realized it—that changing that vision of his future felt like leaving a peaceful harbor for uncertain and turbulent waters.

He ran back to midfield, turned, noted the line toward Scott and bolted with the ball straight at him. Just before he shot, his foot slipped and he nearly stumbled, then went a few extra clumsy steps before he got the kick off. The ball shot full force from close range right at Scott's head. Luckily he was a damn good goalie and punched it away before it hit him.

"Geez, Ryan, trying to kill me that time?"

"Sorry. I'm off today." He jogged up to make sure his friend was okay and slapped him on the shoulder. "Nothing's working."

"Yeah? You want to go grab a beer?"

Ryan grinned, appreciating Scott's implicit offer to listen, or just to provide company. Guys were simple. He liked that about them. Women like Christine were simple, too; maybe that's why he'd been drawn to her.

Jenny was anything but.

"I need to get going, but thanks." He low-fived Scott's outstretched hand and went to pick up his sweatshirt from the bleachers, remembering catching sight of Jenny in these stands the day of his last game, looking as if she wanted to eat him whole. His adrenaline had been pumping plenty high from the win, and in one second, she had it going higher.

That day he'd told her he was going to buy a house and move there with Christine, that Jenny wasn't what he wanted. Less than a week later, he'd put down an offer on a completely different house, and hoped someday to inhabit it with Jenny, who, apart from the minutes they'd spent at 46 Willow Street, showed precious few signs of interest in doing so.

How the hell had all this happened? He pulled on his sweatshirt, said another goodbye to Scott and headed to the subway, dialing Christine on his cell. There was no way he could sit through a two-hour dinner knowing he was about to dump her. His tension would ruin the meal for both of them.

"Hello?"

"Christine, it's Ryan."

"Ryan." She sounded anxious and he frowned. Something had been bothering her the last few times they'd spoken.

"I'm calling about tonight."

"Yes?" Said with clear dread. He hated this.

"Is it okay if we stay in? I want to talk to you about something that doesn't play well in public." He waited for her answer. It didn't come. "I'm just finishing a practice. I can get take-out on the way home."

"That's…fine."

"Good." He stopped at the subway entrance, feeling like a complete jerk. It obviously wasn't fine. Had she guessed already? "I'll be by around eight."

"Eight is fine." She spoke with all the enthusiasm of a woman making a dental appointment.

Damn it.

He punched off his phone and clumped down the subway stairs, stopped for take-out on the way home and arrived at his apartment holding a plastic shopping bag with enough Thai food for a small village. Guilt offering? Probably. He ran upstairs, too antsy to wait for the elevator, showered and dressed fast so the food wouldn't end up tepid.

Outside Christine's door, he sighed, thinking back over the past six months. In so many ways she would have been perfect for him. But she deserved a lot more than a man crazy in love with another woman.

He knocked. The door swung open.

"Hello, Ryan."

His heart thudded. She was wearing a soft pink sweater, beige pants, low-heeled shoes and a brave expression that made her look vulnerable and sweet.

She was gorgeous. He was an ass.

"Here." He hefted the bag. "I hope it's not too cold."

"I can warm it up." She gave a strained smile and walked gracefully to the kitchen, chin high, as if she were heading for the gallows and determined not to show that it bothered her. She knew.

He followed her and put the bag on her counter, which was completely bare. No appliances out, no knickknacks or posters or spice racks, no knives in a butcher-block holder. Not what he'd expect from such an expert baker.

"How was your day?"

"Fine." She started unloading cardboard cartons robotically, not commenting on their ludicrous number. "We spent most of it packing."

"Oh, right, your office is moving." He picked up a plastic bag she'd emptied and folded it unnecessarily. "I'll miss having you around."

She raised her eyes to his. Eyes that made him want to jump off a building. Standing next to him without her usual heels, she seemed small and lost, not the kind of woman he should leave unprotected.

"Ryan, can you talk about whatever it is now? I'm not really…" She gestured at the bag which said, "Good Food Fresh and Hot" in bright red letters. "Not really hungry."

"Sure." He was too tied up in knots to eat either. "Uh…you want to talk in here?"

"Oh. No. This way."

He followed her into the living room, decorated with a total of one picture. An old-fashioned trunk served as a coffee table, surrounded by two folding chairs badly disguised by some material, and a sofa that looked as if it had seen many houses before hers. The cushions had been decorated with pillows in such an odd arrangement he wondered if they were each hiding a different hole or stain. Why the hell was she living in this high-rent building if she couldn't afford decent furniture?

A troubling answer offered itself. Had she done it to be close to him? God, he hoped not. He couldn't bear to think of her bankrupting herself for his sake. He could have rescued her from money troubles. Made her life easier. She needed him in a way Jenny didn't.

He made a polite comment about the Chagall print on her wall since he couldn't really compliment the room, and sat gingerly on the sofa, feeling like a gangly adolescent.

She sat on the other end, clasped hands gripping her knee, looking so miserably expectant that he wanted to take her in his arms and tell her everything would be okay.

"I, uh." He cleared his throat. *Come on, Ryan.* "I've been doing a lot of thinking."

"Yes?"

"About you, and me, and the future."

"And?" She was outwardly calm, but her eyes held sadness, and worse, a glimmer of fear.

"It's…not going to happen for us."

Her breath whooshed out; she sucked it back in. "I see."

"I'm sorry, Christine." He moved closer and took her hand, looking at her earnestly, willing her to understand how difficult this was for him, not just because it was awkward, but because he really had wanted to marry her, really thought they could be happy and it wasn't easy letting that go. "You're an incredible woman. Incredible. It's just…"

"Jenny."

He froze. She'd only seen Jenny that first night at Café des Artistes. How did she know?

He nodded, unable to come up with any line that would smooth the way, feeling as if a knife was twisting in his chest.

"I thought so." She didn't pitch a fit, didn't try to sock him, didn't call him names. She got up, dignified and beautiful as hell, and walked away, as if she couldn't stand to be near him anymore.

He followed her to where she stood, staring at the Chagall. He put his hands on her shoulders, drew her back against him. "I'm sorry, Chris."

"Christine." She laughed, but not as if she found it really funny.

"I know I made it seem as if you and I would—"

"No." She stepped out of his hold and turned to face him. "I knew what was going to happen the second she called you over that first night at Café des Artistes."

He opened his mouth to protest, then closed it. He probably had, too, though he hadn't been ready to admit it to himself. "I'm sorry."

"You said that already."

"I did, didn't I." He stared down at her in helpless frustration, and she looked so miserably confused something swelled and broke in him. "Christine."

He took her in his arms and bent to kiss her soft mouth, offered willingly, generously, sweetly, for him to take…and kissing her only confirmed what he already knew.

There was no one and most likely would never be anyone for him but Jenny.

DAMN HIM TO HELL and back, and back again to hell. Christine pulled another tissue out of the family-size box she'd hauled from her kitchen to her pathetic excuse for a dining set.

Death. Being dumped by Ryan, even though she'd seen it coming, was like a death. The death of her beautiful dream of living in that beautiful house with that beautiful man and having beautiful children who could play in the beautiful gardens out back while she floated angelically through the white kitchen baking perfect cakes and pies and food Ryan and their children would love. It was all she'd ever wanted, to make a really good life with a proud strong man.

Jenny already had beauty, fame, success and sex appeal. Now she'd have Ryan, too. And Christine, stuck in this too-expensive place with her checking account almost wiped clean, would have nothing. All the plotting and planning and efforts she'd gone to over the past six months were for shit. Total shit.

What could she do? Where could she go? Heaven forbid she go home to Charsville with her tail between her legs. But if she wanted to stay in the city, she'd have to rent a place she could afford, a crappy apartment way out some-where, an hour's commute from her job. No boyfriend and no hope of one, either. After Ryan, who could measure up?

Her heart gave a flip as thoughts of Fred stuck up into her consciousness, like moles in an arcade game she needed to whack back down with a mallet.

When Ryan had called and said he wanted to talk, she'd known immediately what was coming. But along with fear and the suffocating sense of doom and panic had been a deeply buried swell of relief and a few traitorous thrills she was furious at herself for feeling.

Marrying someone like Ryan, living the life he could have given her, had been her dream since childhood. She wasn't going to give up that easily. Maybe Ryan and Jenny would crash and burn. Maybe all she needed to do was wait.

Another tissue, to dab her eyes, then she flung it onto

the ugly cheap office table. Who was she kidding? She couldn't afford to stay here across the hall from him any longer; she'd have to break her lease or find someone to sublet. Since her firm was moving, she wouldn't bump into Ryan naturally anymore. And she couldn't realistically arrange to bump into him anywhere else more than once a month before he'd start getting suspicious.

If he and Jenny didn't work out, there would be plenty of willing females within arm's reach no matter where he was. He wouldn't come back to Christine.

She'd probably reached too high above her. She probably needed her head examined to think a man like Ryan would fall in love with a hick girl from Georgia. Jenny was from his town, his life, his league. She could do the whole country-club New England thing. Christine would have been an outsider no matter what. Maybe he knew that. Maybe that was why he'd chosen Jenny over her. Or maybe it was the sex issue. Maybe Christine should have gone that route from the beginning instead of trying to win him with friendship.

Or maybe he and Jenny were just meant to be.

But if he bought that beautiful white house and moved in there with her, so help her, Christine would go up to Southport—walk if she had to—and torch the place.

A new wave of misery rocked her, and she got up, unable to stand her own sniveling anymore. She had to do something. Anything. She had no money to go out with. Maybe a walk?

No. She wanted someone to talk to. A friendly voice, someone who would understand.

Fred. As soon as the name came into her head she shook it, as if she were trying to pry the thought loose. Not Fred. Fred was sweet, but he wasn't what she wanted.

She blew her nose and forced her mouth into a smile, then picked up the phone. Who would she call?

It came to her in a rush and she fumbled trying to dial too fast and had to hang up and do it again. Mom wouldn't understand, not really. She'd never understood her eldest daughter, but she was Mom, and that counted for a lot when you were miserable. Even at age twenty-seven.

"Hello?"

"Mom." Her voice broke as if she were in high school again, passed over for the big spring dance by every boy in school—the price she'd paid for being not only aloof, but intelligent and ambitious and not afraid to hide it.

"What's wrong, Teeny?"

She laughed through more tears. The stupid nickname had never sounded so sweet. "Man stuff."

"I should have known. It's the only thing you've ever cried over. Everything else just makes you mad. Is this the house-in-Connecticut guy?" She clucked her tongue sympathetically. "If he didn't want you, he wasn't worth it."

Christine laughed again, expecting that cliché and doubtless others, thinking wryly that if her mother saw Ryan she'd probably change her mind. "This one was."

"Nonsense. None of them are. Even your father, much as I love him. If he kicked off now, I'd pick up and move on, same as anyone. It's all you can do."

"True." Only it didn't feel true. She felt cut adrift, like her chunk of earth had broken off and drifted out into the ocean and there was no hope of ever reconnecting with the mainland.

"There's other fish out there, honey. In fact, do you remember Harry Slater's boy?"

"Jordan?"

"Yuh-huh. He's back in town after Harry's heart attack.

Got some big techno job out in California, making money hand over fist. He was asking about you, too. Always does when he comes to visit his daddy, but I figured before this you wouldn't care. Now maybe you would."

Christine sniffed and wiped her eyes. Jordan? She pictured him—tall, blond, decent-looking. Big-nosed, but in a way that worked. Maybe she'd like California....

"Come on down for a visit. You haven't been home in years. A little country living will do you good after all that time stuffed in the city. Jordan'll be here a week or so, and I bet he goes to New York once in a while. Travels a lot he says, to Europe, too. Last month he was in London and Paris."

"Paris." She repeated the word dreamily, eyes drawn to her Chagall. She took a step toward it and knocked something off the little shaky table she kept the phone on, which landed with a loud *thwap* on the floor.

What was—

She looked down. Jenny's book. She scowled, wanting to mash her heel on the cartoon cover. Why had Fred thought she'd want to read trash like that? Trash written by trash—though now that she'd seen the town Jenny grew up in, she couldn't really call her that anymore.

"You keep him in mind. When the horse throws you, get back in that saddle and ride like you mean it. You hear me?"

She sighed. "I do, Mama. Thanks for—"

"Good. Your father's hollering at me for more coffee, I gotta go. But you take care."

"Thanks, I—"

"And come see us. That city's no good for you."

"Right. Bye, Mom." She hung up the phone and blew out a breath. Her mom could never could understand why Christine made life sound so complicated when every idiot knew it wasn't.

Mom had no idea.

She twisted one side of her mouth, thinking. Jordan Slater. California. Paris…

One step forward and her foot bumped the book. She gave it a vicious kick that sent it whizzing along the floor.

"What have I done for me lately?" She sneered at the grinning woman on the cover. "If I'm Jenny, I've stolen another woman's chance at happiness."

She stalked over and glared down at the book. *What Have I Done for Me Lately?*

Stupid question.

So…what had she?

She couldn't remember. Maybe going down to Fred's apartment that day when she'd so desperately needed someone to talk to.

She needed someone to talk to now. But if she went to Fred and told him Ryan had broken up with her…

Well, she wouldn't have much of an excuse to resist him. And she couldn't give up her dream just like that because she'd failed once.

What had she done for herself lately?

She half bent down, jerked herself back up. No, she couldn't. The book was ridiculous and Jenny Hartmann was a selfish bitch. Christine had done things for herself. She'd planned a good solid future with Ryan, who she couldn't talk to or be herself with, and whose kisses left her cold. And she'd tried to look attractive and live healthily and be charming…to please Ryan. And she'd rented an apartment so expensive she was on the verge of bankruptcy…for Ryan.

The Chagall caught her eye again and she winced. Even her favorite art involved a fantasy of a man carrying her off somewhere better.

What Have I Done for Me Lately?
Christine sighed. Nothing. Not a blessed thing. She bent down, picked up the book, went over to her battered old sofa, opened it and started to read.

12

To: Jenny Hartmann
From: Natalie Eggers
Re: Getting desperate

Jenny, things are getting so hard! My husband is so furious at me. We've been married eight years. I was eighteen and he was much older. I guess I was wowed that he even noticed me. But now he can't stand to let me out of his sight, he can't stand my clothes, he can't stand anything about the new me. I don't know what to do. I feel so trapped and suffocated.

Help!

Natalie

"THANK YOU, ATLANTA! I love you! Good night!" Jenny gave an enthusiastic wave and strode off the raised platform stage in the Renaissance Hotel ballroom and out the door, to the familiar roars of the crowd. In the hall outside, Sherry, the organizer of the event, was so jubilant, she grabbed Jenny in a fierce icky-perfume-smelling hug that nearly broke one of Jenny's ribs.

"You were fabulous!" Sherry released her and gave her a

shove back toward the ballroom. "They're still cheering. Go!"

Jenny strutted in again and leapt onto the platform, wearing her most tremendous smile, waved once more, blew kisses and strutted off, avoiding a second Sherry hug by shaking hands with the stage manager.

Nothing had felt the same tonight. Nothing had felt… right. Not that she'd done a bad job. By no means. Her energy had been high, she'd gotten the usual words out with the usual timing, had led the crowd through the usual routine, had laughed, joked, had been upbeat and…

Just not that into it.

In fact while she'd been performing—since it was practically more a show than a lecture—she'd been listening to herself through other ears. Not Ryan's, not Mrs. Cornstone's, not her parents'. But someone else's, like a disembodied other version of herself. This other person wasn't quite so taken with the preening and the strutting and the hoopla. This other person would have been just as happy at home in bed watching TV.

Maybe with Ryan next to her.

In the house at 46 Willow Street.

Uh-oh.

Reaching this height, being able to broadcast her important message to women everywhere had been the most fulfilling, validating, empowering thing she'd ever done. Now she wanted to turn her back on it? Because of a *man?*

A man she'd been away from for not even twelve hours and she missed him.

Double uh-oh.

Dinner in the hotel restaurant, with huggy-Sherry and a few of her close friends felt like déjà vu, whereas usually she enjoyed herself tremendously. It was a great chance to eat good food—and of course, dessert—unwind some and, heck, she'd admit it, enjoy a little flattery and the attentions of people who admired her and what she stood for.

Tonight, halfway through dinner, in spite of the cheerful easy chatter and laughter and compliments, she started longing for her hotel room—and Ryan—with a ferocity that scared her.

After dessert—hot fudge brownie sundae with extra whipped cream—and as soon as it was polite, she excused herself on the pretense of being tired and went up to her room. She was dying to kick off her black stilettos and tight orange skirt and sink into a hot bath.

Except when she got into the room, she noticed her message light blinking and only got as far as kicking off the shoes before she lunged across the room to grab the receiver and play the message.

Ryan.

She smiled dreamily—a completely involuntary reaction to the sound of his voice—and rolled over onto her back, wiggling her feet to ease the ache of them being stuffed into pointy-toed misery.

He was thinking about her. He missed her. He couldn't wait until she got home to New York. He wanted her to call him when she got back to her room.

She deleted the message—after wanting to save it to listen to again and again just for the adrenaline rush—and marched determinedly into the bathroom. Jenny jumped for no man. She was glad Ryan missed her—she missed him, too—but she'd come up here to take a bath and that's what she was going to do.

Except once she'd sunk blissfully into the warm pool of water—lavender-scented, thanks to the bath oil she always traveled with—she found herself eyeing the phone just out of arm's reach. She wasn't that wild about the idea of phones in bathrooms, because the thought of talking to someone while involved in most bathroom activities didn't seem particularly tasteful. But here she was, naked and warm and content—except that she wasn't talking to Ryan, and she wanted to be.

Geez, was she never satisfied? When she was with him, she was fighting her feelings, fighting her longings. When she wasn't, she was doing the same. When he'd said he loved her, a joyous thrill had shot through her as if she'd been given a thousand volts. She'd been about to say, *Ryan, I love you, too,* when the panic had started, the fear of losing herself, the fear of loving too much, and she'd lain there, mouth open, probably looking like a fish out of water.

He'd been wonderful, reassuring, gentle and patient. But the only thing stronger than her desperate happiness at being with him had been her desperate need to get away.

Maybe instead of Ryan right now, she should be longing to talk to a therapist.

Except she didn't want to talk to a therapist. She wanted—

Okay, okay. In exasperation, she rose and reached for the phone, which had a plenty-long cord and buttons in the handset. She dialed his number, ashamed that she'd memorized it already, and waited impatiently for him to pick up.

"Hello."

She beamed at the deep husky tone in his voice that told her he knew it was her.

"Hi there." Her voice was also deep, and equally husky. Oh my lord, she was nuts for this man.

"How was your day?"

She beamed harder, practically splitting her face in half.

Until this second she hadn't realized how desperately she missed having someone who cared each and every day how hers had gone. "It was fine. Tiring."

"I thought you got pumped up doing those shows."

"Oh. I do! I do." She sighed. Why bother pretending? "Generally. Tonight everything felt a little off."

"Everything felt a little off here, too, with you gone."

She closed her eyes and grinned and tipped her head back, sinking lower into lavender bliss until she nearly got the phone wet. "Yeah?"

"Yeah. What time do you get back tomorrow?"

"Oh, I thought I'd spend a few extra days here." She stifled a giggle. She was so-o-o bad. "See the sights. You know. Hang out."

"Oh." He sounded so disappointed, her enjoyment from teasing him dropped dead on the spot.

"No! I was kidding." She pitched her voice lower. "I prefer the sights in New York. One tall male sight in particular."

"Glad to hear it."

He sounded *really* glad to hear it, which made her heart triple-beat. "So how was your day?"

"Productive. I identified a possible new investor for the fund. If the Baxters are in, this could be the last one we need."

"Do I have to have dinner with him, too?"

"Her. Meg Keating, CEO of Brandy Cosmetics. And…why don't we start with the Baxters and see how that goes?"

Either her bath water had suddenly chilled several degrees or she had. "Is this some kind of test?"

"Of course not." Only he sounded more contrite than reassuring.

She sat back up, cooling lavender water running off her body. "You want me to liven things up with them, right?"

"Not…really." He started sounding like a man in a roomful of eggshells. "They're…liberal in politics only. Conservative in other ways."

"Meaning…"

"Meaning, your definition of livening things up might not fly with them."

"And what would your guess be as to my definition of livening things up?"

He sighed and she could tell he was resigning himself to a showdown. Which made him a very smart boy, because if this was headed where she thought it was headed, he was going to get one.

"Okay, I'll be blunt here, because I don't want to bullshit around."

"Yes, please."

"The way you dress will bother them."

A sick feeling took hold in the pit of her stomach and started spreading a root system through her intestines. "The way I dress."

"You can play offended all you want, but you know exactly what I mean."

She did. She knew exactly what he meant, but it resonated a little differently on her end than his. "Yes, I think I do. What else?"

"You're pissed."

"I'm not pissed. What else?"

"Okay then, blundering on…some of your bawdier remarks would be out of place. And Mr. Baxter is into hunting, so your views on that sport are better left unsaid."

"Undoubtedly." Oh, hurray. First what she should wear, now what she should say. "Any worries about what I might want to order? Because you might as well let me know now."

"You're furious."

"I just want to know."

"Okay. Here it is then. At our last meal, Mrs. Baxter said she was on a strict diet and she didn't like watching people eat dessert."

"No dessert. Gotcha."

And there it was, the unholy trinity of male domination. What not to wear, what not to say and what not to eat. Thank God he hadn't touched on what she should or shouldn't be thinking while she was sitting there. Or maybe that was next?

This was why he'd wanted to marry Christine. This was why loving him might not be enough. She could be about to waltz happily into making the same mistake she'd already made and swore she never would again. She already knew Ryan would want her to move out of the city she loved, into the house in Southport. Once there, cut off from her lifeline of independence, she'd revert. She knew herself so well. She'd revert into exactly the woman she'd been with Paul, and eventually Ryan would run screaming to someone with more spunk, exactly as Paul had.

No. She couldn't become that bland again, not after having come this far. Could she? How did she know? Already her career choice was feeling like an imposition on time she wanted to be spending with Ryan. Already she was longing for bed and TV instead of the excitement of her speaking tour. She knew how slowly and insidiously she could surrender herself to a man in the name of love because she'd already done it.

So now she had a decision to make. Be the woman the Baxters—and Ryan—would want her to be. Or stay the woman she was, and to hell with what they thought.

There was her choice. Simple, clear-cut, elementary, my dear Hartmann. Either she'd risk losing Ryan…

Or she'd risk losing herself.

CHRISTINE RAISED her hand and knocked firmly on Fred's door. Six-thirty Monday morning, she hoped to have caught him after he'd woken up, but before he'd gone out to work.

She'd been up all night last Thursday, reading Jenny's book, then feverishly pacing her apartment, thinking, planning. The following days had been an exhausting round of errands and loose-end tie-ups, quitting her job, finding someone to sublet her place, writing letters, making calls to airlines. She should be exhausted, but she hadn't felt this powerful and resolved in years—if ever.

She'd misjudged Jenny badly. Her jealously had formed an opinion for her. The woman was amazing. She might as well have written the book starting out, "Dear Christine, here's what I think of you and what you should do about it." No wonder Ryan was drawn to Jenny. And no wonder once Jenny showed up in her sexy I'm-me-and-refuse-to-be-otherwise vibrancy, he hadn't wanted a puppet woman like Christine.

Everything Christine had done in her adult life, she'd done to please the men she wanted. Her mother was the same way. Whatever her father wanted, her mother would immediately subvert her needs or wants so he got his way.

Christine's dream of coming to New York had not been to make it big on her own, but to find a man who had, so she could benefit. How she dressed, spoke, ate, all of it was calculated to fit whatever man she was with—and she'd made sure there always was one. None of it had to do with her true self. Hell, she was twenty-seven and wasn't even sure if she'd met her true self.

But she was going to. Soon.

"Yeah?" Fred's gruff voice came through the door.

"It's Christine."

He opened the door, smiling, dark eyes hopeful, and in spite of her burst of don't-need-men power, her heart beat a little faster, from the thrill of seeing him and from guilt at how her plans would hurt him. But she couldn't let that stop her. This was about her now. She needed to do this.

"Did I wake you?"

He shook his head. "Just haven't had my coffee yet. Come on in."

She walked into his beautiful, comfortable living room and spoke before she lost her nerve, before she transferred all her need to please from Ryan to yet another man and started trying to figure out who she could be for Fred. "I came to say goodbye."

He stood still for a moment, the hope fading from his eyes, then he turned and walked to his kitchen. "Want some coffee?"

She didn't. She wanted to make this as fast and painless as possible. But it seemed rude to refuse, and he'd—

Christine, if you don't want coffee, don't have any.

"No, thank you."

"Okay." He reappeared at the entrance to his kitchen, holding a white mug that read, *I Love NY.* "So you're going to move to Connecticut, eh? Ryan got the house?"

"No." She laughed and clenched her fists. This would be the first time she'd say her plans out loud, and that made them more real, and a little scarier. "I'm going to sublet my apartment, blow my last few thousand on a trip to Paris for two weeks, and move home to Georgia until I get back on my feet and find out who I am and what I really want."

He looked at her as if he'd never seen her before. "I'm stunned."

"I read the book you gave me." She laughed again, a

high nervous laugh that sounded as if it belonged to someone else. "It was amazing. A life-changing experience. I can't thank you enough."

He took a sip of coffee, staring at her over the rim. "Paris, huh? By yourself."

"I've always wanted to go. It's been a dream since I was a girl."

"Then back to Georgia."

Her stomach gave a lurch. That part she couldn't avoid. "Yes."

"That's what you want."

"Of course it's what I want. Why would I be doing it otherwise?" Honestly, the man could not be more irritating. Though it occurred to her that at least she could be openly irritated with Fred in a way she never would have allowed herself to be with Ryan. So maybe she wasn't totally hopeless.

He took another sip, not taking his eyes off her. "I don't know."

Her irritation grew. As if this was his decision to make. "Well, then I'll tell you. This is the first thing I've done for myself in so long I can't even remember the last time."

"Won't you miss New York?"

"Yes." Her voice cracked and she took a deep breath. "But it's not going anywhere. Maybe I'll come back someday. But I'll come back knowing what I want and how to get it. And whatever I decide I want and whatever I go after, it's not going to be a man."

"I see."

If he took one more meaningfully silent sip of coffee, she was going to…too late. "Why don't you say something?"

"I have been saying plenty."

"No, you haven't said what you think."

"Why would you care what I think?"

Right. Right, of course. "I shouldn't. I don't."

"Good." He turned and leaned into the kitchen, then came back around without his mug and stopped a foot away from her, hands on his hips, staring, making her incredibly nervous. "I gave you that book so you'd see how you were changing yourself to please Ryan."

"And I do see. It was…pathetic. But I didn't know how to do anything else. Now I want to learn how to live for myself, entirely apart from men."

"Chris, cutting yourself off from love, is not going to make you happy."

"Oh? What would then?"

He dropped his head and laughed bitterly. "Right. Nothing I can offer. Not staying here. Not moving in with me—"

"Moving in with you?" Her heart stopped, then leapt with something that felt too close to joy and hope. No. *No.* She was not going to allow herself to be rescued. Especially by a man.

"To save money. Or I can lend you some, or help you find a cheaper place. Let me help you, Chris. I can—"

"No." She was so horrified she backed away from him, because the thought of moving in with him, being able to rely on his solid support, was too tempting. It was eroding her confidence in herself when she most needed it to be strong. Once she was on the plane to Paris, she could relax, with no more room for backing out. "I've made my decision. I'm deciding things about my life on my own now. I don't need your help or—"

"It's not normal to want to be totally alone." He took another step toward her. "Humans are built to need—"

"Stop it, Fred."

"—each other. It's how we survive, how we keep the species going."

"Stop." She held up her hand, made her voice come out strong, before she gave into her desire to run to him, feel his arms around her and beg him to protect her for the rest of her life.

She might have done that last Thursday after Ryan had dumped her, if Fred had come knocking or if she'd gone down to see him as she'd wanted to. Moved in with Fred just because he was here and she had no one else. Moved in with him and let him take care of her, bring her cups of coffee, massage her feet after work, spoil her with flowers and chocolates. She'd immerse herself in pleasing him, adapting to his routines and his likes and dislikes. And she'd be gone, before she even had a chance to get to know herself.

"I have to go. I have a plane reservation tomorrow night, and I have plenty of details to take care of before then."

"Right. Okay." He put his hand out for a shake. "Good-bye."

She gave him her hand, tears welling, feeling as if she were cutting her lifeline. "Goodbye, Fred."

"Don't cry." He pulled her to him, wrapped his big arms around her, and held her tightly. "I'm always here if you need me. Always."

"Thank you." She barely got the words out through throat muscles that burned with the effort not to sob.

He let go and took a step back, looking as miserable as she felt. For a second her knees nearly buckled with the fear that she was doing something impulsive and stupid. The next second she found her resolve, managed a smile and turned to leave. What had she done for herself lately?

Soon, *very* soon, she'd be able to say, "Plenty."

13

To: Natalie Eggers
From: Jenny Hartmann
Re: The Husband
Natalie, doll, there is no way I can decide for you what to do with your marriage or your life. But I think if you reread the e-mail you sent me, you'll see that you already know what to do.
Good luck, girl. Stay strong and always be yourself!
Jenny

DINNER WITH the Boring Baxters.

The reminder popped up on Jenny's laptop calendar with a discreet chime and she wrinkled her nose, abandoning any pretense at working on her book. As if she needed reminding. If Ryan had mentioned the dinner one more time yesterday, she would have gagged him with one of his neckties and run screaming from his apartment.

After she'd gotten back from Atlanta, she and Ryan had enjoyed a fabulous weekend. A wonderful dinner at Babbo Restaurant Friday night, delicious food, romantic setting, and boy did they manage to work a lot of it off at his place afterward.

Mmm. Could that man ever make her…day.

Saturday had been rainy and cool, the kind of weather that made lying around in bed mandatory. They'd cooked spaghetti and meatballs—Ryan's favorite comfort food— and rented *Dances with Wolves*. Sunday she'd insisted she go home for the morning—a girl could only take so much sex and happiness—and she'd met him in the afternoon for the Yankees game against the Seattle Mariners. The weather had been perfect, sunny and cool, the Yankees had won, Ryan and Jenny had stuffed their faces with junk food and gotten mildly buzzed on beer.

Everything had been right with the world. And if she worried she was spending too much time with him or getting dependent on him or…well, she hadn't been worrying. She'd turned off her fret machine for the whole weekend and didn't know when she'd had such a good time.

But then they'd lived only in the present, hadn't touched the future, hadn't talked about the relationship. He hadn't told her he loved her again, and she hadn't told him yet, either. It had all been light and easy and fun and damn did she enjoy his company.

Then…as Sunday afternoon had drawn into Sunday evening, the subject of The Loathsome Baxters had come up again and he'd started in once more with the instructions. She wasn't to go into specifics on her book; he got the feeling the Baxters espoused the traditional male-dominated marriage. And again with the don't-eat-dessert thing, since Patty Baxter never did.

In short, Mr. Masterson had become rather tense. And then Ms. Hartmann had gotten rather annoyed and defensive. And the dinner tonight had started to feel more and more like a test of whether she was suitable to be Ryan's girlfriend in front of other people.

So now that her computer had reminded her, she was face-to-face with the choice she'd been putting off making. Dress like Christine and act like Christine and earn his undying gratitude and charm the pants off Mr. and Mrs. Texas?

Or stick up for who she was, dress the way she would for any night out by herself or with friends or with him, say what occurred to her, eat what she wanted and stay true to everything she believed was important and right about being a woman in the twenty-first century?

Put that way, it almost sounded as if there was no choice to be made. Not really. If she sold her soul and acted the happy housewife, then she was betraying herself.

But…if she stayed true to herself, then in a sense she was betraying Ryan. And if that were the case, were they really going to be any good together? Wasn't one's true self a hell of a price to pay for good sex and good times and shared history and attitudes?

She opened her closet door and frowned at the contents. She did have one conservative black suit she'd bought for a job interview years ago and kept in case she needed to attend any funerals. Just looking at it made her feel dowdy and caged. Her eye lit on a fabulous long black gown, with a neckline that did a high dive down to her navel and a hemline slit nearly to her waist.

Oooh, did she love that dress. But that would be sticking it to Ryan pretty obnoxiously, and even if he deserved it…she wasn't sure she had the balls. Or the right.

Then there was her Dolce & Gabbana knockoff, with a relatively modest neckline—as long as you didn't lean too far forward—made from a floral material that clung deliciously to every curve and dip from breast to mid-thigh. Or her shockingly red dress, discreet in front though pretty faithfully following her shape, and more or less absent in back. Or her favorite little-black-nothing dress, barely more than an extended camisole…

She took the suit out and gave it a long hard look. Maybe she could wear a scarlet cami under it and survive okay. She even had a scarf with a good amount of red and black in it, in case even the cami was too much…or rather too little.

Ugh. She sighed and sank down on her bed, holding the suit. Just the thought of putting it on depressed her.

The door buzzer rang and she frowned. Had Jessica forgotten her key again? Was Ryan coming by to make sure she didn't wear anything inappropriate? Oooh, she'd absolutely *kill* him.

She stalked to the intercom and jabbed the speaker. "Yes?"

"Jenny Hartmann?"

Jenny frowned. The female voice was unfamiliar. Better not be a weird fan who'd managed to track her down. "Who's this?"

"Christine Bayer. Ryan's…friend."

Holy petunias. What did *she* want? A cat fight? Though Jenny doubted she was spirited enough for that. To plead for her man? Maybe. Ryan had told Jenny about their Big Talk and Jenny had managed genuine sympathy for Christine, though she wasn't wild about Ryan's protective tone or the tiny wistful light in his eyes. Given her and Christine's polar differences, if he thought he could slip easily from thinking Christine was the perfect woman to thinking the same about Jenny, then he had a lot more thinking to do. And they had a lot more negotiating ahead of them.

"What's up?"

"May I speak to you?"

"Uh…" Jenny frowned. How could she say no? "Can I have some idea what about?"

Soft laughter. "Don't worry. Not Ryan."

"Good enough." She buzzed her in, curious in spite of herself. What would Christine want to talk to her about that didn't have to do with Ryan? Unless she'd lied and would come tearing up the stairs toting a machine gun. Doubtful. The heavy gun might break one of her nails.

Giving in to an attack of female paranoia, she ran to check the bathroom mirror—okay, so she was competitive—and came back to the foyer in time for Christine's knock.

Ready, set, gracious smile, open door…go!

She blinked. Whatever she'd expected to see from Ms. Barbie Doll perfection, it wasn't this. Instead of linen/silk/wool finery, Ms. Bayer was decked out in tight straight jeans over high-heeled boots and a white scooped-neck sweater. Her long blond hair was down, tousled and free. She looked casual and sexy. More than that, her face looked different. Was it makeup? Rosier lipstick? More blush? Had she changed her brow shape?

"Can I come in?"

"Sure, sure." Jenny stepped back from the door and gestured her in, thinking this had to be the most surreal encounter of her life. *Step into my parlor, Ryan's almost-fiancée. Let's chat.* "Would you like some tea? Coffee? Something else?"

"No, no." Christine laughed nervously. "I just wanted to say…thank you."

"Okay." Jenny closed the door. *Thank you?* For ruining her relationship? "For what?"

"Your book." She put a hand to her chest. "It changed my life."

"Wow." Okay, *now* it was the most surreal encounter of her life. She pointed to the sofa where she and Ryan had, er, gotten reacquainted. She was dying to hear more. "Come in and sit."

"No, no, I can't stay. I have a million things to do, but I had to come see you. Ryan gave me your address—I hope that was okay."

"Sure." *He did?* He could have told her. More to the point, he should have asked her. She glanced at her answering machine and saw a message light blinking. Maybe he'd called earlier while she was in the shower?

"I can't tell you what this book meant to me. It was as if you'd written it for me. Before this, I…well, let's just say 'men' were the answer to all my questions."

Jenny smiled. She knew this speech. She'd lived it. "And now?"

"I'm going to Paris, something I've dreamed of doing my whole life, but I realized I was waiting until I had a man to take me." She beamed and threw out her arms. "Not anymore."

"You're incredible." A lump formed in Jenny's throat. She meant it. Christine positively glowed. "Good for you."

"I'm going to Paris by myself." She laughed breathlessly. "I keep saying it out loud just to hear it."

"You go, girl."

"And if someday I want a big house in the country, I'm going to buy it with my own damn money."

"Ha!" Jenny applauded furiously. "I'm proud of you."

"I've never felt like this before." She put her hands to her flushed cheeks, eyes wide and bright. "It's amazing. I feel so free."

"Honey, I know *exactly* what you mean." Jenny grinned, unable not to, and it suddenly hit what was so different. Christine looked alive. Energized, confident, powerful, about a one-eighty turn from the way she'd looked back at Café des Artistes, icily disapproving of Ryan talking to Jenny, but not willing to move or speak on her own behalf.

And now look.

Pride swelled. She couldn't help it. Look what she was doing for women everywhere. For every Christine or Natalie, there might be dozens, hundreds or thousands of others she'd helped to set free. Look how Christine had changed, blossomed, nearly overnight. Because of Jenny's message.

Hot damn.

"I have to go." Christine took a few steps toward the door. "I know I'm crazy barging in like this, but I just had to see you and say thanks."

"You're welcome." Jenny's throat tightened. She stared at Christine, who stared back awkwardly. At the same time they both laughed and moved in for a spontaneous hug, the kind of affection women can summon for virtual strangers from a shared experience.

"Good bye. *Au revoir.*" Christine opened the door, turned for a cheery wave, and left, striding brisk and sure, off on her new adventure. An adventure Jenny had made possible.

She closed the door and moved to the tiny table in the foyer, then hit play on the answering machine.

Ryan's voice. "Just another reminder about tonight, I'll pick you up at five-thirty. And Christine called. She was very anxious to talk to you about your book. I gave her your address, didn't think you'd mind. Try to be nice to her. See you at five-thirty, in please-the-Baxters mode."

The machine started to announce the date and time of the message, but Jenny was already hitting delete.

She turned and marched back into her room, picked up the suit from her bed and hung it back in the closet. Ryan was not the answer to "Who am I?" Neither were the Baxters.

She was Jenny Hartmann, celebrity author of *What Have I Done for Me Lately?*

And she knew exactly what she was going to wear to dinner.

IF HE REALLY WERE IN HELL, he'd have a pitchfork, wouldn't he? Red suit, arrow-tipped tail, something like that? Wouldn't flames be crackling cheerfully around their table? Wouldn't the restaurant be filled with the despairing screams of other damned souls?

He'd think so. Certainly. So he wasn't actually in hell.

It just felt like it.

After all his careful hints about what type of people the Baxters were, about how maybe her usual style of dress wouldn't be appropriate to the occasion, Jenny had showed up dressed like a jungle princess from the Paleolithic era. What there was of her dress was leopard print, with straps so thin they looked as if they could snap if she moved wrong, and a tattered lace hem. Her heels were so high she towered over Mrs. Baxter and nearly over Mr. as well.

Thanks, Jenny.

Now he understood why she'd insisted on meeting him at the restaurant—a casual Italian family-run place on East 50th Street he thought might be more the Baxters' style—instead of being picked up. When he'd taken off her coat, she'd turned around slowly and her eyes had met his with unmistakable defiance.

As far as he was concerned, the dress wasn't a dress. It was a large extended middle finger.

From there, his incredulity had descended into seething rage, which hadn't done much for the conversation. When Mrs. Baxter, wearing a long-sleeved dark green blouse buttoned up to the lowest of her chins and grey wool pants, had taken one look at the dress, her eyes had shot open and her mouth had dropped, then snapped shut. There had been fewer than a dozen words out of her since. Not that she was chatty Patty last time, either.

Mr. Baxter, however…

Ryan sighed.

"So-o-o, little lady." Mr. Baxter addressed himself to Jenny's breasts, as he had been doing more frequently the more alcohol he consumed—which would have made Ryan want to sock him if he didn't already want to sock Jenny. "Tell me more about this book of yours."

"Well, Mr. Baxter…"

"Jed."

"*Jed*, right, sorry." She beamed at him. "My book is a warning to women whose identities are defined by what the men in their lives—"

"So, Jed and Patty…" Ryan turned up the sickly smile that had been pasted to his face all evening, aware Mr. Baxter and Jenny were staring at him—Mr. Baxter in puzzlement, Jenny in annoyance. "How is New York treating you?"

"It's crowded." This two-word wonder from Mrs. Baxter.

"Have you seen the sights?"

"Well sure, we've been up the Empire State building, seen a bunch of shows on Broadway—you loved *Lion King,* didn't you, honey?" Jed beamed at his wife.

"Yes."

"Done lots of shopping, eaten out too much." He patted his bulging stomach. "Several museums. Heck, you never run out of stuff to do here, do you? 'Course a man gets to missing open spaces. Come fall I'll be up to Vermont for hunting season. You ever been hunting, Miss Jenny?"

"Definitely not."

"Why definitely?"

"Because I don't see how anyone could—"

"Jenny," he all but growled.

"Yess?" she all but hissed back.

This was so much fun. "Did I tell you Patty is a champion needleworker?"

"A champion?" Jenny moved her grimly frozen smile to Mrs. Baxter, thawed it and winked. "You compete in the Knitting Olympics?"

Mr. Baxter snorted and had to put his martini down. Beside Ryan, Mrs. Baxter jerked, then turned from stone to…whatever was harder.

"I'm sorry, Patty." Jenny leaned forward, genuinely contrite, but pushing a nearly complete view of her breasts closer to the silent woman. "I was joking. I think it's great you do needlework."

"I knew you were joking."

"She's a wonder at it." Mr. Baxter became more intimate with the contents of his martini glass. "You do any needlework, Jenny?"

"No, no, I'm a washout with anything requiring manual dexterity."

"I bet that's not entirely true, eh, Ryan?" Mr. Baxter guffawed loudly.

"Jed."

Mrs. Baxter's soft tone hinted at homicide. Jed stopped guffawing.

"So, Patty." Ryan searched frantically for any new topic that might interest Mrs. Baxter and came up empty. "Have you started any new projects?"

"No."

It was amazing how that one little word could stop an evening in its tracks. Though given that this evening had been barely inching along in the first place, it shouldn't have surprised him.

"Patty's a bang-up decorator, too. You should see our house." Mr. Baxter whistled. "Back home in Texas we were on the cover of *Better Homes and Gardens* twice."

"Wow. That's great." Jenny nodded encouragingly at Patty. "I'm impressed. I just don't care about that stuff. I wish I did."

"Your home is an extension of yourself." Patty managed an entire sentence. She must be on fire with passion—or with the need to put Jenny in her place.

Good luck to her.

"Now that's an interesting view." Jenny's eyes lit up the way they always did when she was gearing up for a good argument, which was the last damn thing she should be doing with Mrs. Baxter. "I've always thought—"

"Coffee anyone?" He hunted desperately for the waiter, who—thank God—came right over.

"No coffee for us, thank you." Jed was clearly content with gin.

"Anyone care for dessert?" the waiter asked.

"Patty and I won't have any." Mr. Baxter turned to Jenny's breasts. "But maybe—"

"No dessert," Ryan said to the waiter. Loudly.

"Hey, there, now, you didn't ask Jenny if she'd like any."

Ryan took in more breath than he needed. "Jenny. Would you like to have some dessert?"

"I always have dessert." Jenny met his eyes dead on, and he knew without a doubt that if they did any rolling on the bed tonight, it would be trying to reach each other's throats. "But tonight I'm full. Thank you."

He let the breath out, noting zero increase in warm

fuzzy feelings because of her backing down. "No dessert. And I guess no coffee, either."

"Just the check?"

"Sure." He pushed a lock of hair back that had come about as unraveled as his mood. Might as well cut his losses. If the Baxters invested now…well, they wouldn't. End of story. He wasn't sorry he'd ended his relationship with Christine. He understood that he loved Jenny and that he didn't want to be with a woman he didn't love. But he could have used Christine here tonight. And if Jenny's idea of helping him was to openly flaunt everything he'd asked her to avoid, then he had some serious questions to ask her…and himself.

"Jed," Mrs. Baxter prompted.

Mr. Baxter took his eyes off his martini, fixed them on his wife, then nodded. "We need to get going. It's been a splendid evening. Splendid. Lovely meeting you, Jenny. I certainly hope we'll get to see you again."

"Me, too." She beamed at him and let him kiss her hand, then nodded to Mrs. Baxter. "It was really nice to meet you."

"Same here." Said without even a hint of enthusiasm.

Mr. Baxter gave Ryan a firm handshake. "Damn good to see you again, Ryan. We'll be talking again soon."

"I look forward to it." Right. If he ever heard from Jed or Patty again, he'd run right outside and test his water-walking skills because it would take that kind of miracle.

One more lustful glance at Jenny's cleavage and Mr. Baxter all but staggered out of the restaurant on the arm of his wife.

Ryan dropped back into his seat, more angry at Jenny than he could ever remember being, and fumbled for his wallet to pay the bill.

"Well." Jenny folded her hands and thumped them down on the table in front of her. "That was unpleasant."

"Yes. It was." He practically tripped the waiter to get his attention, and shoved a credit card into his hand. "We need to leave. *Now.*"

"Certainly, sir." The waiter flicked a glance between Jenny and Ryan and bolted for the cash register.

"Gee, you don't want to stay and—"

"No."

"Oka-a-ay." She lifted her chin. "You're pissed about the dress, aren't you."

"Pissed doesn't even begin to describe it. And it's not just the dress."

"No? Let me guess." She looked off to one side as if deep in thought, tapping a finger on her chin. "Ooh, I know! I disobeyed you and didn't act like the woman you wish I was."

"It's not about obeying me. It's about respecting my job and my position."

"And not about respecting who I am?"

He gave the dress a contemptuous glance. "That's who you are? A leopard-print dress? I had a deeper sense of you, Jenny. As someone who wouldn't stoop to sabotaging my business relationships."

"Oh, is *that* what I was doing?" She dropped any pretense at pleasantness, brown eyes flashing. "I thought I was trying to have a decent evening."

"By offending my guests at every turn?"

"How could I possibly have offended them? I barely got a word out before you squashed me. Like I was some disgusting bug that showed up at the table."

"Because each of those words was carefully aimed to hit every topic I asked you to avoid."

The waiter came back and put down the receipt, clearing his throat nervously in the icy silence. Ryan signed the copy and handed it back to him. "Thanks."

"Thank *you,* sir." He half bowed and fled again.

"Look." Ryan leaned forward and lowered his voice. "I'm not asking you to like the Baxters. I'm not asking you to believe what they believe. All I was trying to tell you was that this evening, unlike everything else in your world, was not…about…*you.*"

She rose to her feet, proud and straight, color high, and it occurred to him that if he wasn't ready to throttle her, he'd probably want to tumble her right here onto the table. The woman drove him to those kinds of extremes.

"Of course it wasn't about me. How could it be when you invited someone else to this dinner?"

"I wasn't asking you to be someone else."

"You know what?" She stepped from the table and pushed her chair in, put her hands on its back and leaned forward. "You need to find another Christine."

"For the last time, this is not about Christine."

"But oh wait!" She held up her hand. "You can't *have* the original back, because guess what? She read my book and realized what a doormat she's been. Get it, Ryan? Not the perfect woman. A *doormat.*"

He stood up, not about to stay seated for a scolding. "Let's take this outside."

"Fine." She whirled, grabbed her coat and stalked out of the restaurant.

Yeah. Fine. Dandy in fact. He followed, people turning to stare on the way out, probably thinking he was causing all the trouble. Was this what the rest of his life would hold? Public scenes? Nasty arguments? Not what he wanted. Not by a long shot.

On 50th Street they fell into a fast angry march, the evening air as chilly as their moods.

"I have never asked you to be a doormat, Jenny."

"That's what's so sad. You don't even know you have."

"You're dumping *your* baggage at *my* door."

"The New Christine is leaving for Paris right now." She gestured to the east and nearly decked a passerby. "On her own, happier and stronger and more confident than I've ever seen her, because she's finally being herself, something you and your gender don't seem to understand women rarely get to be."

"You're mixing me up with Paul."

"No. I'm just recognizing him in you in time to save myself." She stepped to the curb and raised her hand for a cab, then turned to face him. "Go find someone who hasn't read my book, marry her and live happily ever after in your big white house in Connecticut."

"I am not going to—"

"With a woman who will be everything you want and nothing she is." A taxi pulled up, she wrenched open the back door and turned to face him for what would no doubt be her exit line. He had no illusions that he was going to be invited back to her place. And with the anger and frustration he had going right now, there was no way he wanted to be in an enclosed space with her, either.

"Because I have been with men who tried to change me my whole life." She got into the car, rolled down the window and poked out her head. "And I am *not* going back there again."

Predictably, with perfect timing, the cab zoomed away, leaving him alone on the curb. He let out a bellow of frustration that caused even hardened New Yorkers to turn and stare in alarm.

Damn it. Damn her. Damn everything.

Of all the women in the world, he had to fall in love with one who thought men were only slightly better than toxic waste.

He'd made a stupid mistake assuming she would try to please him by fitting in with the Baxters. He'd made a stupid mistake taking her to Connecticut and dreaming she could fit into the life he wanted. A stupid mistake going to her apartment that night and jump-starting more passion between them, passion that had brought them to yet another bitter dead end.

He was tired of making stupid mistakes. Yet it seemed when his life intersected with Jenny's, that was the only thing he could do.

14

CHRISTINE OPENED the window in her quirky, nearly seedy hotel room on the left bank of Paris. Paris! The room was barely big enough for a bed and the toilet was down the hall, but she could see Notre Dame if she leaned out far enough and looked to the left. She never got tired of looking at it. Especially late at night like this, when it was lit, spires and gargoyles and flying buttresses glowing against the night sky. The most romantic awe-inspiring sight she'd ever seen. Think of all the people for thousands of years who had set foot inside to worship or wonder. Royalty and nobility, people who helped shape human society and culture…and among all of them, Christine!

Everything in Paris was beautiful. Everything. She'd never seen a city so clean and orderly and kept up. Considering it was eons older than New York, the order and shine were even more amazing.

She was constantly astounded. Walking along streets lined with majestic low white buildings that housed modern shops on their street level, she'd turn a corner and encounter a church or monument built by Napoleon himself. The real man! Not some legendary figure who existed only in the dry-as-dust pages of a social studies book. Right in the bustling everyday heart of the city!

Mercy. Did Parisians realize what they had or were they

so used to it that the incredible loveliness around them seemed normal?

Even the shops were gorgeous. Pastries and colorful fruit tarts and loaves of bread arranged just so in every bakery window. Fish markets with shrimp put out meticulously, tails facing the same direction, forming a perfect pattern. Produce the likes of which she'd never seen, in open air markets, piled so appetizingly as to make her mouth water. And shops devoted entirely to cheese! So many different shapes and sizes and textures, lord, she had no idea cheese could take so many forms and taste so delicious.

And the food in restaurants—she hadn't had a bad meal yet, whether she went into a corner café or splurged on a bistro meal. Even bread, ham, fruit and chocolate she got from a supermarket and took to eat in the Luxembourg gardens tasted better than food at home.

There were cafés on every corner, where you could buy a glass of wine or hot chocolate or a cup of tea and sit reading or people-watching for hours and no one made you feel it was time to move on. How civilized. How leisurely and indulgent.

As far as she was concerned, the place was paradise, everything she'd dreamed of even in her most romantic fantasies, and then some. She loved her country, loved New York, but these people took living and turned it into an art form. Coming here, strong with her new understanding about herself, had been the smartest thing she'd ever done.

Except…

Even though she filled her days with a combination of tourist activities and leisure, determined not only to see the sights, but to taste the real Paris, too, she had a niggling sense of idleness, of a lack of purpose she hadn't had since she was a child.

She wanted someone to share Paris with.

Now, even with Notre Dame claiming its glowing share of the night sky so close by, the loneliness she'd been trying to keep at bay finally overwhelmed her. Fighting tears, she turned from her neck-craning view of the Ile de la Cité and stepped back into the tiny, spare room.

Nearly midnight. It would be evening in New York, commuters bustling home, tired and crabby, fighting crowds and traffic. Where was her newfound heroine, Jenny? Was she with Ryan right now? Were they on their way to see each other or making plans for dinner?

A tear rolled down her cheek. She crossed to the phone next to the saggy bed, and stared down at it, not sure whom she thought she was planning to call. Her parents would panic and insist she come home immediately. They thought all foreign countries were overrun either with rats, terrorists or both.

She could call Jenny to tell her what a wonderful time she was having, and thank her again. Jenny had been very sweet receiving Christine in her home and wishing her well. But if Christine kept contacting her, Jenny would think she was unbalanced or a stalker.

Ryan? Her heart grew soft and a little wistful. She'd like to know how he was doing, whether he'd decided to move to Connecticut, how he'd feel about her transformation.

Honestly. She let a puff of self-derisive air whoosh between her teeth. She'd been gone less than a week and she was acting as if an entire lifetime had passed since she'd seen these people.

The bed squeaked when she plopped down onto it. Another tear slipped quietly from her other eye. She didn't want to talk to Mom or Jenny or Ryan. They'd never been able to talk, not really. None of them would understand what she was feeling.

Not the way Fred would.

Her soft heart dissolved the rest of the way into mush. She laid her hand on the phone and lifted it, not having really decided to call yet. A little like watching herself as someone else, and not being sure what that person would do next.

She pressed the button for the front desk and told the nice man who worked there in her dreadful French that she'd like to make a call to the United States. Could he help?

She listened to his instructions and made him repeat part of it slower—she couldn't translate numbers from French to English fast enough. Eventually she got it, thanked him and hung up.

So. Was she going to call Fred? And why? To whine to him that she was lonely so he'd make her feel better? Using him again for her own selfish needs? Not to mention she'd be breaking The Laws of Jenny going to a man for strength that she needed to be able to provide herself.

She pictured him—stocky, short, balding, with the kindest, deepest, darkest eyes she'd ever seen. He'd be there for her, understand her feelings, help her in a way Ryan wouldn't begin to know how to do.

And it hit her in a rush that she'd been a doormat for Ryan because that's what she'd thought he wanted her to be. But she hadn't tried to be anything for Fred but herself. In a way she hadn't been able to. Even when she tried to hold back, he would poke and prod until he got to honesty. Amazingly, he still wanted her that way.

Even Jenny couldn't find fault with that.

She dialed the number and waited nervously. Of course he wouldn't be home.

"Hello. You've reached Fred, building super. Please leave a—" The machine cut off and she heard the fumbled sound of a phone being picked up. "Hello?"

She jumped, euphoria lifting her sinking disappointment, just at the sound of his gruff voice. "It's Christine."

"Chris, geez 'o Pete, where the heck are you? Are you okay? What's wrong?"

She closed her eyes over the freely flowing tears and laughed. She'd said two words and already he knew she wasn't happy. Even if she did try to be someone or something she wasn't, Fred saw right through it. "Nothing serious."

"Are you back early? Are you here?" His voice was so hopeful she wanted desperately to be there, not only to please him, but herself as well.

"I'm still in Paris. It's beautiful here."

"I bet." He waited, and she realized it was up to her to explain why she was calling him transatlantic after midnight.

"I'm calling because…" For a second, she thought of a wild tale of checking on her apartment, making sure everything was going fine with the woman subletting.

She shook her head. She was Jenny's woman—no, even better. She was her own woman now. In a way she always had been. She'd always known what she wanted, and wasn't afraid to go after it. But this time what she wanted didn't involve changing herself to be happy. "I called because I…wish you were here with me."

Silence for so long she was afraid he'd changed his mind about her. "You do?"

"Yes."

"How come?"

"I…miss you."

"Chris." He sounded genuinely astounded. "Why did you wait until you're three thousand miles away to tell me this?"

"Because—" she smiled wickedly "—if I was there with you, I wouldn't be missing you."

He laughed, and the sound of his laughter made her giggle and feel lighter than she had in weeks. Or years. Or ever.

"If you *were* here with me, what would you do?" His quiet voice held a note of hope that showed she had more convincing to do.

"I'd look you in the eye and tell you I've been a fool for most of my life."

"And?"

"I'd tell you that you're one of the wisest men I've ever known."

"And?"

She smiled and turned toward the night sky of Paris. "Then I'd probably kiss you until you couldn't breathe."

He gave a soft groan. "*When* are you coming home?"

"Another week and a bit."

"I'll never make it."

She laughed again, loudly, not trying to suppress it, though she probably should since the hotel walls were made of paper as far as she could tell. "You'll make it."

"I won't. I'm dying already."

"Dying?"

"For you. To hold you, and to tell you how I feel about you."

"How do you feel about me?"

He clucked his tongue. "Listen to her, greedy girl. Call me tomorrow. And the next…no, wait. Not tomorrow."

"No?" She was disappointed already.

"No. Tomorrow's going to be nuts for me. The next day, though?"

"Yes. I will. Good night, Fred."

"Good night, sweet Chris. Sleep well."

She hung up the phone and danced to the window, facing west this time, not interested in Notre Dame but what lay far beyond the city, sending her love out across the vast dark ocean.

Paris was wonderful. But New York with Fred Farbington in it was perfect.

To: Jenny Hartmann
From: Natalie Eggers
Re: The next step
Yes. I know what I have to do.
Thank you, Jenny.
Love, Natalie

"HI THERE." Jenny's smile by now was so painful that she felt like the back of her head was about to split open. She'd been signing books for two hours and the line still stretched out of Barnes and Noble. Great, fine, lovely, she was happy, the bookstore manager was elated, but somehow she couldn't summon her usual enthusiasm.

Being away from Ryan, being at odds with him, tossing and turning night after night, trying to go over and over and over the Baxter evening and the issues, had left her totally drained. She missed him with a ferocity that exhausted her and kept her awake and kept her from enjoying...pretty much anything.

"I'm Linda."

"Hi, Linda." She signed the book to her and handed it back. Linda reminded her a bit of Patty Baxter and that reminded her of the evening and that reminded her of Ryan and that reminded her of how much she was hurting.

She'd done the right thing. She knew she had. Dressing and acting like herself had brought out a truth about Ryan she'd suspected but still fervently hoped would not surface. During the course of the evening, he must have cut her off half a dozen times. Even Jed had started looking at him strangely. Patty might not be garrulous, but she didn't strike Jenny as all that fragile, nor had she seemed offended by anything Jenny wore or did or said. She'd reined in her breast-obsessed husband once, but had seemed more embarrassed than hurt.

If Ryan had been able to grasp Jenny's point of view, they could have chalked this one up to a learning experience and moved forward. But she had to walk away from Ryan before squashing her became a habit—and before being squashed became such a habit she stopped noticing. It was her only option.

"Hi." Next in the endless suffocating lineup stood a man, which wasn't unheard of, but was certainly unusual. Even more unusual, he was glowering at her. And he was big. And hairy. And icky. "You Jenny Hartmann?"

She looked pointedly to the right at the life-sized cardboard cutout picture of herself holding her book. "That's what the sign says."

"I got something to say to you."

"O-kay." She glanced around nervously, pretty sure this would not be fun.

"You know my wife? Natalie?"

Oh, crap. She briefly considered not being able to remember which fan Natalie was, but she had a feeling this guy wouldn't appreciate bullshit. "Sure. Natalie."

"She left me. You know anything about that?"

"I…that is…she mentioned…"

He leaned close, right up in her face, which wasn't pleasant, but beat him standing there screaming at her. "Do you have any idea how much I love that woman?"

Jenny's stomach turned icy. "I'm sure you—"

"Let me tell you."

Uh-oh. *Uh-oh.* She glanced anxiously around for the store manager. "I'm kind of busy right—"

"I took a night shift and stayed home with our kids during the day so she could go to nursing school. Did she tell you that?"

"Uh…no." She started feeling sick. No, Natalie hadn't told her that.

"Since she got your book she's out four nights a week with her girlfriends, doing God knows what. Comes home stinking drunk, has spent thousands on new outfits, money we should be putting away for our retirement and college for the kids. According to her, she deserves this. Is that what your book is about?"

"No. God, no."

"Well, maybe you better be a little more careful what kind of shit you say to people."

Jenny's nerves started disappearing under the weight of some serious irritation. "I was saying what I believe."

"Are you married? I bet not."

She glared up at him. "What does that have to do with anything?"

"I thought not. You in love with someone?"

Yes. "Not your business."

"How's that relationship going for you?"

It wasn't. Her anger dissolved. She stared at the stray hairs creeping out of his tangled beard and inching up his cheek.

"Let me tell you something." He pointed a big puffy finger at her nose. "Love and marriage are about compromise, give and take, two people trying to get along through the crap life dishes out. As soon as it becomes about one person doing what she wants, the marriage is over. You getting this?"

Jenny nodded, cold perspiration breaking out all over her. She was pretty sure she didn't have a shred of color left in her face. Had someone sent this man to put her evening with the Baxters in a new and unpleasantly harsh light? She hadn't compromised her ideals. Neither had Ryan.

Maybe, rather than the issues, their stubbornness was keeping them apart.

She had an instant vision of herself and Ryan on the couch in the house in Connecticut, private and snug, snow falling, fire crackling…and she wanted it desperately.

Mr. Natalie put his pointing finger down and straightened. "So if you think this girls' club stuff is fun, think again. Because you single-handedly ruined my life, Jenny Hartmann. You left my kids with a broken home and me with a broken heart, and I hope you're satisfied with all the money you're making off us people."

He threw what was probably his wife's copy of her book contemptuously on the table, turned and shouldered his way out of the store.

Somehow, Jenny made it through the rest of the signing. The other people in line rolled their eyes at the crackpot and murmured disapproving things about his behavior and grinned extra wide while she wrote her name over and over in their books. She had no idea how she made it, how she smiled or, hell, even managed to spell Jenny. Thank god she hadn't eaten lunch, because no way would it have stayed down.

Back at her apartment she gave a prayer of thanks that Jessica wasn't home, because she needed to cry in a big, big way.

She did. All the grief and anger and now thanks to Natalie's husband, shame, that had been building for the past week burst out of her.

An hour later, finally peaceful, looking like death warmed over, she blew her nose into the last tissue of the box next to her bed and sat up, grimacing at the wet stain on her pillow.

Okay. She gave a long shuddering sigh. Now that was over, she had to think this through rationally. Natalie wasn't every woman. Many had benefited from her book in important ways. Christine for one. Jenny couldn't be held responsible for the breakup of Natalie's marriage. If Natalie was a lying shallow party girl at heart, another excuse to duck out of her responsibilities besides Jenny's book would have come along. She didn't blame Natalie's husband for being furious with her, but she couldn't feel responsible for their troubles. Not entirely.

Never mind that the guilt was still making her sick.

But something else he'd said had struck home, deeply. *Love and marriage are about compromise, give and take, two people trying to get along through the crap life dishes out. As soon as it becomes about one person doing what she wants, the marriage is over.*

If someone had said that to her even last week, she would have shrugged and responded intelligently with, "Well, duh." Because everyone knew that, didn't they? You couldn't pick up a magazine or listen to a talk show without hearing that same old relationship mantra over and over and over. Except obviously she hadn't internalized it very well.

Ryan had asked her to behave in a way he thought would make his guests comfortable for one evening, and she'd refused. Worse, she'd taken great pains to do the opposite. *Boy she'd shown him.* Yeah, she'd shown him that she cared much more about herself and what she wanted than about him or what he did. She could have lost him the money the Baxters represented. And she could have lost him.

Way to go! Major victory! Would it have killed her to go a little easy on the Jenny aura for one night? Did she think putting on a suit would change her back into her old self? Did she have that little faith in her transformation? Ryan had given her no reason to think he wanted her back that way permanently. Hadn't he wanted her, pursued her, said he loved her as her new self?

She jumped off the bed and a page of her hyper-edited and stalled manuscript lifted from the desk as she blew by on her way to the phone. *Jenny's Guide to Getting What You Want.* All the book needed was a subtitle: *Without Hurting Those You Love.*

As for Ryan, she was going to call him right now and see if he'd meet her tonight. She caught a glimpse of her puffy, blotchy, slit-eyed face in her bedroom mirror.

Um…make that tomorrow night.

And she'd show him exactly the woman she could be. For him.

"I'M OPEN!" Ryan pounded toward the opposing team's goal, shouting to his teammate Mike, who was involved in a furious struggle with a member of the Jaycees' defense. Mike cut back and to the left, giving himself enough time for a beautifully placed kick across the field. Ryan adjusted his position and launched himself into the ball, smashing it with his forehead toward the goal, catching the goalie by surprise and scoring his third goal of the day to end the game with a win for the Bombers.

He threw his arms up and shouted. His teammates surrounded him, congratulating him with back slaps and high-fives.

"You were on fire today."

Ryan nodded, still breathing hard, shoving the hair out

of his eyes. Yeah. Pain and rage would do that to a guy. He responded to a hug—a manly one, of course—from Mike, and over his teammate's shoulder caught a glimpse in the stands of a tall brunette in a tight red sweater, and nearly forgot to let Mike go.

Jenny.

"Dude!" Scott shoved Mike aside and held his hand out for a shake. "Good game."

"Thanks." Ryan glanced at the stands again, more adrenaline going now than when he'd made the shot. She was here. She still wanted him. She must have had as hard a time as he had trying to conceive of the relationship being over.

In fact, now that she was here, even the thought that it could be over seemed as ludicrous as—

The brunette turned. It wasn't Jenny.

His teammate Drew slapped him on the back, jolting him forward, and he forced a grin over the disappointment sinking inside, then lined up to shake hands with the Jaycees.

Great. Now he was hallucinating.

He needed to call her and deal with this, since obviously the situation wasn't going away on its own. Five days since the disaster with the Baxters and he'd forgotten a person could be in this much pain. Ironically, last time he'd been grieving like this, Jenny had been the one to help heal him. Doubly ironically, she could easily be the one to do it again.

But damn it, what then? Their reconciliation would be so good, passionate and thrilling, emotionally full—but only until they ran into another situation like last Monday night. She'd done her best to provoke him the entire evening. Was that how all their conflicts and differences of opinion would be handled? Jenny's way or not at all?

He'd called the Baxters to lie through his teeth and say he'd enjoyed the dinner. He'd had to leave a message, and, predictably, they hadn't called back. He doubted they were on the road to a knitting tournament, either. The enormity of Jenny's defiance costing him investors was too much to ignore. Couldn't she have put on a suit and calmed herself down for one evening? He didn't think it was too much to ask.

Out with the team for beer to celebrate their victory, he stuck to soda. Adding alcohol to his mood would be lighting the fuse on a stick of TNT. He yucked and yacked and yee-hawed with the rest of them, but to say his heart wasn't in it was like saying outer space was bigger than Toledo.

After an hour of faux-jollity his patience wore thin and he said goodbye, accepted more congratulations for a victory that felt hollow now and headed home.

His apartment was silent in the oppressive way it had been all week. He'd lived alone nearly all his adult life and one weekend with Jenny here had made the place feel built for two.

Three messages blinked on his machine. He forced himself not to hope, tossed his keys on the table and hit play, bracing himself not to be disappointed if none of the messages was from her.

"Hi, Ryan, Sally Granger." Sounding extra cheerful. "Just wanted to let you know your offer was accepted on the house at forty-six Willow! Congratulations! It's such a lovely property. Give me a call ASAP and we'll work out details. Talk to you soon!"

The house. He was thrilled. He loved that house. But he'd just been sucker-punched in the gut again. How long would he have to live there before he could stop imagining Jenny sharing it?

He had it bad. He needed to call her. He was just too damn afraid of what she would, or wouldn't, say. Vulnerability wasn't his favorite state of being and Jenny had cornered the market on making him feel that way. She also made him feel alive, and he'd felt more alive in the past two weeks than he had in way too long.

The second message began to play.

"Ryan, Jed Baxter. Meant to get back to you sooner, but we were out of town." Ryan's eyebrow lifted. So they *were* at a knitting tournament. "Patty and I enjoyed dinner and meeting Jenny, and want to come to your office soon to discuss details of the fund. We've had a talk with our investment counselor and he thinks it's as good an idea as we do. Oh, and Patty dug up some of her easy sweater patterns and said she'd love to teach Jenny. She got a real kick out of her. Said she wants to know where Jenny shops."

Ryan's jaw was in danger of hitting the floor. He hit replay and listened to the message again. Were they talking about the same evening? He ran over the details, the conversation—such as it had been—and the number of times he'd had to jump in and...

Stop Jenny from being herself. He thought of the number of times in the preceding weekend he'd reminded her what not to do, what not to say. The Baxters had enjoyed her. Even Patty.

A sick feeling grew and spread in his stomach. Maybe Patty was always like that. A woman of few words. Maybe her reaction to Jenny's outfit had been covetous, not horrified. Maybe her reaction to Jed's flirting had been embarrassment for him, not jealousy and censure.

Why had he been so quick to assume Jenny would be and had been a problem? Since when had he become as uptight and judgmental as the people he'd rebelled against in his youth?

Yeah, Jenny had been deliberately sticking it to him. But admittedly he'd created a high-pressure situation where there hadn't needed to be one. If he'd left her to her own devices, shown he'd trusted her taste and judgment, maybe she would have shown up dressed and acting less outrageously.

He hadn't given her the chance to be herself. Damn it, she was right. He was a nightmare right out of her book.

He reached for the phone to call her, when the third message started playing.

"Ryan. It's Jenny." He froze. She sounded so sexy and sweet he wanted to grab his keys and rush wherever she was. "I'll be at Café des Artistes tomorrow evening at the bar, around six. We should talk about what happened. Not on the phone, though. I want to see you in person."

Before she'd finished, a grin had taken over his face, and hope rushed up to do a crazy dance in his chest. Tomorrow night, Café des Artistes. He'd be there.

And if the plan forming in his mind right now worked, they'd have a lifetime of hot dates ahead of them.

15

THE SUN WAS POURING spring warmth over Paris. The sky was the deep blue that reminded everyone summer was around the corner. A light breeze wafted the tantalizing smell of freshly baked bread down the narrow cobbled street. Outside, the city beckoned: every shop yet unexplored, every museum, every restaurant, every café, every beautifully preserved reminder of past centuries.

Christine was going home.

She'd spent the past two nights tossing and turning, imagining the rest of her trip even lonelier, even less satisfying, having finally admitted to herself where she really belonged. No matter where she went, what splendors presented themselves, she'd always be looking somewhere else—to the day she could go home to Fred.

That morning, she'd called her airline and been told she had a good chance of flying standby on the flight that afternoon. With another few hours left, she'd spent the morning strolling the streets, drinking in every detail to share with Fred. Maybe they'd come back here someday. Maybe they'd get married and come here for their honeymoon.

Out of the brilliant sunshine and into the relative gloom of the tiny lobby, she smiled at the man behind the desk, Jean-Claude.

"Ah, Mademoiselle Bayer." He pronounced her name Bay-ay, which she loved. It sounded exotic instead of like aspirin. "I'm happy you are returned. We have had a small problem with your room."

She blinked. "A problem? I'm about to check out."

"There was water from the room above. We had to move your things to a new room to avoid damage."

"Oh, well I don't need another room, because I'm about to check out."

"My records say you are staying the full next week. You will like this room. Much bigger and with a bathroom."

"But I'm leaving today." She took a few more steps toward him and leaned her elbows on the narrow wood counter. "You've made a mistake."

"No mistake," he said with typical French confidence. "Room seventeen. Here is the key. Your things have been moved for you. Enjoy your stay."

"Jean-Claude." She tried to keep the irritation out of her voice. "I'm *sure* that I am—"

"I suggest you go up and see the room, then we can talk." He looked as if he was enjoying his hotel's ineptitude, which was beyond her understanding. "Yes?"

"No. I—" She sighed. She needed her bags one way or the other. "Fine."

"Perfect." He dropped the key onto her outstretched palm and grinned.

She turned, making a childish face he couldn't see, and took the tiny winding staircase to the second floor—which they called the first floor here. Number…seventeen. There it was. She fit the key in the lock hoping Jean-Claude wasn't completely mental.

She pushed open the door. *Oh no.*

He was completely mental. A suitcase on the bed, not

hers, and water running in the bathroom. Immediately she pulled the door toward her as softly as she could…

Except as her view of the room narrowed to a slit, she saw her suitcase. Both her suitcases. What the—

Honestly. She opened the door again and tiptoed inside to make a grab for the cases and bolt downstairs where she intended to rival a true Frenchwoman for screechy outrage. Three steps inside, the bathroom door to her right opened.

Lord have mercy, no! She turned, backing toward the door, brain scrambling for a suitable apology in French.

"Pardon moi. Je—" Her terrible French froze on her lips.

Fred.

In Paris. *Fred!*

"Oh, my lord!" She put her hand to her mouth and started laughing. "Fred. My God, what are you doing here?"

He put his hands out in a typical New York gesture. "What the heck kind of welcome is that? I came to see you. Why else would I be here?"

She couldn't stop laughing. "Fred. Oh, my God. You came to France. For me."

He scratched his head, looking bemused. "I did say all you had to do was let me know, didn't I? And you did."

"Is this why you told me not to call yesterday?" She put her hands to her mouth, shaking her head. She couldn't believe it. She could *not* believe it.

"Yeah, I had all the arrangements to make, and then I didn't want you to call and not get me while I was on my way."

"I was going to come home today. I told them I was checking out and he—"

"That Jean guy?" He grinned. "Took a lot of convincing to get him to move your stuff. Against hotel regulations and all that. But then he looked up that you'd called me last night. That helped. Bunch of euros didn't hurt, either."

"You bribed him?" She gaped at him. "Just to surprise me?"

"You're worth anything, Chris."

Tears started without warning. She took the few steps between them and threw her arms around his neck, bursting with joy and gratitude. "Thank you, Fred."

His arms came around her. He pressed her close against him. "I love you, Christine."

Her heart stopped at the sound of his deep husky voice, then swelled, bigger and bigger until she thought it would burst in her chest. "It's Chris. And…I love you, too."

She could only manage a whisper, but by the way his arms tightened so she almost couldn't breathe, she guessed he'd heard her.

"I can't wait to show you Paris." She spoke into his shoulder, joy nearly overwhelming her. "I can't wait to take you everywhere. How long can you stay? Tell me you can stay the whole week. I want to show you everything. You won't believe how wonderful it is. Oh! There's this place I found on the—"

"Whoa, wait a second." He looked down at her, dark eyes tired, but warm and full of love and dearer to her than any eyes she'd ever seen. And the reverence in his smile made her suddenly sure this man would be with her the rest of her life.

"I'm sorry. I should have done this first." She kissed him, gently, slowly, savoring the shape and taste of his mouth—and the thrilling response in her heart.

"Honey." He reached out and shoved the room door closed behind her. "You should have done that a long time ago."

"I know." She kissed him again and again, the sweetness in the kisses slowly turning to heat that spread through her body and took her mind in directions other than sight-seeing. "Fred?"

"Mmm?"

"Remember how I said I wanted to show you the entire city?"

"Yeah?"

She gave him a saucy look and moved backwards toward the bed, pulling him with her.

"Right now I'd rather show you something right here."

JENNY WALKED INTO Café des Artistes fifteen minutes before she'd told Ryan to meet her. She wanted to be there when he arrived, as she had been before. Only this time she was dressed to seduce him in an entirely different way. Not sexually. Emotionally.

She was wearing her in-case-of-funerals suit: black, with a narrow skirt, one-button jacket and very slightly flared peplum. Under it she'd worn a burgundy cotton-cashmere blend sweater with a modest scooped neckline that displayed only her collarbones.

On her feet were sensible black pumps; in her hand she clutched a demure burgundy handbag; from her ears hung garnet and gold drops, dangling only a half inch under her lobes. On her face, she wore discreet makeup; mascara, blush, burgundy lipstick. Her hair was up in a neat French twist.

And...truth be told, when she'd looked in the mirror expecting to see her grandmother looking back at her, she'd been surprised—and happy—to find that she looked nice. Really nice. She even found she missed looking like this. It almost seemed more grown-up than dressing outrageously, not that she'd pushed the boundaries of the fashion world by any means.

But she looked sleek and polished and yes, even sexy. She hoped Ryan would think so. And she hoped he'd get the message when he saw her at the bar. She'd screwed up the night of the Baxters. She should have dressed like this, and was prepared to dress like this again when he needed her to. Not because she was reverting to being a slobbering man-pleasing gutless wonder…but because she loved him.

"Hello there, George." She slid onto one of the chairs at the bar, grinning at the bartender.

"Hi…?"

Obviously he was drawing a blank. He could very well just not remember her. Or he could not recognize her. Plenty of men turned blind and forgetful when there were no longer T&A jogging their memories.

"Jenny. I was here a few weeks ago, sent a drink to my friend who was—"

"Right. Right." He tapped the side of his head and looked exasperated with himself. "Sorry. You…look different, though."

She smiled and batted her eyelashes at him. "Ya think?"

He grinned back. "What'll you have?"

A no-brainer. "A seven and seven."

"Coming right up." He poured Seagrams into an old-fashioned glass. "You meeting someone here again?"

"Same guy who walked in last time."

"No kidding. So the woman he was with…"

"Was a friend."

"Excellent." He topped the glass off with 7-Up and handed it to her with a flourish. "Enjoy."

"I will, thank you." She took the first sip, grimaced slightly at the sweetness, but sighed with pleasure over the memories the taste resurrected.

And here she was, waiting to find out whether the man

who starred in those memories would show up. And whether he'd accept her apology. And whether they could move forward. And whether her future might include the crazy possibility of moving to Connecticut and living in that wonderful quirky house.

Not that there was a lot riding on the evening.

More and more the thought of a move to Connecticut filled her not with fear or claustrophobia, but the notion that it might suit her, as long as she could commute frequently into the Big Apple. She loved New York, would always love it. But she was starting to think she'd used the city to define her the same way she'd used clothes. Maybe she wasn't as one-dimensional about noise and bustle any more than she was about exposed thighs and cleavage. Maybe she needed to look farther inward to define herself and make it less about how she appeared.

Oh, those lessons sounded so obvious once you figured them out. It was as if the human brain had a comprehension time-lapse. She'd heard all your life, "It's what's inside that counts," but until she was in a situation that tested her and made her realize what that truly meant, the phrase was only so many words to spout at a cocktail party.

A tall man in a dark suit entered the bar and she didn't need to see more than a glimpse in her peripheral vision to know it was Ryan.

She didn't think she'd ever been so glad to see anyone in her life. And unless she was entirely wrong, the fact that his face lit up at the sight of her meant he was feeling roughly the same way.

Oh, my goodness. A silly sob rose in her throat and she laughed to cover it, not realizing how tense she'd been until the relief affected her like an hour in a hot tub.

"Jenny." He sat next to her, smiling warily, and it

occurred to her his eyes were cautious, as if she was the one who needed to do the forgiving and he was anxious about whether she would.

Huh?

"I'm really glad you're here."

"Yeah?" His wariness dissipated and he did a slow appreciative once-over of her outfit that made her want to remove it immediately and stretch out on the bar. "You look…amazing."

"I'm wearing this retroactively."

"To what?"

She sent him an apologetic smile. "Last Monday."

"Monday? Oh, the Baxters." His eyes warmed. "Actually, about that—"

"Wait. Me first." She winced. "Sorry. No more 'me first.' After you."

"Hello." George put a cocktail napkin in front of Ryan. "What can I get for you this evening?"

"George, this is Ryan. He'll have what I'm having."

"I guess I'll have what she's having." He glanced at her glass after George took off to make the drink. "What *are* you having?"

"A seven and seven. And doubts."

His smile dimmed. "About seventh heaven?"

"No. About me." She fingered her napkin, too nervous to meet his eyes. "I was a brat that night with the Baxters. I was so anxious not to be who I used to be that I wasn't even paying attention to who *you* are. It was—"

"Wait, wait." He accepted his drink from George with a nod of thanks. "That was *my* speech."

"Your speech?" She stared stupidly.

"About being so anxious not to be who I used to be that I wasn't even paying attention to who you are."

"No, Ryan." She wiggled around in her chair to face him. "I shouldn't have acted like that. It didn't matter what I was wearing, not for one night. And I ruined your chances with—"

"I didn't have to stomp on you every time you opened your mouth."

"Hold on a second. *I'm* the villain." She put her hands on her hips in mock indignation. "Stop trying to make this about you."

He burst out laughing, then hauled her close and kissed her so passionately and intimately that she was actually embarrassed when they broke apart, imagining George and his buddies pointing and whispering.

And since when did she care?

Wait, more importantly, since when did he stop caring? Oh, this was good. This was really, really good.

"I've got news for you." He brushed her forehead, then traced a line tenderly to her jaw.

"Mmm?"

"The Baxters loved you."

She did an exaggerated double take. "The who? Whah?"

"They not only want to invest, but…" He lightly punched her shoulder. "Patty wants to teach you to knit."

Jenny grimaced. "To knit? Me?"

"I don't know. Might come in handy someday. You know." He looked casually away. "Little *knitted* things. One of these days…"

She blinked. Blinked again. Imagined little Ryans and Jennys tucked upstairs asleep in the house in Southport, and her blinks became more about keeping tears back than shock. "Oh, gosh. Well. Yes. Knitted things could come in handy, couldn't they?"

He turned and grinned, threading his fingers through hers and holding her gaze, while she sat and gazed back, too full of emotion to speak.

"How are those drinks?"

"Perfect." Ryan was talking to George, still gazing at Jenny. "Exactly as is."

"Seven and seven and seventh heaven." She didn't take her eyes from Ryan's. "Don't change a thing."

"Uh…yeah, good. Okay." George probably walked away. Who really cared about anything but the man next to her?

"Ryan, next time we go out with Baxters or anything resembling them, I'll leave the leopard print at home and wear the funeral suit."

"You look as sexy in that as you did in the leopard dress. Just in a different way." He ran a finger over the taut skirt covering her lap, and managed to send a warm vibration through it and down to where she didn't look remotely proper. "So, um, what do you have on under there?"

"Hmm." She uncrossed her legs and moved them slightly apart. "Would you care to go somewhere you can find out?"

"Definitely." He emptied his drink and fixed her with a steady gaze that started her hormones doing the happy dance. "In a bed or in public?"

"Hmm." She pretended to consider deeply. "Well since we're all about compromise now, how about both? A bed in public?"

"Mattress department at Macy's?"

She finished her drink and thudded the glass down. "You're on."

He stood and threw down bills for the drinks. "Bye, George."

"Gotta run?"

"Important business. See you soon."

"Bye, George." She winked and followed Ryan, who was all but dragging her out of the bar and onto the street.

"Did you drive?" He pulled her along at a pace that made her very glad she'd worn sensible shoes.

"No, subway."

"Excellent." He swung around, pulled her close and kissed her. "Wait here."

"I don't mind walking. These shoes are—"

"Wait. Here."

She giggled. "Yes, *sir*. I'll wait here, *sir*."

Two steps away he wheeled back, grabbed her and kissed her until she could barely think straight. "I love you. Don't leave with anyone else while I'm gone."

"As if." She gazed into his eyes, his dark and fabulous blues that made her shiver from the inside out. "I love you, too."

"Will you move to Connecticut with me?"

"Yes," she whispered.

"I have another important question to ask but not tonight. I want to do it right, dinner, champagne, the works. Okay?"

"Oh, yes. Very okay." Tears rose in her eyes and as he kissed her again, she closed them, immersing herself in the moment, soaking in everything she was feeling and tasting, all of it centered around Ryan, all of it the right thing for her.

"I'll be back in a second." He winked again, released her and strode off.

She stepped back, looking around for a light pole to lean against since her knees had gone on strike. A few minutes later, they'd stabilized and she started watching in the direction Ryan had gone a bit more anxiously. Where was the Lexus? How far away had he parked? Of course given it was New York, he could be blocks and blocks away. She wished she could have gone with him.

Another few minutes, still no Lexus. Taxis, yes. But he said he'd driven.

A motorcycle stopped in front of her, the rider wearing a black leather jacket and tight jeans. She glanced absently at the machine. It was a beauty. A Yamaha Virago, like the one Ryan had owned when he—

The driver took off his helmet. Dark hair hung in sexy strands over his forehead. Blue eyes blazed at her. He turned, picked up another helmet from the back seat, and held it out.

Three seconds to get over her total astonishment then she grinned, laughed, put the helmet on and climbed behind him, her tight skirt riding up so he could glimpse the bad-girl red lace garters she wore underneath.

She put her arms around him, pressed herself close to his back, and made all sorts of evil plans as to what her hands could be doing along the way.

Her wild man was back. And she was going to be his wild woman—and her own woman—forever.

Ryan pulled in the clutch, kicked the bike into gear, revved the motor a couple of times for good measure…

And they were off on the ride of their lives.

*Romancipation

ro·man·ci·pa·tion *noun*

The freedom for women to love whom they choose
whilst retaining their own space and identity

Maggie is living the life she's always wanted.
Her career is taking off and, thanks to Japanese
straightening technology, her hair is lying down.
Maggie even has a funny, caring boyfriend – but
there's one problem: he wants Maggie to move in.

Maggie's not sure she's ready to move from "me" to
"we"… As she examines the relationships around
her, Maggie has to decide: is she ready to face her
fears and embrace her own romancipation?

Available 17th August 2007

MIRA

FREE!

2 Books
and a surprise gift!

We would like to take this opportunity to thank you for reading this Mills & Boon® book by offering you the chance to take TWO more specially selected titles from the Blaze® series absolutely FREE! We're also making this offer to introduce you to the benefits of the Mills & Boon® Reader Service™—

★ **FREE home delivery**
★ **FREE gifts and competitions**
★ **FREE monthly Newsletter**
★ **Exclusive Reader Service offers**
★ **Books available before they're in the shops**

Accepting these FREE books and gift places you under no obligation to buy, you may cancel at any time, even after receiving your free shipment. Simply complete your details below and return the entire page to the address below. You don't even need a stamp!

YES! Please send me 2 free Blaze books and a surprise gift. I understand that unless you hear from me, I will receive 4 superb new titles every month for just £3.10 each, postage and packing free. I am under no obligation to purchase any books and may cancel my subscription at any time. The free books and gift will be mine to keep in any case.

K7ZEF

Ms/Mrs/Miss/Mr ....Initials ....
                                                         BLOCK CAPITALS PLEASE
Surname ....
Address ....

....Postcode ....

Send this whole page to:
UK: FREEPOST CN81, Croydon, CR9 3WZ